On the Battlefield at Malabon, Philippine Islands.
Copyright 1899 by Underwood & Underwood

Insurrecto

Insurrecto

Gina Apostol

SOHO

Copyright © 2018 by Gina Apostol

Jacket art: *Woman with Fan*, acrylic on canvas by BenCab,
2001 BenCab Museum collection

Published by
Soho Press, Inc.
853 Broadway
New York, NY 10003

Library of Congress Cataloging-in-Publication Data
Apostol, Gina.
Insurrecto / Gina Apostol.

ISBN 978-1-61695-944-9
eISBN 978-1-61695-945-6

International PB ISBN: 978-1-61695-946-3

I. Title.

PR9550.9.A66 I57 2018 823'.914—dc23 2018027922

Interior design by Janine Agro, Soho Press, Inc.

Printed in the United States of America

10 9 8 7 6 5 4 3 2 1

Insurrecto

Gina Apostol

Copyright © 2018 by Gina Apostol

All rights reserved.

Jacket art: *Woman with Fan*, acrylic on canvas by BenCab,
2001 BenCab Museum collection

Published by
Soho Press, Inc.
853 Broadway
New York, NY 10003

Library of Congress Cataloging-in-Publication Data
Apostol, Gina.
Insurrecto / Gina Apostol.

ISBN 978-1-61695-944-9
eISBN 978-1-61695-945-6

International PB ISBN: 978-1-61695-946-3

I. Title.

PR9550.9.A66 I57 2018 823'.914—dc23 2018027922

Interior design by Janine Agro, Soho Press, Inc.

Printed in the United States of America

10 9 8 7 6 5 4 3 2 1

For Arne

Grief is a nation of everyone,
a country without borders.
I roam the avenues of it
out of habit. Summoned to testify
on everyone's behalf, I'm sticking
to my story. It's better not to talk
about the wounded, or the moist remains
of the disappeared. But there's always one
who can tell, in the packed
amplitude of crowds.

We are so many bodies, my friends.
We all move in the same direction.
As though someone had a plan

from "DMZ" in *Amigo Warfare* by Eric Gamalinda

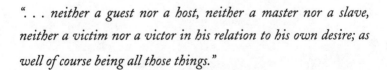

". . . *neither a guest nor a host, neither a master nor a slave,*
neither a victim nor a victor in his relation to his own desire; as
well of course being all those things."

from *Becoming Freud* by Adam Phillips

Cast of Characters

and some other figures

(in order of appearance, for the most part*)

Part One. A Mystery

MAGSALIN	Translator
STÉPHANE RÉAL	Writer
WIFE OF STÉPHANE RÉAL	Mourner
LUCIA/CHIARA	Names

ALCOHOLIC WRITER FRIENDS IN FLUSHING, QUEENS

JOE FRAZIER	Boxer
MUHAMMAD ALI	Boxer

ASSORTED CLOWNS FROM FIESTA CARNIVAL

CHIARA BRASI	Filmmaker
LUDO BRASI	Filmmaker, father of Chiara, husband of Virginie
OLIVER STONE	Filmmaker
FRANCIS FORD COPPOLA	Filmmaker
VIRGINIE BRASI	Wife of Ludo, mother of Chiara

OLD WOMAN CLUTCHING AN EMPTY PAIL IN LAS VEGAS

GUS	the famous polar bear of Central Park Zoo
CHAYA SOPHIA RUBINSON	Née Chazanov, also known as Madame Rubinson, also known as Cassandra Chase, mother of Virginie Brasi, grandmother of Chiara

HOLLYWOOD TYPES IN THE CATSKILLS

AMPARO MUÑOZ	Miss Universe of 1974
MISAY	A cat
TOMMY O'CONNELL	Protagonist of *The Unintended*, cult film by Ludo Brasi
JACOB "HOWLING WILDERNESS" SMITH	US commanding general in Tacloban, Leyte, 1901
PROFESSOR ESTRELLA ESPEJO	Filipino scholar on Philippine-American War
SMITTY JAKES	Protagonist of *The Unintended*, cult film by Ludo Brasi
THOMAS W. CONNELL	Captain, US Ninth Infantry Division, Charlie Company, Balangiga, Samar, 1901
JUAN LUNA	Painter who murdered his wife
PAZ CHICHING LUNA	Juan Luna's murdered wife

EWOKS SPEAKING TAGALOG

FILIPINO FARM WORKERS IN PAUL THOMAS ANDERSON'S *THE MASTER*

WAITRESS AT ALI MALL

SECURITY GUARD AT ALI MALL

TRUANT SCHOOLBOY AT ALI MALL

TRICYCLE DRIVER AT MERRY-GO-ROUND NEAR ALI MALL

STEVIE WONDER, MICHAEL JACKSON, KAREEM ABDUL-JABBAR, GLORIA GAYNOR, ETC., BLACK IDOLS OF FILIPINOS ON MURALS AT ALI MALL

WOMAN EMPLOYEE OF COMMISSION ON AUDIT

EXTRAS IN CUBAO WHO NAB TWO CLOWNS

TRAFFIC COPS

SMARTASS FILM BUFF

FIONNUALA AND OTHER IRISH FILM INTERNS

MAID IN HOUSE OF MAGSALIN'S UNCLES IN PUNTA

NEMESIO, EXEQUIEL, AND AMBROSIO, MAGSALIN'S UNCLES IN PUNTA

ELVIS AARON PRESLEY

PRIVATE FIRST CLASS EDWARD   Guard

PRIVATE FIRST CLASS GOGOBOY   Guard

RESORT WORKERS

BERNARDO GUSTAVO RANDOLS   Policeman

UNIDENTIFIED MEN RIDING IN TANDEM

FATHER AND CHILD

Part Two. Duel Scripts
Script I. Balangiga, 1901

CASSANDRA CHASE	Photographer in Balangiga, Samar, 1901, and protagonist of film set in 1901
FREDDO OF GUBBIO, ITALY	Art director of film set in 1901
ADMIRAL GEORGE DEWEY	Hero of the Battle of Manila Bay, 1898
FRANCES BENJAMIN JOHNSTON	Photographer of Admiral Dewey, 1898
MAJOR EDWIN GLENN	Water cure specialist, US Army officer court-martialed in 1902
SENATOR ALBERT J. BEVERIDGE	Republican of Indiana, imperialist, 1901
SENATOR GEORGE FRISBIE HOAR	Republican of Massachusetts, anti-imperialist, 1901
WILLIAM MCKINLEY	US president, killed in Buffalo by an anarchist in 1901
WILLIAM JENNINGS BRYAN	Democratic candidate for president, 1900
THEODORE ROOSEVELT	US vice-president in 1901, US president upon McKinley's death

THOMAS EDISON	Inventor
GENERAL EMILIO AGUINALDO	First president of the Philippines
MARK TWAIN	Writer, anti-imperialist

AMERICAN SOLDIERS IN BALANGIGA IN FILM SET IN 1901

THOMAS W. CONNELL	Captain, US Ninth Infantry Division, Charlie Company, 1901
MEYER THE BUGLER	US Army soldier, Ninth Infantry, Charlie Company, 1901
RANDLES THE SERGEANT	US Army soldier, Ninth Infantry, Charlie Company, 1901
BUMPUS THE LIEUTENANT	US Army soldier, Ninth Infantry, Charlie Company, 1901
GRISWOLD THE SURGEON	US Army soldier, Ninth Infantry, Charlie Company, 1901
SEWARD SCHEETHERLY	US Army soldier, Ninth Infantry, Charlie Company, goes insane, 1901
FRANK BETRON, AKA PRANK VITRINE	US Army soldier, Ninth Infantry, Charlie Company, 1901
BENTON FRICK, AKA PRICK	US Army soldier, Ninth Infantry, Charlie Company, 1901
WALLS THE COOK	US Army soldier, Ninth Infantry, Charlie Company, 1901
SERGEANT IRISH	US Army soldier, Ninth Infantry, Charlie Company, 1901

FILIPINOS IN BALANGIGA IN FILM SET IN 1901

VALERIANO ABANADOR	Chief of police in 1901 and Hero of Balangiga
PEDRO ABAYAN	Mayor of Balangiga in 1901
ANDRONICO BALAIS	Vice-mayor of Balangiga in 1901

PADRE DONATO GUIMBAOLIBOT	Parish priest of Balangiga in 1901
FRANCISCO	Orphan, servant of Captain Connell
CASIANA NACIONALES	Revolutionary, also known as Geronima of Balangiga
BENITO NACIONALES	Farmer, father of Casiana Nacionales

JAILED MEN OF BALANGIGA

DOLORES ABANADOR, FELISA CATALOGO,

PURING CANILLAS, MARGA BALASBAS, DELILAH ACIDRE,

AND ALL THE HEROINES OF BALANGIGA

Script II. Forest town in Samar used as a film set in film set in 197-

CAZ	Schoolteacher in film set in film set in 197-
LUDO	Director in film set in film set in 197-
MESSENGER	Carpenter in film crew of the director Ludo in film set in 197-

PETER HORN (OR HEARNE) AND OTHER ATTENDEES OF WAKE IN

MAGALLANES VILLAGE IN FILM SET IN 197-

FREDDO OF GUBBIO, ITALY	Art director in film crew of director Ludo Brasi in film set in 197-

CHINESE TODDLERS IN SAMAR FOREST TOWN USED AS A FILM SET

IN FILM SET IN 197-

DONATO	Cockpit boss in Samar forest town used as a film set in film set in 197-
VALERIANO	Tuba maker in Samar forest town used as a film set in film set in 197-
KAPITAN ABAYAN	Mayor of Samar forest town used as a film set in film set in 197-

CHIARA	Foreign child in Samar forest town used as a film set in film set in 197-
FOREIGN WHITE WOMAN	Mother of Chiara
SEWARD	American actor in Samar forest town used as a film set in film set in 197-

AMERICAN FILM CREW IN SAMAR FOREST TOWN USED AS A FILM SET IN FILM SET IN 197-

FIONNUALA	Assistant director in Samar forest town used as a film set in film set in 197-

ORPHANS IMPORTED FROM S.O.S. CHILDREN'S VILLAGE, NULA TULA, TACLOBAN

FRANCISCO	Brother of Caz, on film set in film set in 197-
PIERO DELLA FRANCESCA	Painter from Umbria, Italy, 1415–1492

written by

Chiara Brasi & Magsalin

or

Magsalin & Chiara Brasi

directed by

Chiara Brasi

Based on a Mystery

*A selected glossary of characters, settings, and other matters pertaining to the characters listed above can be found at The End Notes, and at the website of cultural curiosities praxino.org.

Insurrecto

Part One. A Mystery

Cubao, Quezon City;
and Punta, Santa Ana district, Manila

20.

The Insoluble Puzzle at the
Heart of the Labyrinth

For the mystery writer, it is not enough to mourn the dead. One must also study the exit wounds, invite the coroner to tea, cloud the mind with ulterior motives.

The translator and mystery writer Magsalin has undertaken (yes, no, pun) some of the above at previous incidents. But the insoluble puzzle at the heart of the labyrinth, the secret within the secret, is not hers to bemoan. That is up to the dead man's kin, who are, fortunately or not, also dead. It is said, for instance, that the writer Stéphane Réal's mother died in Auschwitz, his father of shrapnel wounds before the war started. The writer Stéphane Réal had a wife. She is a widow. Her heart must be broken. (Magsalin cannot do that for her.)

For the mystery writer, there are clues. Sheaves of paper with marginal notes, clippings of newsprint events of general interest, such as the Tunis–Marseille ship schedule, lottery numbers, and election results for the mayor of the commune Ivry-sur-Seine, 1979 (the winner is a communist). Everything could be a sign, and a word has at least two meanings, all of them correct. And it is not right to jump to conclusions, especially when it becomes apparent that one's sorrow is misplaced in this instance.

First, the writer Stéphane Réal has been dead for some time. Second, Magsalin has read only two of his books. Third, it turns out he does not figure at all except as premonitory prompt, place holder in this story of disappearance Magsalin is about to tell as she slips a hoard of facts into her duffel bag (leather, made in Venice, aubergine with olive handles, always admired by salesladies): to wit, the writer's income tax returns, an unmailed box covered in pale blue whorls, doubled postcard-size photographs, books with slips of paper falling out, index cards slipping from loose envelopes, a stash of library books the writer thought he would have time to return.

Her protagonist, what do you know, is female. The dead male writer that prompts the story waves goodbye. It turns out the woman is a filmmaker of moody artistry whose scandalous father precedes her fame. The woman's name has an arbitrary Italian flavor—Chiara or Lucia, with the first *C* glottal and the last *c* a florid *ch*: she is Kiiiara, or Luchiiiia. Magsalin has yet to decide the name, an act that must occur without the reader's noticing. Both names mean *clear*, or *lucidity*, or something that has to do with *light*, something vaguely linked to *eyesight*, hence to *knowing*, thence to blindness, or paradox.

Choosing names is the first act of creating.

2.

At Ali Mall

Magsalin gets the dossier from the filmmaker herself, who emails Magsalin. Microsoft Outlook warns: *Mail thinks this message is Junk.* Magsalin likes that her Mail thinks, but she doubts it. The subject line is intriguing.

Translator needed, meet me at Muhammad Ali Mall.

The message must be from a foreigner. No one in Manila calls the mall by that name. Some Filipinos do not even know that that seedy building in the traffic hellhole that is Cubao is named for the greatest—Muhammad Ali.

Magsalin ignores the message.

She is jet-lagged. She has just arrived from New York, on vacation in her birthplace, and she has no time for paid work. She is trying to unwind in Manila, hoping to continue a task that she believes has great spiritual payback, though the rewards are yet to surface.

She has begun her mystery novel.

She arrives with her baggage. A balikbayan box for her uncles, whose home she is visiting on this trip. The box is packed with vinyl records from bargain bins in a shop on Bleecker

Street—Neil Sedaka, Ray Conniff and His Singers, the elegies of Karen Carpenter, and for good measure a new press of their favorite, Elvis, *Aloha from Hawaii*, still in cello-wrap, plus bottles of Johnnie Walker Black Label that she thought might appease them. She has been gone for so long. All wrapped up in bath towels from Marshalls and stuffed with bags of Hershey's Kisses in the extra spaces. Another suitcase, filled with books. In her duffel, aubergine with olive handles, a square box, covered in pale blue whorls.

When Magsalin finally opens the email message, it only repeats its subject line, run-on included.

Translator needed, meet me at Muhammad Ali Mall. Signed.

The curtness of it, Magsalin thinks, is rude. She thinks the message is a joke, a hoax drummed up by her writer friends, a bunch of alcoholics hiding out in pork-induced stupor in Flushing, Queens.

Not even her mother's phone call had moved her to return home.

"I cannot go home," Magsalin had told her mother a long time ago.

"Do not come home," her mother had said on the phone. "If you feel you cannot do it, inday—do not return."

So she had not.

The reasons for return need not be sentimental: they could be an intellectual project, a way to deal with writer's block, or a respite during a cheap-airfare month. For a mystery writer, it is correct to return to soak in the atmosphere, to check out a setting, to round out a missing character, to find the ending.

Later, of course, she searches the Web for the filmmaker's name.

The search results include an item only eighteen hours ago mentioning Chiara Brasi's arrival in Manila. The report is an innocuous piece with a photo of the filmmaker at Ninoy Aquino International Airport, wearing huge shades and what looks like a safari outfit. Chiara is scouting locations for a movie, but no quote emerges from the director herself.

Magsalin checks praxino.org, her website of choice for cultural curiosities. A Philippine tour operator reports in a news update that Tom Cruise was sighted in August at a resort in the Ilocos, sporting an ugly ingrown toenail revealed by beach flip-flops. Sandra Bullock did not buy her black baby in the area near the old US Air Force base in Pampanga. Madonna's orphanage in Malawi is losing money, its website hacked by teenagers. Eric Clapton's late son's former nanny, a Chabacano, is said to be in seclusion in Zamboanga, an island in the far South, near the pirates—she still mourns her single lapse. Once again, Donatella Versace did not slap her maid. A video of Chiara Brasi shows a wan and wavering figure, in one of those canned interviews to promote a project. This detail appears in FabSugar, the *Emory Wheel*, the *Irish Times*, romania-insider.com, the *Kansas City Star*, the *Prague Post*, gmanetwork, inq7.net, and Moviefone: at age five Chiara rode a helicopter over Manila with her father when he was filming his war movie about Vietnam. A fond memory, in 1976. Someone had unhinged the helicopter's doors, and she looked out as if the sky were her vestibule.

Magsalin goes back to the email message.

She hits SEND.

3.

A Decrepit,
Cramped Cement Block of Shops

During the best of times Ali Mall is a decrepit, cramped cement block of shops hosting rugby glue sniffers, high school truants, and depressed carnival men in their off-hours. It was built in 1976, after the Thrilla in Manila. Ali Mall is across from the Araneta Coliseum in Cubao, site of the match that destroyed the career of the heavyweight champion of the world, Joe "The Gorilla" Frazier, and the source of our modern discomfort perhaps—a faint unease over earthly striving—whenever we remember the power and beauty of Muhammad Ali.

Even at noon Ali Mall is creepy. The circus is nearby, and a cranky carousel rounds out a tiresome concept of eternity. Magsalin enters by the basement annex through the Philippine Airlines office toward the Botak shop and a trinket store selling Hello Kitty barrettes. A security guard is texting by some plywood boards. A clown stands by, also holding a phone, his fingers in the act of reply. Magsalin heads straight to the bakery selling cinnamon buns and pan de sal.

Magsalin notes, like a skillful detective, that the woman, her likely protagonist, is wearing a felt-banded panama hat and tan wedges. It is the incognito look. But the designer shoes (Clergerie) and her giant shades (also French: Chanel) are amateurish, and even an idiot knows she's rich. Magsalin does not live in New York for nothing. People exist there only to shop, and everyone develops a third eye for noticing the fashionable cut of a stranger's pants, or someone's too-youthful chukka boots. Some are tourists, frantic and passing by, but worse are the residents, a candid lot who will demand the make, the time, and the place you bought your bag, which Magsalin clutches, that aubergine and olive duffel, made in Venice.

She pats the square contours of the pale blue box inside her bag.

The duffel is clunky, and Magsalin feels foolish, like a tourist, unable to leave her valuables behind.

This woman at the counter, drinking bottled water and eating no bread, has the luxury of looking underdressed. Magsalin would not be caught dead in a tank top in Manila. It is indecent, so her uncles say. Chiara is slightly naked but no-nonsense. She's flat-chested. She is clutching an envelope. Chiara is muckle-mouthed. An errant grimace mars her beauty, rendering her ordinary at disarming moments, despite the glamour fame reports. In fact, Chiara has a fugitive charm, now you see it, but then it passes. Her shyness makes you uncomfortable. At least that is what Magsalin feels until she recognizes that the faraway gaze (obvious even behind Chanel), the averted angle of her chin, the awkward pose on the stool, the determined and surprisingly uninteresting monotone are signs of indifference.

Magsalin considers leaving. How dare this filmmaker in too-short designer shorts ask urgently for her help online but in person look so apathetic about her reply?

But then, Magsalin thinks, the woman also looks sedated, stoned.

What does she know? Magsalin's own buzz of choice is cheap Chilean pinot noir.

Anyhow, Chiara's past is full of shady anecdotes. At least, her father's is. Magsalin did not need to Google the details. There was a time newspapers in Manila were full of Ludo Brasi's escapades. His famished look belied his monstrous appetite. Even in preproduction, traveling around southern Luzon for his film, he was notorious, expending not just cash but also his spirit in wastes of shame. Oliver Stone, coarse-mouthed and demanding, shooting *Platoon* in the rice fields of Laguna, was a saint compared to Chiara's father. So reported foreign bums around Olongapo whose claim to fame was being Dead Body Number 2 or Long-Haired Soldier with Venereal Disease in *The Unintended*. Wasn't it in Lubao, Pampanga, that Ludo Brasi had an affair with both a costume designer and a local props woman, or was it a schoolteacher, during the filming of his Vietnam War movie, now more or less forgotten, though at one point it was thought *The Unintended* would challenge the genius of Francis Ford Coppola's *Apocalypse Now*—except be less commercial? He and Coppola are practically the same age; both grew up in New York. But while the one has a genial, paternal aura, even in the documentary by his faintly bitter, long-suffering wife, the other is satyric, greasy, saturnine, and unstable. Unlike Coppola, after his film's triumphant premiere, Ludo Brasi disappeared. The initial reports were muddled. Was it an accident? Was he killed by rebels while on location in the wild? His disappearance, a critic said, made the existential weariness in his film, *The Unintended*, even more burdensome.

It is no wonder that Ludo Brasi's daughter has the aura of someone only intermittently aware, as if she has a learned disinterest in the questions people will ask. She could be thinking about a swatch of fabric she once saw in Umbria, or the time she smoked opium in Thailand with a famous pop star, a drug-addled childhood friend, the way she looks so distracted while she explains to Magsalin her semi-urgent business that brings her to this pastry shop in Cubao.

21.

Everything in the World Is Doubled

In Las Vegas in 1969, everything in the world is doubled, the chandeliers, the plush of the blackjack tables, the old women in furs and mohair caps with rhinestone hatpins, the sheen of the noiseless slot machines. Even the song sounds like a broken record, a desperate loop. *We can't go on together! With suspicious minds!*

"It's a comeback hit!" says the d.j. "The King is baaaaack," the d.j. crows. Virginie has no idea what he is talking about.

Virginie is staring at an old woman holding on to an empty pail, the name THE SANDS somewhat erased, its huge S an eroded snake, a molted shadow of itself. She stares because she and the woman are wearing the same Schreiner brooch: a pink rose. It is a coincidence. The woman's mouth is open in silent despair.

But the only sound Virginie hears is the scratch of Ludo's pen (it is an antique 1940s Esterbrook, a miniature in pale green, one of hers).

Her husband is so young.

This fact touches Virginie, though she is six years younger than her husband.

Virginie's diplopia has the odd advantage of centering her focus only on the sound of Ludo's writing.

She sees double but hears nothing but *scratch*.

As she watches her husband, she does not even hear the King.

Scratch scratch scratch scratch.

The woman sobbing in the elevator with her empty pail makes no sound for Virginie.

4.

Chiara Affirms She Is the Daughter

Chiara affirms she is the daughter of the director of *The Unintended.*

Magsalin confesses she saw the film several times in her teens.

At one point, memorably, she recalls watching it frame by frame in a muggy class along Katipunan Avenue, for a course called Locations/Dislocations, about the phantasmal voids in Vietnam War movies shot in equally blighted areas that are not Vietnam. The disturbing web of contorted allusions, hidden historiographical anxiety, political ironies, and astounding art direction resident in a single frame, for instance, of a fissured bridge in the Philippines, in real life dynamited by the Japanese in 1943 and still unrepaired in 1976, and rebuilt specifically and reexploded spectacularly in the film's faux-napalm scene against a mystic pristine river actually already polluted by local dynamite fishers—the movie, for whatever reason, kept putting Magsalin to sleep.

But she omits that detail before the filmmaker's daughter.

There was something both engrossing and pathetic about it, about reconstructing the trauma of whole countries through a movie's palimpsest, and what was most disturbing, of course, was that, on one level, the professor's point was true, our identities are irremediably mediated, but that does not mean Magsalin has to keep thinking about it.

Chiara seems unconcerned, however, by the scholarly implications of her father's cult classic. She nods absently at Magsalin's recall, as if she, Chiara, has heard it all before, as if she needs another Adderall.

What she really needs, Chiara says, almost upsetting Magsalin's cup of chai, is someone to accompany her on a trip.

"Where to?" asks Magsalin.

"I need to get to Samar."

22.

Why Samar?

Ludo pours out his dreams to her, and Virginie restrains her own, as if hers should be checked so his can run free, though no one has established the rules. She knows it will be no honeymoon because he is still thinking, a terrible condition, the way he pores over and picks through his scraps of demented plots before settling on the one: an epic about Rotarians; a love story involving Gus, the famous polar bear of Central Park Zoo (one of his obsessions), also known as The Bipolar Bear; a musical about dwarves in space (a physicist's dream); an Italian soccer fantasy film with himself in a cameo, of course, as a deaf-mute goalie—a perfect life condition, he says, a state of pure passion!; a murder mystery set in Vietnam but in fact about pyromaniac grief, gruesome and unconsoling; an adaptation of *The Tale of Genji* in a World War II Japanese internment camp (also a musical).

From his jumble of ideas he zooms in to his desire—his stubborn cathexis, a four-leaf clover that, on her part, she overlooks. It is admirable how his desire just cuts through the brush, when Virginie can barely figure out which pin to wear: the Schreiner rose, a fabulous fake, or her mother's choice, an antique pearl in an abstract coil.

The Colt .45 was invented to kill the Filipino juramentados, violent insurgents out of their minds, during the Philippine-American War. That much she is told. She has learned more than anyone will ever need to know about the Philippine-American War in the years she has been married to Ludo. The genealogy of the genocidal Krag-Jørgensen rifle (Norway, 1896), obsolete prop of a dirty war; the melancholy artistry of local bamboo snares (Samar, 1899), makeshift prop of a hopeless war; the advent of photography (Underwood & Underwood Photographic Company, founded 1881), propaganda tool for the imperial wretchedness of this war; the terms for the enemy (katipunero, juramentado, nigger, insurrecto), interchangeable names in a confusing war. Ludo keeps the gun on his desk as he researches, poring over maps he has ordered from the Library of Congress. He litters the desk with his doubled cards, sepia tones in disarray. His mute histories on pasteboard. As he shows her the trail they could take, using the gun to make his point, from the infernal streams of Samar's interior to the mountain passes beyond the Caves of Sohoton, she wonders if her husband has imbibed it, the spirit of his juramentados.

Still, she knows she will go.

Virginie, too, has a sense of the wild, though it is not apparent in her outfit. She is dressed in brocade and gold. She glitters like a sunfish. She wears the metallics and embroidered clothes that she wore in the days when she had first met him. Her mother, Chaya Sophia Chazanov of Sosnitsa, near the Dnieper, Cassandra Chase to immigration authorities, and now Madame Rubinson of Rubinson Fur Emporium on Park Avenue, had always favored old-world props, lace and lamé. Madame Rubinson was a former set designer who, not quite by intention, married rich.

It was Virginie's secret that she bore a sense of trauma that the world around her mocked—she was coddled from birth, showered with toys, after all; but she has long had this subliminal perception of a wound without root or reason, which not even she could see. She had gone to the zoo that day in one of those bouts of boredom that took teenage girls like her, who had an excess of time and indolence, into parts of the city that enthralled children and manic-depressives.

It was September. She lived only a few blocks from the animals, the hippos and the bears and the penguins, but she had never seen them up close. It was not proper, said her aunts, to do things without companions: the devil stands in ambush for lonely minds. Anyway, zoos were for the vulgar. Every day, once school started, passing the zoo, she would hear the chime of its hours, tinkling in a sunlit, dying fall, like the charmed suspiration of the endless tedium that lay ahead. That day, playing hooky, she found herself next to the sea lion tamer, magnetized by the sleight of hand with which he fed the animals their midday fish.

The act's doubleness struck Virginie—the way she believed absolutely in the spectacle of beastly affection, at the same time that she saw the bait that fed it.

She needed to go out more.

She failed to see the filmmaker catching her figure, out of place in her sequined outfit and spotted coat from Rubinson Fur Emporium. She had intruded onto his picture, but it was semi-neorealist anyway (i.e., done on the cheap). He was filming his pro-animal masterpiece, tentatively called *Maniac in the Ark*, about an insane killer who turns out to be a zookeeper (of course) who wreaks mayhem to extort funds from the mayor of New York to find a cure for his great love (Gus the Polar Bear, of course, dying of the loss of his own great love, Ida, another polar bear). No distributor bought it. Ludo still thinks of the plot fondly. He likes its themes of civic duty matched with violent redemption. Ludo caught her like this, a truant in his mise-en-scène of constructed magic, and when he asked her to sign away her right to privacy, also asking for her phone number, she did not see the symbolism—the tamer at play with a hungry beast.

She took his bait.

The life of a filmmaker is one of scraps of plots sandwiched between the lack of means to fulfill them. The life of a woman in the fifties is one of scraps of plots sandwiched between the lack of means to fulfill them. It is hard for Virginie to grasp that she has agency, just as in those old films of femmes fatales dying in grisly circumstances (Garbo in *Camille*, or Garbo in any other role), the viewer starts shouting at the doomed woman, who fails to grasp that she has agency—don't fall for that lousy count, you nincompoop!—and she dies of consumption or jumps in front of that speeding train anyway. Eloping with a bearded artiste she meets at the zoo does not strike Virginie as a cinematic cliché. It feels like freedom. In the dark of the screening room, she watches the shreds and patches of the scene he has just filmed. The polar bear swims in despondent figure eights, over and over again, a whitish impression of unrest. She clutches his hand during the scene of murder in the Arctic cages, as the killer raises his bloody axe. She screams. He tells her—look, it's just sleight of hand. All of your terror lies in the cut. No penguins were harmed in the filming of this movie. She does not look. But she keeps watching him rolling his film, feeding his reel.

He stops and starts and cuts and discards, including her scene with the sea lions (he says the metaphor is sublime but the lighting is not). And the power of that—the certainty of his director's vision—gives her *invidia*: a disease of empathy. It's that envy of the artist that arises in certain readers: a visceral connivance with his dreams matched only by the desire to kill him for fulfilling them.

5.

Chiara Crafts a Movie Script

It turns out Chiara is a member of a group of Hollywood types who gather every few years or so in the Catskills. In a woodsy agricultural setting, Chiara's group plays parlor games and captures ghosts in séances and commands lunar apogees and exhibits all sorts of megalomaniac tendencies, in small and unreported doses, usually in April, the cruelest month only if you are a poet, not a millionaire.

At one of the revels, Chiara's cabal gathers for lunch at the giant liver-shaped kitchen table in the eighteenth-century manse owned by Chiara's mother, a dreamer in constant convalescence whose absence from her mansion goes unremarked. The artist guests spontaneously carry in their arms, as if lifting ritual Byzantine icons, their identical fifteen-inch, quad-core, silver MacBook Pros.

People barely look at each other or even check the wine list (one of them has been in AA since age fourteen). Instead, they *all* begin typing memos or searching the difference between heirloom or heritage apples or opening their email at the *same* audible *incredible* momentous *freaky* time! Snapping her head up at the moment when everyone else understands that the room has just exploded into one eerie propulsive CLICK, all together, twenty-first-century robots come to life—Chiara laughs.

They begin to eat the free-range duck confit with organic pea shoots and Roxbury Russet compote (heirloom, not heritage) and drink the local cabernet franc, which has no sulfites. But a pall comes over the afternoon, though no one mentions it.

Perhaps only Chiara had this recognition that something terribly gauche had just united them, wistful, emerging auteurs. After dessert, still sipping espresso, the group comes up with a parlor trick. It occupies them for the next few days, in between yoga and once again watching *Mulholland Drive*.

Each moviemaker chooses a search term, and from information produced by a single Google search—from the Web's constraint—each will write a movie script.

6.

Why Samar??!!

By the time the game starts, Chiara is drowsy, and the lethargy that seems to accompany feelings of nonexistence, as if she is only borrowing her body and sometimes floating above it, uncomfortable feelings that have plagued her, off and on, since she was six, wash over Chiara.

So she takes the easy route and goes Oedipal.

She types in the name of her father's most celebrated film, *The Unintended*, and the year production began, 1975.

She has never done this before—looked up her father online.

Her childhood was in analog.

For a long time, in her teens, she had made an effort to forget.

But Chiara has pleasant memories of the times she spent with her father in the tropics. Specifically, she was in Quezon City, then in Makati, then in Angeles, Pampanga, but she will learn that only online. She was four in 1975. She remembers a skating rink, being crowned Miss Philippines in games with tiny beauty-contest-obsessed girls who in excessive gestures of companionship always made her, the white girl, win, and getting lice in her hair from goats owned by a visiting tribe of mountain people.

She has a memory of one blackout night during what she now understands are Manila's seasonal, spectacular rains. Her mother, usually all nerves, a Ukrainian Jew brought up on stories of pogroms, who turned to Roman Catholicism then hatha yoga in the aftermath, is agitated, sitting down and getting back up to protect a flickering flame. Oddly, the Philippines has driven her mother's persecution complex underground, and in the Philippines she lives in an almost Buddhic calm amid the lizards on the ceilings, monstrous cockroaches in the toilet, sewer animals in the garden, and nubile prostitutes promenading all around the seedy areas near the American military bases. Chiara's mother grew up spoiled. She is used to getting her way. She gave her husband his Hollywood start. But it is as if the desperate indignities of living in a perpetually fallen state, among lives she shares and witnesses and attends to with a perplexed gaze, has lent her peace, a converse calm, that she has not regained since.

Perhaps this explains Chiara's sense at times that a vulnerable world could be an oasis.

The shadows of her mother's single candle and the sounds of a gecko on the wall are the night's only cartographic points. Otherwise, she and her mother and her father are suspended, the only people in a universal void, rocking in a gigantic cradle hanging above Manila's awful monsoon winds. But Chiara is happy. Chiara is lying with her curly four-year-old head on her strong, sweating father's lap. An athletic man in soccer shorts and blue and yellow rugby shirt. The famously methodical director is picking lice, one pinch following another, a rich rhythmic tug mauling her along her tender scalp, each tug pleasingly soporific, a victorious bloodbath on her father's hands. She doesn't remember her father cursing every time he finds a pest and crushing it with his purple thumb, though her mother has pointed out those gross details. It is the most pleasing memory of her childhood, that blackout night, her father picking out lice from her hair until she falls asleep: it is pleasing to recall her dad, a man busy with so many things, determined to rid her of all the bugs he could find, to use his magical director powers to seek out the vermin touching her body, to squash the blood out from each creature's abominable veins.

True, it is as if the concentrated frustration arising from the calamities of his unsteady enterprise, the making of his cursed monumental film, has bubbled forth, you know, and he is crushing his fate as much as he is crushing the Filipino goats' lice.

"Lice do not come from goats," Magsalin interrupts. "They come from people."

Chiara ignores her.

Wikipedia, IMDb, praxino.org, Rotten Tomatoes, reviews from the usual sources, the *New Yorker, Asia Week,* the *Guardian, Time,* come up in quick succession in her Google search.

It occurs to Chiara that the world of her childhood might be compressed in this single click, a mass of news and memory with not even a rough cut.

She keeps scrolling.

Chiara does not click on the obvious items.

She has read them before: reviews of her father in newsprint, cutout items in her mother's boxes.

She thinks she knows his ephemera by heart.

Once, she had tried to search him out, her father. She had studied his movies, gone through boxes in her mother's home in the Catskills, full of books and files and note cards, and read through his scripts. Even his last, his unfinished one.

She had carefully read that.

But the effort to find him during an unstable time, how old was she, eleven?, was a confounding quest—a shambles—a heap and a mess and a horror—the horror—that led only to tailspin, collapse, her inability to retrieve herself. Without medication, asylum, or retreat.

She came through by a huge effort of will. She pats herself on the back mentally for that fact. She is proud of herself. Rising up by her bootstraps—and her mother's money. She keeps talismans—a few of her father's effects, a camera, snapshots, a bunch of library books he never returned, stuffed in a box in her mother's home.

But she never went back to his films.

She made her own.

Art is her asylum.

She has hubris, that afternoon in the Catskills, scrolling through Google.

Maybe she thinks she can traverse it—the Googling of her father's name—she can seek him out now, after all these years, with no pain attached.

And it is true: there is something comforting about it.

This Oedipal fix.

Chiara keeps scrolling.

The piracy sites, the Cyrillic pages, the Chinese message boards, the links to Paypal to download the movies for free, these boxing matches that keep coming up.

Chiara thinks she will never find anything of interest, and she will surely lose her group's game.

Then she starts clicking.

Muhammad Ali's historic match against Joe Frazier on October 1, 1975. Miss Universe Amparo Muñoz is stripped of her crown and becomes a soft porn star. The bells of Balangiga, some religious items stolen from a Philippine island, remain missing.

More piracy sites, more voodoo video games that have nothing to do with anything.

The construction of the first multilevel shopping mall in the Philippines rises in tribute to Muhammad Ali's victory. Then another article on the ambush in Balangiga of American soldiers of the Ninth US Infantry Regiment on an island called Samar in 1901.

What is going on?

Her father's film is being ambushed online by an unrelated disaster.

Balangiga, Samar, keeps coming up, neck and neck with Muhammad Ali.

23.

Before the Weeping

In 1969, they are still childless. Virginie hates leaving Manhattan but wishes to appreciate her husband's way of life. In Las Vegas Ludo prefers the Grand, but she chooses the Hilton. There are lines of women in beehives and stilettos. It distresses and pleases her to see so many women looking like her, all in a line to see a show. The rows of women give Virginie this rush. She is scared of crowds. She hides behind her husband's growing fame, his vitality. In the photographs, she always strikes this sub-alar pose, like a puffin cub taking cover. She hates going to premieres. She discovers too late that she hates the movies, a detail that amuses Ludo. The visual effects strain her nerves. She always imagines, as the train rushes straight at her, that she will fall with the hero into the abyss.

This neurological defect draws her husband to her. Her sense that fantasy is never an illusion and that the purpose of art is hypnosis, a form of body snatching, arouses in Ludo both tenderness and calculation. She is the ideal viewer for whom he makes his thrillers.

Also, a reliable investor.

It might be fun to see the shows, she says.

Sure, Ludo says, why not. Grist for the mill.

Ludo can write anywhere.

He prefers the casinos. By the baccarat tables, he likes to spread out his 5 × 8 note cards, ruled. Security and waiters leave him alone. They are used to oddballs with money. He ponders a sequence, then he shuffles, inserts a note card into a middle set, moves a top card to the second column. He's an orderly man and scratches his reconfigurations of the plot in a neat list of rearranged numbers with corresponding new scenes. Like playing solitaire with a set of laws that he is inventing. He can see the scenes coming together; then he doesn't. The end is elusive. His wife taps him on the shoulder.

I got the tickets, she says.

WHEN SHE THINKS of it years later, she wonders—was that it? She stood among the crowd, a well-shod woman with a starving look, cigarette in thin hand, staring entranced but also distracted (as one can see in a brief pan over the concert crowd)—was it then that in a flick of his white, flashing tassels her life turned?

She remembers standing up to watch the singer, mesmerized.

To get a better view.

Ludo sits bemused by the rhinestone-and-sequin world of Las Vegas, because, after all, he would always be an immigrant kid from Cutchogue, some no-name town on Long Island,

indifferent to the material world, even annoyed by its require-
ments—suits and ties and matching shoes.

At dinners on Park Avenue, with the Rubinsons, Ludo has a
hard time keeping a poker face among her parents' friends until
the theater people arrive, Madame Rubinson's Broadway crew,
their old-lady musk and antique-store sweat bringing back their
lost world—fashioning muslin toiles or quilting woolen bouclé
suits with silk charmeuse linings, their painstaking manual labor
for others' sleights of hand—and Ludo can sit listening to their
music-hall gossip all night long.

Magsalin can see in this couple their shared solitudes.

Chiara can see in this couple a daughter's loyalties: divided.

The man bends down to the concert floor to do his karate-move
dancing. The precarious sight of a grown, sweating man in white,
sequined suit slowly splitting in front of Virginie's eyes—becoming
two people at once, straining to seduce this crowd that has no need
for such attention (a mere glance from the white-robed singer is all
the screaming women want)—the world blacks out for Virginie.

That stage effect—the sudden dramatic darkness before the
lights turn back on—is so corny that any thought beyond stupor
does not flash through anyone's mind.

Ludo notes the crowd's crazy suspension of its disbelief.

He stands up. He takes a picture with his Polaroid. Ludo is a
showman. He envies mass hallucination.

Something to study, he thinks.

Ludo does not notice Virginie shaking, tottering. The women

gasp. The spotlight turns back on. Virginie realizes it is a visual effect, not a snap in her brain, and she sees the man being rearranged, put back together by the strobe lights. A constructed and reconstructed figure, produced by his audience's screams.

And he becomes who he is—a fused, patched, and growling man breathing into a microphone—

Now even Ludo is back up on his feet, by Virginie's side. She clutches her husband's arm as he brings his fingers to his lips, blowing through them a long, ardent hiss, whistling for Elvis.

Is it her mind failing her, or is it her bad eyes? At the sight of a figure straining to become whole before the crowd that fragments him, she feels something crawling under her bones, the pain of a rip in her own shell: a snail-house disassembling, coming unglued from her skin.

She thinks she will topple over, a dizziness not new to her, but strangely liberating just the same.

What a show, says Ludo. He is drenched, wiping at himself— Don't know how you can pimp yourself like that every night and not go goddamned crazy, he says.

And Virginie feels she has been slapped.

She freezes.

She wishes to say to her husband, standing there wiping off his sweat—but she does not speak her thoughts—*You think you're so smart. You have no clue how people feel.*

It sounds self-righteous, improper, and dumb.

Her response to Ludo, her lover, over this gyrating, growling stranger in a sequined costume, embarrasses her. Her aunts are right—the devil stands in ambush for hungry minds. It is a passing thing, her revulsion for Ludo, her shame for herself, that moment in Las Vegas. Ludo's remark means no harm, and in time, though she remembers it, she forgets the point.

She watches the same show eight more times during that stay in Vegas. Ludo sits in the casinos, reorganizing the index cards, figuring out his film. That is a craftsman at work, that is a showman, he speaks in approval to his wife who returns to him late at night every night the entire time they are in Las Vegas.

The way she arcs her body toward Ludo, wanting herself to want him, makes her shudder even before she comes. The way she arcs her body toward Ludo, wanting him to want her, makes Ludo smile, I have married a child, he thinks, and a warmth comes over him, and he pretends she is a lion in a cage, and he is the tamer, and she screams as he snarls, clutching her at her wrists—she is unmovable—and he laughs as if he has invented the act that will follow and that, soon enough, swallows him. Virginie sits awake late at night, next to her snoring husband, who looks frail, hungry even in his sleep. And the next day, Ludo is recalculating his show's purposes, shuffling his pliant cards. She does not quite know how to put it, this fragmenting sense of herself, except that it is the only way she can get at who she is.

7.

There Is Always an Alternate Story

So Chiara's search reveals.

It turns out a Filipino scholar has written a paper linking the massacre of civilians in Balangiga, Samar, 1901, to the 1968 Vietnam massacre that frames her father's film. As some viewers might recall, *The Unintended* is a memoir, or as the *Guardian* describes it, "a sterile mystery wrapped in spiral flashback," about a teenage kid, Tommy O'Connell, who fails to be court-martialed for acts he has committed in a South Vietnamese hamlet, code-named Pinkville (the name of the actual village is never mentioned). The boy Tommy, along with his fellow soldiers of Charlie Company, razes the hamlet to the ground. He tells his story so that the world does not forget the horror he, Tommy, cannot leave behind.

The Balangiga incident of 1901 is a true story in two parts, a blip in the Philippine-American War (which is a blip in the Spanish-American War, which is a blip in latter-day outbreaks of imperial hysteria in Southeast Asian wars, which are a blip in the infinite spiral of human aggression in the livid days of this dying planet, and so on).

Part One: An uprising of Filipinos against an American out-post in Samar (the exposition here would be a fascinating movie in itself, though with too many local color details) leads to forty-eight American deaths, with twenty-two wounded and four missing in action.

Part Two: The US commanding general demands in retalia-tion the murder of every Filipino male in Samar above ten years of age. Blood bathes the province. Americans savage—"kill and burn" is the technical term—close to thirty thousand Filipinos, men, women, and children, in a rampage of such proportions that the court-martial of the general, Jacob H. "Howling Wilderness" Smith, causes a sensation when the events become public in 1902.

The scholar, Professor Estrella Espejo of the University of the Philippines in Diliman, points out that the Samar incident also implicates a Charlie Company (though of the wrong regiment, the historic US Ninth Infantry, the Manchu Fighters, a glamour brigade). And as in the Vietnam incident (and in other similar times, e.g., in Afghanistan and Iraq), barely a handful of Ameri-cans are tried for the homicidal affair.

The infamous General Jacob Smith ordered the Filipino deaths by making memorable staccato statements: "I want no prisoners. I wish you to kill and burn. The more you kill and burn, the better it will please me."

The general's resonant phrase made his name: "The interior of Samar must be made *a howling wilderness.*"

According to Professor Espejo, the repulsive yet fascinating

Smitty Jakes, the Kilgore-like lieutenant whose pathological patriotism is the most troubling yet truest aspect of Ludo Brasi's film, is a nod to the butcher of Balangiga.

The movie's hero, the guilt-ridden wraith Tommy O'Connell, Espejo concludes, resting her case, is clearly the West Point–educated commander of the Samar outpost, twenty-six-year-old Captain Thomas W. Connell, a moralist whose meager ethics measured in full the absurdity of the American cause.

24.

The Monsoons of Manila

The monsoons of Manila give Virginie a thrill. Frogs from the garden leap onto her soaking carpet and into the borrowed house's Chinese vases. The rain traps her in the sala. Catfish swim toward her shoes. Her baby daughter's Wellingtons come splashing down from the dusty ottoman while the feral cat, a castaway, casually invades the kitchen. Virginie thinks a tadpole is tickling her toes, but she does not dare to look. The cat, Misay, is completely dry, like the perfectly coiffed maid in the corner cutting up the mangoes with utter calm. She is staring at Virginie's legs. "Ma'am," she says. An obscene dead cockroach, its genitalia splayed out for the world to see, is coming and going in waves, like an upturned boat with frail masts. Virginie looks. She screams. The cat pounces. The baby claps, and the maid bustles about. The cat almost has the cockroach in its grasp, but the maid swipes at the cat, who runs off, and she sweeps the dumb flaccid bug easily into the dustbin, with a nonchalance that her mistress's embarrassment observes. It is odd that it is so sunny outside, Virginie thinks, when for all she knows the world has turned upside down. It is a sinking ship that was once a home. Her toes are cold.

VIRGINIE DOES NOT know what to do with her time in Manila while Ludo is off in Pampanga. It rains for weeks on end. Now it escapes her why she allowed herself to leave New York. With a baby. To live in this drowning city. But she remembers that feeling she had when she had stepped out onto the tarmac in the oppressive heat, as if she were conquering something, as if despite her blindness, under the dazzle of the sun, she had been given this gift of vision, a vista into a strange world she would one day know.

That feeling of anticipation, of something about to happen, comes upon her as she watches the crowd outside the windows of her car, driven by the chauffeur. It is after the storm. The storm had shuttered their lives because Magallanes Village is its own oasis, alert and alive and intact because of its obscenely anxious regard for itself—the way it exists at the expense of others. As she leaves McKinley Road, she watches children swimming in and out of a culvert, paddling through submerged streets. She thinks—how far away I am from home. The city is a vast and bulldozed wreck of upright palms and floating goods and moving, haunting homes that have survived. It is a city of survivors. (It turns out it looks that way even after the rainy season.) She feels unmoored. And in a sort of kindness toward herself, the thought strikes her—her isolation is deserved. This thought is a comfort.

She is going to buy shoes for her daughter. The shoe store is an apocalypse of boxes. It is a cement atrium of stacked shelves and smiling saleswomen before glass cabinets that also contain lace fans, shell trinkets, and embroidered handkerchiefs under lock and key. Are the items sheltered for their cost, or for their fragility, or for their propensity to catch dust? She wishes to know things but is also bored. People speak English to her as if she were a child, as if she does not understand their language. They take extra care with their vowels and sound out their diphthongs with precision, saying the sound *ste-re-o*.

Paul Anka, ma'am? Barry Manilow? Art Garfunkel? Neil Diamond?

The shoe store sells everything, including albums of Christmas carols and plates with touching epigrams: SWEETS FOR THE SWEETS ONE, one dish setting says, its tender affection unedited twelve times. She thinks she stands out, with her wild hair and her cheeks sweating under sunglasses then freeze-drying in the air conditioning, and she wishes she were shorter. She is glad to stoop down over the sneakers presented to Chiara.

Chiara is in love. With the display and plenitude of the shoe shop, this cavern of merchandise, also unedited, and she touches everything she sees—the ceramic pigs with bobbing heads, the satin dots on the bows of the salesgirls' uniforms.

It turns out, wherever she goes, soon everyone crowds around Chiara. Virginie's beauty is problematic, people politely turn away from it as if embarrassed to be observers. She has a movie star face, a white woman's profile that creates a stir, registered to her only as discomfort. But the child is like a magnet to the tidy, starched women with straight backs and exquisitely made-up faces and prim hair stretched tight into neat buns. Their stiff, smiling poise turns into abandon around four-year-old Chiara, their hairpins loosened, stockinged heels separating a precarious inch from their pumps as they bend on tippy toes and leave their positions in their departments, at Beach Sandals or Charles Jourdan, to bend down to the height of the child, looking for all the world as if they are falling over laughing, as they come cooing around the girl.

"So pretty, ma'am," they say, and they brush Chiara's fat cheeks and touch her light-filled hair.

"Are these real?" they ask about Chiara's curls. "They look like a munyika's, a doll!"

Virginie marvels at her daughter, how at ease she is in the world, as if everything is her due, sometimes answering the sales-girls' questions, sometimes not, running off to pull out from the Disney display a plush toy, a cat.

"Misay!" Chiara returns with the animal, calling out the name of her cat, and the salesgirls think this is so funny it is difficult for them to get back to work and look for other sneakers that fit the child, they keep repeating the word Misay and laughing.

"Wow, she's Visayan," says one.

"She speaks Waray," giggles another.

Virginie frowns, not understanding, then she gets the joke.

The name of their cat Misay means "cat" in that language, Waray. A Wonderland world, she thinks, where the names you give are jokes to others, and your ignorance is the moral lesson of the story.

Finally her daughter chooses her pair of shoes. A pile of pastel sneakers lies spilled at her feet. The salesgirl takes the mother and child to the woman who peers into their chosen box, cataloging a number on her mimeographed sheet. Another girl stamps a receipt on the box. Then a girl takes her to a line to pay.

Virginie is afraid.

She is afraid of her freeze-dried mind in the air conditioning as she stands above the shopgirls, her spine straight. To complain is a sign of a small mind. Any minute she will scream, she will throw this bunch of tissue-paper money into the cashier's smiling face, she will throw a tantrum in this labyrinth of inexplicably multiplying shoebox warrens.

And no one will fault her for her rage.

She is very tall; she has dominion.

She is tired. Mainly she is tired of herself.

Her knuckles are tight around her bag, her fingernails dig into her palm.

So this is life, Virginie thinks. Her world in Manila is not so different from the terror of her girlhood, the life she had escaped when she married Ludo. She is taken from one shopgirl to another in a snaking, frozen tundra full of glass countertops and boxes. She cannot see her way out of the labyrinth of stations that comprise the paying of the shoes. The line of salesgirls playing with Chiara is growing longer. Then the cashier counts out the pesos Virginie offers with a doubtful air. Then the cashier in another line counts Virginie's cash again. She gives the box of shoes to yet another girl. The other girl wraps the box. Virginie is following the sequence, moving with the box, she thinks she will go out of her mind.

Where is Ludo?

He is up in the sky over Pampanga, directing his new world.

How does he describe it?

—You look out, Virginie, he said to her on the phone, above Arayat—and it is as if the sky is your vestibule.

The idea of Ludo ruling the world with his borrowed money— his loans and banks and her cash infusions causing him all sorts of headaches and euphoria, cash being the engine of his art— gives her a bloated, bruised feeling, of a tenderness in the offing, a wound of affection coming to the fore in this freezing place.

The wrapping girl places the box of shoes into a bag. The stapling girl staples the bag shut. But when Virginie is shown the way to the next line, the salesgirls' heels click-clacking on the cement floor, to one more glass counter where one more girl will take out one more receipt and stamp one more symbol onto the wrapped box of her daughter's pastel shoes, Virginie begins to cry.

The sound surprises even Virginie.

She is wailing.

She cannot help it.

She is a monsoon wind that will never stop.

Virginie's hair is wet and hanging from her face, and her sunglasses are askew, and Chiara hears her mother cry—*Aiiiieeeeee!*—falling down into her rabbit hole, the cavern of boxes that is the mall.

The salesgirls gather around the lady.

Finally, they look straight at Virginie.

They leave the child, they scuttle around, they open a glass cabinet, they fan her with the lace fans from the magic glass shelves, they cradle her head gently, they soothe her with their talcum breaths.

"She's so pretty," they say, "like a munyika, a doll."

Later Virginie will smell that whiff, a mix of baby cologne and that odd ammoniac fragrance, Tiger Balm, on an airplane, and she will turn to the woman bearing the perfume, a complacent passenger staring at the airline menu, and ask the stranger: *Do you remember me?*

Get me out of here, Virginie weeps to her daughter in the mall, *get me out.*

The child combs the hair of her mother with a pearl-encrusted object, also from the magic glass.

"Mamma," Chiara remembers herself saying, "Mamma, it's okay."

8.

A Film with a Void at Its Heart

Chiara says that a visit to Samar is necessary for her spiritual journey.

"You know that's not a normal thing to say about Samar," Magsalin advises.

Chiara ignores her.

Chiara says she had a conversion online.

This is the part when, to Magsalin, as Chiara tells her story, the filmmaker lets down her guard.

Chiara gains a hint of, let's say, *embodiment*, shedding that slightly offensive look of tactful sedation. She finally takes the proffered pan de sal, buttering it up on all sides, crust and filling both, eating a lot, and her straight, bronzed hair gets caught in her shiny, jutting, expensively symmetrical upper teeth.

That is the effect she wants for her next movie, Chiara says.

It will be a film with a void at its heart.

Emotion will lie in the film's structure, like a silent grenade.

It will be set in 1901, or maybe 1972, or maybe 2018, in any case not quite her father's '68—no one will be the wiser. There will be unapologetic uses of generic types, actors with duplicating roles. Anachronisms, false starts, scarlet clues, a noirish insistence on the pathetic pursuit of human truths will pervade its miserable (quite thin) plot, and while the mystery will seem unsolved, to some it will provide the satisfaction of unrelieved despair.

After clicking on all the Balangiga items in her Google search, as far as page 102, Chiara says she cheated and began a new search. She finds fifty-seven articles by an Iranian journalist named Samar, and twenty more by her Jordanian counterpart also named Samar, before she narrows her search to "Balangiga Samar 1901." It is embarrassing to note Chiara's unscholarly search habits, but I imagine no one is unfamiliar with her process.

She had a conversion into the world of the Filipino insurrectos of 1901, Chiara says.

That is not the correct term, Magsalin says.

What?

They were revolutionaries, Magsalin says. It was not an insurrection.

Chiara ignores her.

It was as if, Chiara explains to Magsalin, she had entered a portal and become the body of a Filipino farmer disguised as a devout Catholic woman carrying a machete inside his voluminous peasant skirt and hoping to kill a GI.

"You were hallucinating," Magsalin points out. "Do you know what was really in the heirloom apple compote in your mother's castle in the Catskills? You know—too much limoncello has been known to go directly to the brain. In any case, the whole thing

just sounds, well, lame. An unearned case of white guilt. I'm sorry
if that is offensive."

"Oh. No worries. No offense taken."

Professor Estrella Espejo's papers on Balangiga, "*The Unintended*: A Consequence," parts 1, 3, and 6, were on kirjasto.com,
on two WordPress blogs by the same tenure-track assistant professor in San Diego, and on a remote server that, when clicked
upon, apologized for the inconvenience but due to copyright
questions, et cetera, et cetera. Chiara's efforts to find the scholar's
contacts were fruitless until she found an exchange in a Com-
ments section on inq7.net involving Espejo and Magsalin.

"Wait a minute," Magsalin demands. "When was this?"

Chiara takes out a leather-bound notebook from her huge
Hermès bag.

"August 15, 2000. You likened the, quote unquote, bitter,
essentializing determinist, Professor Estrella Espejo, to the
coyote in the Road Runner cartoons, saying, quote, like Wile
E. Coyote you keep setting your traps though it is only you
who bites, unquote."

"That was in reference to her loony-tunes theory that Juan
Luna, the Filipino painter, could be Jack the Ripper, you know,
like Juan the Ripper, just because he was also in Europe, like
the Ripper, around the same time Juan Luna killed his wife, Paz
Chiching Luna. She thinks that the death of Paz Chiching Luna
is the last Ripper death. Estrella Espejo is insane. For one thing,
Luna killed his wife in Paris, not London."

"You had another run-in with her in 2004."

"She gets these history worms in her head and won't let go."

"It was about my father's film."

"Yeah, yeah."

"You read closely the scene in which Tommy O'Connell shoots a woman and her daughter, who are hiding something in a rickshaw."

"They were hiding a book."

"It was a diary. You noted that the camera panned over a few quick words, meant to be in French, or maybe Vietnamese."

"It was supposed to be the diary of the woman's dead husband. It was supposed to be a list of his descriptions, his affecting trifling observations of his kid, the girl Tommy has just orphaned. The kid rides a merry-go-round; the kid won't get out of the swimming pool; the kid creates a pun, on the words *moon* and *comb*. There are receipts that fall from the book, there are photographs. And it is clear that the now dead mother and her child had only been trying to keep the father's personal possessions intact. That is what Tommy reads, in the sentimental scene that follows his murder of the kid's mother. Tommy had shot her in her gesture of self-defense, as mother and child tried to save the dead man's papers. In my view—that scene is the crux of his story. And onscreen, the actual words of the page in the dead man's journals, if you stopped the frame, are in Waray, my language—the language of Leyte and Samar."

"Your idea was that the sentences in my dad's film were actual pages from a diary of a revolutionary soldier in Samar in the Philippine-American War."

"In truth, no such diary has ever been found. The extant published records of the Philippine-American War are, as you know, in the words of the colonizer. But yes, I imagined your dad was alluding to the other war and making a connection. I wondered then why the Philippine diary, a red herring in his text, was so repressed in his film? Why was it that in his press conferences your dad made no references to the 1901 incident in Balangiga at all? I mean, as I said, look at the names in his movie: Smitty Jakes, Tommy O'Connell. Read *The Ordeal of Samar* and you have your dad's movie right there."

"I did."

"Read *The Ordeal of Samar*?"

"I got the Joseph Schott book, yes. It was disturbing, but not in ways that could make a good movie."

"So you cheated way more. You went off the Internet and read an actual book."

Chiara laughs. Then she asks: "So I want to know. Are you Professor Estrella Espejo?"

Magsalin almost topples off the stool. She starts coughing. The waitress offers her water and a napkin.

Magsalin takes a long sip.

"Hell, no," Magsalin says, putting down the glass. "I wouldn't be caught dead being Estrella Espejo. She's a lunatic with astasia-abasia tied up in IV tubes on an island in the South

China Sea. I mean the West Philippine Sea, depending on your disposition."

She stares at the filmmaker, daring her to contradict.

"Yeah, I know," says Chiara. "Estrella Espejo is something else. She told me to get in touch with you if I wanted to go to Balangiga. She said she could not help me because she's on an IV drip and unstable."

"You can say that again. Did she give you my email?"

"And cell."

"She's a shit."

"Pardon?"

"She makes things up in her head and won't let go. Take the details of your father's film. First, Charlie Company: the third company in every goddamned battalion is called Charlie. Or Charmed. Or Chicken. Anyone who took Citizens Army Training, as Espejo did, since she lived under Marcos's martial law, knows that. C Company just means third! It's not significant. Second, Smitty Jakes, Jacob Smith. Okay, sounds like. Tommy O'Connell, Thomas Connell—the similarity of the names is convincing. Clearly, one text is lifted from another. And she goes on and on making a case about *names*. But the point is not the coincidence of the naming, or even their intentional equivalence. The one-to-one correspondence between history and fiction is not so interesting. It's a logical fallacy to mistake the parallel with the important—it is not yet clear that God, you know, exists between parallel lines. I mean, if you are going to steal my idea, at least make something useful out of it. The question, it seems to me, is how to keep the past from recurring. I mean, what the fuck is the point of knowing history's goddamned repetitive spirals if we remain its bloody victims?"

"Do you think there are parallel universes and we are stuck in the one made up only of the bad movie plots?"

"I wonder if we are stuck in the bad movie plots we make ourselves," says Magsalin.

"I think we are stuck in someone's movie," says Chiara.

"Pardon?"

Magsalin looks hard behind Chiara Brasi's Chanel shades. Chiara will not take them off, even when she accidentally gets butter on them from the cinnamon buns. Now that Chiara has already buttered the pan de sal, she starts buttering the cinnamon buns, which are already buttered.

"I think we are stuck in someone's movie," says Chiara, "and the director is still laying out his scraps of script, trying to figure out his ending. He does not have an ending. Everything around him has the possibility of becoming part of his movie, his love for his wife, that seventies song, the fly over there licking the sugar on the bun, the clown in the corner playing with a knife, a moment in a mirror store in New York when he sees himself replicated through his camera lens in all the mirrors, except he cannot see his eyes, that schoolboy folding carefully a white shirt and tucking it neatly into a brown paper bag lying on a bench, an anxiety attack he has in 1975 when his movie is still not done, when it has a beginning and an idea but no end, and two million feet of unedited film, with takes, retakes, and other duplications. That is what we are: hundreds of thousands of feet of unedited film, doing things over and over, in a recursive spool, and we are waiting for the cut. But who is the director? What is our wait for? I would like to make a movie in which the spectator understands that she is in a work of someone else's construction, and yet as she watches, she is devising her own translations for the movie in which she in fact exists. It seems as if *The Unintended* were constructed out of the story of Samar, but the reverse is also true. *The Unintended* also produces, for us, the horror of Balangiga. We enter others' lives through two mediums, words and time, both faulty. And still, one story told may unbury another, and the dead, who knows, may be resurrected. At least, that is the hope. Recurrence is only an issue of not knowing how the film should end."

"So it's a zombie flick?" Magsalin asks.

"Well," Chiara hesitates, "it is not as meaningful as that."

Magsalin takes an index card and reads aloud the first Big Question:

"But is it about knowing how a film should end or not knowing its shape?"

"A film has no shape if it does not know its end."

Magsalin takes an index card and reads aloud the second Big Question:

"But is it about knowing how a film should end or that its end could be multiple, like desire's prongs?"

"*Touché.*"

Magsalin takes an index card and reads aloud the third Big Question:

"Why does a film persist at all?"

"A film exists only when it has an observer."

Magsalin takes an index card and reads aloud the fourth Big Question:

"Do you know that a clown is going to kidnap you?"

"In a mystery, clowns are always significant."

Magsalin takes an index card and reads aloud the last Big Question:

"What is in the manila envelope?"

"If you take it, you will see."

9.

The Thrilla in Manila

"Okay," says Magsalin, taking the envelope. "I'll see what I can do. I know some people. At the very least, maybe they can help you get to Samar, if I will not."

"Thank you," Chiara says, in that shy, nasal voice that is so annoying. "How do you get out of here?"

"Just follow the signs. There are detours for the exits. They're renovating, you know."

"Are you leaving too?"

Magsalin thinks she will take her up on it, on the forlorn implication in Chiara's little-girl voice that she would like some company, that Chiara is scared of Cubao and her impulsive clueless spiritual adventure to get to Samar, an idea that only people as rich and thoughtless as Chiara suddenly get in their heads and then stupidly follow through; and yes, Magsalin will lead her to the exit and get her safely through Cubao and then onto Roxas Boulevard (formerly Admiral George Dewey) straight down the length of the ancient bay to Chiara's rooms in the MacArthur Suite at the Manila Hotel.

"I want to take a spin around the mall," Magsalin says. "I'll hang around here a bit. Here's my address and phone, if you need me. Or I can see you sometime later at your hotel."

The waitress offers the check. Chiara offers her a credit card to pay. The waitress shakes her head. Magsalin takes out her non-Hermés bag, aubergine and olive, made in Venice.

She unzips the duffel and, carefully fishing around corners of the pale blue box that takes up too much space, she finds her wallet.

"I like your bag," Chiara says. "I have one exactly like it."

Sure you do, thinks Magsalin.

Magsalin pays with cash.

"Thanks," Chiara says.

"No problem."

They both stare at the poster of Muhammad Ali, sandwiched between sandwiches, as Magsalin waits for her change.

"My father saw that fight, you know. Ringside. They used to watch all those shows in the States, in Las Vegas. My dad liked boxing. My mom preferred Elvis Presley."

"You know, Ali and Elvis were friends. I think. I read that somewhere. Elvis gave Ali a sequined robe so they would look like twins when Elvis watched Muhammad Ali in Las Vegas."

"The robe said PEOPLE'S CHOICE," says Chiara.

"I know! But Ali was People's Champ," says Magsalin.

"I remember my mother sobbing when Elvis died," says Chiara.

"Everyone's mom sobbed when Elvis died. Even in Manila,"

says Magsalin. "You know, a woman journalist once met Muhammad Ali at an Elvis concert, and she asked him, so what are two African Americans like us doing in a concert like this, and Ali said, what are you talking about, I'm from Louisville, Kentucky—we listen to this music all the time! So, you know, you never know where the borderline of your own life is, the journalist said. Elvis could be in you."

"Sounds like a good thing," says Chiara.

"Actually, come to think of it, it was a Johnny Cash concert, not Elvis. Ali grew up with country. He listened to Johnny Cash."

When the waitress comes back with her change, Magsalin is not sure about the protocol, about when and how she can leave the filmmaker.

At Ali Mall, is she, Magsalin, the guest, or is it Chiara?

Magsalin clears her throat. "Um, it's amazing, though. What a thrilla that your parents saw Ali-Frazier in Manila in 1975."

Chiara perks up.

"Yeah. The Thrilla in Manila. At the time, we lived nearby in—let's see. I have it here in my notebook. Magallanes Village."

"That's in Makati, not Quezon City."

"Oh. The Internet was wrong."

"Figures."

"The Thrilla in Manila," Chiara repeats, and then she gets up, just like that, leaving Magsalin and the pan de sal shop without any warning.

Bitch.

Chiara is in the dark hallway, and Magsalin has to follow behind. The filmmaker is blocking Magsalin's exit and gazing, as if mentally noting its pros and cons as a film location, at the boarded-up space beyond Philippine Airlines, the scaffolding that might be a promised escalator or remnant of someone's change of mind.

"Muhammad Ali Mall. What an interesting tribute."

"Ali Mall," Magsalin corrects, wondering if Chiara will ever budge from the door. "That's what people call it. Its name is Ali Mall."

"I like it," Chiara turns and smiles at Magsalin. "I like tributes."

"I guess," says Magsalin.

"I once read all these books about the fight," Chiara says. "After my father finished *The Unintended*, you know, after the movie was done, my mother left Manila. He had this idea for another film. But my mother left. She was always doing that, leaving, then coming back. I was always with my mom. When he died, we kept moving. All over the place. New York. The south of France. She could not stay in one place for too long. Places suffocated her, she said. She had dizzy spells. I kept missing my father. I think she did, too. We lived in hotels. Hotels were her way of erasing things, maybe. She has this saying—about embracing the present. *One must embrace the present, Chiara—it is all we have!* I have never blamed my mother, you know. She did not know the ending of the story. How could anyone know? The last time my mother, my father, and I were all together was in Manila. The Thrilla in Manila. I've watched that match over and over again. On DVD. Round 6. When Ali says to Frazier . . ."

"'They tol' me Joe Frazier was all washed up!'"

"And Frazier goes . . ."

"'They . . . lied!'"

"Hah!" Chiara claps her hands. "You do a mean Frazier."

"Thank you. Were you for Ali or Frazier?" Magsalin asks.

"I love Muhammad Ali."

"Do you think he's real?"

"More real than I," says Chiara. "He's The Greatest."

Magsalin smiles. Just for that, she thinks, she'll do whatever this spoiled brat says.

"I am sorry about your parents," Magsalin says. "I am sorry about your father—"

"*Di niente.* It's my life. When I think of the world around me"—and Chiara's gaze does not wander, does not look at all at the world around her—"why should I complain?"

"Myself, I liked Frazier," says Magsalin.

"Really? But why?"

"Because he wasn't really an ugly motherfucker. He was no gorilla. Except Ali, the director, made him up."

10.

Translations

At first, what puts Magsalin off at the pastry shop is Chiara's voice. It is nasal, and her monotone, a bored flatness, even in the most interesting parts, keeps Magsalin, or the pastry shop waitress, or anyone else willing to listen amid the humid baking scones and moist pan de sal, at bay, as if an invisible wall, maybe socioeconomic, exists between Chiara's voice and your attention.

It is past one o'clock, and outside, the truant boys are shrugging back into their white button-down polo shirts, the uniform of all the Catholic schools that dot EDSA, done with their lunch-hour video games, and the circus men, on break from Fiesta Carnival, are wending their way out of the mall like blind mice, every clown in deep-black Ray-Ban knockoffs, wiping off rice grains and chorizo oil from their greasepaint lips.

And still Magsalin does not know what *she* has to do with Chiara's trip to Samar.

Was Chiara clutching the rough draft of the war-movie script that won her the prize among her peers that April afternoon in her mother's Catskills mansion?

Is Chiara's next project an art-house political film, à la

Costa-Gavras's *Z,* to be shot on location in the actual country in which the plot occurs, a film of dizzying, unheard-of realism, hence the need for translations into the actual language of the hapless citizens in the process of being killed by the occupation forces?

It is clear to Magsalin that Chiara is on a quest. Her elaborate Google search is suspect, a ruse, and the expository setting, the rural mansion of filmmaking bots, even if true, has the feeling of a patch over the real story.

Her arrival in Manila did not arise only from a ludic pastime, this play on her father's name.

In Samar, Chiara wishes to unlock a key.

About her father? About her script? About herself?

But what does Magsalin care about that?

Magsalin's taxable occupation is to translate, hence her professional name: Magsalin. (It means *to translate* in her maternal grandfather's tongue, Tagalog.) Her English-language website, translationsforhire.net, says as much.

Magsalin is aware of those scenes in Hollywood movies when, requiring an actor to speak in a conveniently alien tongue, the character starts speaking an inappropriate one, like Tagalog. The prayer of the Javanese man in *The Year of Living Dangerously.* The possessed woman hissing at Keanu Reeves in *Constantine.* Farm workers who chase the, as usual, somewhat psychotic Joaquin Phoenix far into a senseless desert in one of those unbearably tense movies by Paul Thomas Anderson.

And, of course, the Ewoks scenes in *Star Wars: Episode VI—Return of the Jedi*.

In the trade, there are terms for those short-term projects.

Inversions provide a set of unmatched signifiers that, if understood, do not require logical coherence. This is the case of the Bahasa-Indonesian prayer in Peter Weir's movie. The Indonesian prays the "Our Father" in Tagalog, not Bahasa—that is, he need not be coherent. It's the concept that counts.

Inversions are opposed to *obversions*, that is, providing a set of unmatched signifiers that, if understood, are generally insulting. The Ewok dialogue in the *Star Wars* prequel, a few choice Tagalog epigrams, is a basic Filipino fuck-you to the universe.

Diversions, like the irate Filipino farm workers in Stockton, California, in Anderson's *The Master*, are plausible, though irrelevant in the overall scheme of things.

What Magsalin expects is that Chiara's script will require *reversions*: a set of matching signifiers that, if reversed, will portray the privileged language as in fact the other, and vice versa.

Perversions, of course, produce scant good.

Lastly, *conversions*, in which one exists like a vestigial body, a desiring corpus, occupied by the words of others, is the most difficult of these types of translations: Magsalin simply refuses to attempt them.

What interests Magsalin most about Chiara is not the prospect of a job but the filmmaker's likely disappearance. In her mystery novel, Chiara will leave Ali Mall by a wrong turn, through the plywood board tunnel, a sign announcing the mall owner's promise of a NEW ALI MALL! COMING SOON!—put up ten years ago. The security guard, looking up from his cell phone, will give Chiara clear directions in English, but she will not understand his accent.

Chiara has a sense of being lost amid the warped plywood, the tunnel is so spooky and haphazard it has the impression of not even being lit, though makeshift electrical wires become obvious once her vision adjusts. The tunnel spills into the harsh light of the fluorescent bulbs of the decaying merry-go-round outside, where tricycle drivers waiting for clients pick their teeth on ill-painted horses.

Magsalin knows the area well from her days as a serial bookworm roaming Alemar's and the vaster though soulless National Bookstore, when she went to school nearby. It occurs to her now that the details she has evoked in the last few sentences might bear traces of her memory's obsolescence and Chiara's plaintive future; therefore, her kidnapping by a pair of muscular, Ray-Ban-wearing goons is in fact set among details of a vanished world.

Of course, the goons are dressed as clowns, in matching puffed-sleeve blouses and billowing striped trousers made of sad flour-sack cotton, their look of cheap improvisation a mark of the ongoing decline of Fiesta Carnival, the venerable old circus of Cubao, next door to Ali Mall.

Chiara's struggle will be unseen, though one might expect a stray schoolboy to be lighting a match nearby, polo shirt half on, the gothic logo of the band AC/DC, or maybe Metallica, partly visible on his muscle shirt (he's actually a bit malnourished); but the irony is that the boy, smoking his last cigarette before he's expected in gym class, will be looking at the comic book he has just bought with carefully saved change. Struggling into his shirt and reading his comic, he is in no state to observe a famous film director being shoved into a waiting tricycle, an ordinary passenger pedicab painted in the usual deranged Manila hues.

11.

Magsalin, on the Other Hand, Will Be Wandering

Magsalin, on the other hand, will be wandering Ali Mall. Done with the exhausting interview with the filmmaker and feeling a bit nauseated amid the steamy cinnamon buns (the bakery smog was making her groggy), Magsalin clutches the thick manila envelope Chiara has given her and travels Ali Mall in a daze.

The mall is now quite modern, practically Singaporean; at the same time, its familiarity is distracting. There is a schizoid confabulation between the new upscale fixtures, such as the shiny escalators and neon in the Food Court, which now looks like a strip club, and the ratty hair accessories wrapped in dust-holed plastic that seem to have been in the Cardam's chain of shoe shops since they opened in 1976. What is true perhaps is that, after the vertigo of listening to the story of Chiara Brasi, Magsalin feels unreal, and the world has an illusory aspect, part memory, part script, the split state of a spectator awkwardly providing her own unpaid translations in a movie in which she in fact exists.

25.

Its Molting Spirals

At the hotel in Hong Kong, unknown to her daughter, Virginie sees visions. She is looking for ice. Down the hotel corridor she follows the curls of the carpet's tracks neatly along its molting spirals—once, when she looks back, she is startled to see the zoological humps of her footsteps' former map disappearing at her glance. The whorled carpet behind her has turned white, or fogged. It must be her dizziness (her vision troubles her, but she refuses to wear her glasses), a trick of her strained eyes. She shrugs the vanishing off. As she turns and weaves along the serpentine trail of the carpet's dragon-tail design, tottering along the amphisbaena spines in her insomniac stilettos, Virginie follows the spiral toward the sign that says ICE, in English, then in Mandarin. She has been having these visions, she tells her doctor. It is up to her to contain them, he says. He means, she explains to Ludo, she must patch herself up on her own, without anyone's help. But what's a doctor for? Ludo is perplexed. If you are seeing visions, does your doctor not have a cure? Ludo does not agree: why shouldn't he, her husband, help? Because, she thinks, you are already whole, you will not understand, but she does not tell him that.

She sees the man, in his fractured tassels, all in white, like some specular void slowly transforming, a sweating beast. He is filling up a silver bucket, and behind him, dreamily, she waits in line.

12.

What Chiara Does Not Reveal

Is what Magsalin does not reveal to Chiara—

13.

A Motif of the Postmodern

A motif of the postmodern, renovated Ali Mall is a series of commissioned portraits of the boxer framed in glass at strategic points, like altars. The reflexive signifiers, several of them ugly, are not tongue in cheek. They are serious gestures of commercial veneration. One portrait has a wilted flower on its ledge, left by an admirer (candy wrappers and cigarette stubs also decorate the shrine). The corporate intention of co-opting The Greatest in order to shill shoes is obvious. But the populist beauty of the display—the portraits that modify the mall and the mall that is an appositive of the portraits—is attractive. Sheer presence confounds purpose.

The portraits do make Ali as absurd as the corporation that hopes to promote meaning from public displays of dumb idolatry. But at the same time, passing by the Muhammad Ali altars, at first in horror, at several points laughing out loud, Magsalin is increasingly attached. She spends the afternoon searching the mall for all the altars. One, a giant billboard, painted in painstaking flatness, makes Ali's nose as big as the letter A in the word *CHAMPION*. It has graffiti all around it. But when you look close, expecting obscenity, instead you find sincere compliments, some of them mistaken: *ali is da greatest! I saw the HBO, THRILLA! r.i.p. Muhammad Ali, floats like a butterfly, sings like a bee.* At this point, though in the future it will change, Muhammad Ali is still alive. In these scrawls, even the errors count. In another, a cubist Ali in a relaxed pose, bold and allusive, looks like Pablo Picasso in an early self-portrait, the one in which he is wearing a striped camisa. Another illustrates a Filipino pantheon of assorted black idols, Stevie Wonder, Michael Jackson, Kareem Abdul Jabbar, the kid from *Diff'rent Strokes*, one more idolized basketball player—Magic Johnson, Diana Ross, of course, then Gloria Gaynor of "I Will Survive" fame, and their forefather, Muhammad Ali, descending in order somewhat like Marcel Duchamp's *Nude Descending a Staircase*, but not. To pan on each of these is a slice of time, precious in a movie, so the viewer does wonder at their meanings, juxtaposed as they are with a kidnapping that has been left hanging.

14.

The M.O. of Clowns

Chiara understands that a kidnapping in the open air in a busy city like Manila has many risks. Plus, the country has become an icon of extrajudicial horror, a dystopia of brazen exterminations even in broad daylight, an international emblem of criminal slaughter by fascist police.

Clowns add an awkward design to this brutality.

Already, with her director's eye, Chiara is noting all the problems that will occur in the editing room. Any viewer might mentally record the taxi drivers on the idle carousel as possible witnesses of the initial event: a clown shoving the film director into a passenger pedicab, then following her in. Chiara, trapped in this cramped cab appendage both flimsy and baroque, notes that the slow, clunky spasms of the pedicab indicate that it has no care in the world, as speed makes no money in the city. And the stupid, voluminous clown costume crowding the interior interferes with the position of a knife blade in the clown's hand, which she suddenly feels, jostling at her exposed shoulder.

Then what the hell?

Sitting on a seat she would never have mistaken for one, a padded bump parallel to the driver, perpendicular to Chiara and facing the street—there is a second clown!

Where the fuck did that clown come from?

The spatial logistics in a passenger pedicab in metropolitan Manila are too absurd to bear.

The second clown grabs her Hermès bag.

Magsalin has to decide on the spot whether the driver, too, is integral to her mystery, or only a pathetic bystander worried about making boundary, his daily bread. Whereas Chiara, obviously more experienced at exploiting suspense, sizes up the driver's irrelevance, accomplice or not, and knows she has only a split second—though in the actual footage ideally there should be several camera angles to consider despite the singleness of the decisive moment—and she ups the ante.

Chiara fights for her bag.

It is, after all, an Hermès.

It also contains her notes.

This is not the right thing to do.

Fighting for your bag usually kills you. Self-defense classes always tell you to give everything up, no questions asked. Magsalin, a paranoiac, expecting trouble at the unlikeliest moment like every alert, vulnerable woman in a city, does not even consider it in her story. However, Chiara's desperate gestures catch the attention of a passenger about to get off a bus on a crosswalk on EDSA. Up on the bus, the tired employee of the Commission on Audit happens to have a bird's-eye view of the blonde girl in the tricycle grabbing back her bag.

You see—and the crime statistics in Manila are no mere trope in this mystery, though it is clear Magsalin has overlooked these facts, having been gone for so long—this incident has happened to the government employee before.

Many women riding public transportation in Manila know the m.o. of clowns.

It is one of those miracles that still occur in an overcrowded city, a city of twelve million—give or take the numbers in dawn-versus-dusk traffic, plus the rising death rate in this beleaguered place—where coincidences are just as likely as not. The hyperactive (atypical) policeman at the curb gives chase on the tip from the eagle-eyed woman who has just gotten off the Monumento–Quezon Avenue express. The woman follows the policeman. She is that kind of busybody, always wanting to know the denouement.

Then crowds of extras swell the scene—jeepney riders who impulsively change their minds and decide to catch the next one, vagrants, passing salesmen, fugitive drug addicts, cigarette smokers who always stop for a quick light before taking a bus, sign painters, child flower sellers in the grip of crime syndicates, a pregnant woman, of course, and all of Manila's bystanders who every day dream of being on their favorite detective show, *CSI*.

They are frustrated in their expectation of a chase because of the traffic. The pedicab gets stuck amid a diesel dragnet of belching buses.

An ominous motorbike with two men riding in tandem weaves a remarkable path through the cars, vehicles waving the motorbike through as it beeps an onomatopoeic *tokhang tokhang tokhang*, and the motorbike whizzes away.

But the clowns are trapped.

Needing only to take a few quick anticlimactic steps, the policeman taps the pedicab driver on the shoulder as he is making an illegal move. Three traffic policemen at the corner of Quezon Avenue are now also on the scene, only to discover no one has handcuffs. The clowns understand their game is up, and they try to rush out the cab, but the crowd is up in arms, happy to be saviors, not the salvaged this time, and taxicabs are honking, and the tricycle driver is explaining to the police—there he was, just sitting on this merry-go-round outside of Ali Mall, waiting for customers, when two clowns entered his cab.

In the melee, Chiara is forgotten. Umbrellas, folded news-papers, fragrant sampaguita leis, policeman's batuta, they all rhythmically go up and down in the narrow frame of this thrilling crowd scene, pounding on the hapless clowns, and momentarily one's empathy falls on the criminals, if one is that kind of viewer, until someone, a smartass film buff, recognizes Chiara Brasi and diverts everyone's attention.

"OMG! It's Chiara Brasi! You know. She made *Circular Ruins*, about Stone Age fucking zombies! And *Dr. Quevedo's Columbarium*, the sequel to *The Urn Burial*! You know. She made the videos for the punk group Dwarves in Space! And the last Ukrainian Eurovision entry, Chicks Kiev, a lively a cappella quartet clicking castanets!"

Clearly he is one of those fond Filipino fans, glued to the Internet, connoisseur of the hip and the famous, K-pop stars, cult auteurs, and such, knowing the obscurest points of his idol's IMDb page, including the minutiae embarrassing to the film-maker. He instantly multitasks, text-messaging, trying to get her picture with his phone, but he's low-batt, and his phone makes one of those desperate bleeps that announces it will soon shut down.

Now the crowd has turned from the clowns to the filmmaker, including the policemen, and for a minute there it seems the point of the spectacle will be foiled and the goons will escape in the crowd's stampede to get the celebrity's autograph.

But of course that does not happen. A bunch of urchins saves the day and sits on the costumed criminals, while a policeman comes back with the missing handcuffs to take the clowns in custody, and sundry bystanders look on with their makeshift weapons—tabloid journals and those old-fashioned lace fans that unfold to show watercolor scenes of Spaniards in hair combs and mantillas, doing flamenco dancing.

Everyone is a bit out of breath.

No one knows any of the films the hyperventilating buff is talking about (the elderly among them having spent their lives watching kung fu movies on the Sunday Chinese channels, and Charlton Heston in *The Ten Commandments*, during Lent), but it is clear that Chiara Brasi, rising out of the passenger pedicab, is one to whom the glare of the spotlight is as ordinary as stirring coffee or scratching an armpit. She steps out, her bronzed hair in her eyes, a wan and wavering figure, carrying her bag and a look of command. She stops a news photographer from taking her picture (GMA-7 is the first to arrive, since their towers are nearby), holding up an imperious hand that smartly also covers her face, and with the other she waves: "Taxi!"

She is gone before the traffic cops can get their reward.

15.

The Need to Forget

Magsalin admires Chiara's plot choices as she watches them play out on the evening news.

Ludovico Brasi's Daughter in Streetcar Scuffle! Film Director Sends Off the Clowns in Cubao! If you witnessed the true-crime scene of vehicular drama, text 092172-050916 with your eyewitness account or send your cellphone video!

That heroic gambit with the Hermès bag takes the lead on GMA-7, complete with actor simulations of the bumpy pedicab ride. On Channel 9, the woman eyewitness from the Monumento bus on EDSA narrates the foreigner's trauma, basing the victim's emotions on her own intimate experience with clowns. Technically, it is the eyewitness from the bus who provides all the quotes. She is flustered by the moment. She is the heroine.

Chiara Brasi's fuzzy, half-covered face, shiny hair falling across her vacant gaze (which Magsalin now understands is her regular expression, her RCF: resting celebrity face), shot by dozens of cell phones, flickers across the TV screen, giving legitimacy to the celebrity hour. The movie fan on the spot also counts off with satisfaction the music videos Chiara Brasi has made, adding to the mix the songs of the up-and-coming folkie/ska group, the Osmond Others, and the Muslim-American girl band Averroes's Search (three gorgeous sisters discovered in a mosque in Detroit), and the music of several Nico wannabes, mostly pleasant Scandinavian art students.

And of course, interspersed with the mugs of the bungling buffoons and shots of suspect pedicabs behind Ali Mall are iconic scenes from Chiara's father's famous movie, *The Unintended*: haunting shots of a lush, ravaged Philippine countryside in the seventies.

It is just as well, Magsalin thinks, taking out the sheets of paper from Chiara's manila envelope, as she stares at the computer screen. It is too early in the novel for the heroine to disappear. And the idea of a kidnapping by passenger pedicab is dumb. I mean, in the open Manila air! Transportation is the third most overlooked quotidian detail in mysteries (the two most overlooked: eating and going to the toilet). And tricycles are not allowed on EDSA. Plus, that was too much fun with clowns. Clowns are people, too.

Still, one can learn from it.

The anticipatory anxiety arising from a vulnerable woman's presence in the plot dissipates with the Aristotelian double plot arrangement of kidnapping plus rescue. Any viewer of Disney is wise to the poetic function of such opening scenes. Magsalin admires how the filmmaker accurately predicts the rescue scene's place in the drama, saving her life in the bargain, no mean feat. The episode marks pathos then dissolves it, allowing the viewer time to attach—and then forget. A writer plots even how we forget.

16, also 26.

The Model for the Photographer

Maybe it is Virginie's posture—always a bit slouched, though not quite awkward—that makes her seem unaware of her power. Even in sleep upon a wicker butaka, cheeks checkered by abaca twine, or vigorously gardening in the tropics with her mouth open, red bandana fluttering against monsoon winds that make wild commas of her hair, Virginie has a touching look that her otherwise embarrassingly pampered life fails to obscure.

She is inept rather than thoughtless—those dashes across the ocean, for instance. She is quick to the draw and always has cash. She leaves and comes back to Ludo in his studio, who is rearranging his index cards, reading a book. What is it you want, what is it you want? He gives her a camera, a tripod. She leaves and comes back. How many times has she carried her baby, four-year-old Chiara, in an Igorot blanket onto private, chartered planes? Chiara would find herself all alone in a hotel suite in Hong Kong or Macau, staring at the scarily erect arrangement of three cattleya orchids triplicated in the mirrors, with her small curly head in triple counterpoint to the infinite trinity of her father's absence.

Magsalin lines up with care the vertiginity of the triptych impressions.

Those midnight migrations in grandiose and sterile rooms would haunt Chiara's childhood, though now her memories are blurred, and her mother, emerging in a white bathrobe from her suite and offering her a guava, Chiara's favorite fruit, taste acquired in the tropics, looks for all the world as if nothing were the matter. Virginie's image in white bathrobe and silver stilettos—Virginie looks vaguely like Gena Rowlands, or Mrs. Robinson in *The Graduate* (an involuntary resemblance—but the cheap trick that pop culture plays on her daughter happens to the best of us)—her image burns in Chiara's mind, a warning: her beautiful mother of the bedlam rests, sleeping so deeply after a long day of gardening and watering orchids, slumped with mouth open in that awkward rocking chair in Magallanes Village, in Makati, not Quezon City. If it were not for the occasional spasm of Virginie's slim foot dangling from the creaking butaka, little Chiara would imagine her mother dead.

17.

The Dossier Magsalin Receives

The sheets of paper look like a script. Are there also drawings? Magsalin shakes out prints of Samar in 1901, ordered from the Library of Congress Prints and Photographs Division (the receipts fall out, too, from the envelope): index card–size pictures against yellowed boards—pictures of banana groves, dead bodies in gray trenches, GIs in dress fatigues gazing down as if in regret at a charred battleground.

Each of the pictures is doubled. Each card is a set of thick, twinned prints, the prints pasted side by side on stiff panels. All are roughly postcard-size.

They are late-nineteenth-century stereo cards.

You look closely at the twin pictures as if presented with one of those optical illusions that should come with the caption, *Find What's Missing!* But there is nothing missing to find: the two pictures on each stereo card are identical.

Only a slight time lapse, undetectable, indicates difference.

Difference produces perspective.

On the Library of Congress website, www.loc.gov, search "Philippine insurrection," and you come across them. Archived stereo pairs from the years 1899 to 1913, the bleak years of US imperial aggression before the surrender of the last Filipino forces to American occupation. You may as well just copy and paste the gist. *Soldiers wading across a shallow river, advancing through open country, et cetera. A group of men with crates of food on the beach, et cetera. A burned section of Manila. The burned quarters of rebel president, Aguinaldo. Firefighting measures. Artillery. Ducks swimming. Children wading. Soldier burying a dead "insurgent." Soldier showing off the barrel of his Colt .45. Et cetera.*

Et cetera. A history in ellipses, too obscure to know. Not to mention the words in quotes and not. "Insurgents" are in quotes. Insurrection is not. Rebel is a problematic term. History is not fully annotated or adequately contemplated in online archives.

The puzzling duplication becomes mere trope, a cliché. Photographic captions rebuke losers and winners alike. "Soldiers," for instance, refer only to white males. "Burned" does not suggest who has done the burning. "Firefighting measures" is a generous term, given the circumstances.

Magsalin looks with impatience at the familiar photos among Chiara Brasi's papers falling from the manila envelope.

The pictures of the dead Filipino bodies and the burned Filipino towns are remarkably precise.

But they are hard to see.

The passivity of a photographic record might be relieved only by the viewer the photographs produce. And even then, not all types of viewers are ideal. Photographs of a captured country shot through the lens of the captor possess layers of ambiguity too confusing to grasp:

there is the eye of the victim, the captured, stilled and muted and hallowed in mud and time;

there is the eye of the victim, the captured, who may be bystander, belligerent, blameless, blamed—though there are subtle shifts in pathetic balance, who is to measure them?;

there is the eye of the colonized viewing their captured history in the distance created by time;

there is the eye of the captor, the soldier, who has just wounded the captured;

there is the eye of the captor, the Colonizer who has captured history's lens;

there is the eye of the citizens, bystander, belligerent, blameless, blamed, whose history has colonized the captured in the distance created by time;

and there is the eye of the actual photographer: the one who captured the captured and the captors in his camera's lens—what the hell was *he* thinking?

27.

Elvis Is Polite and Longs for Love

On January 14, 1973, Elvis Aaron Presley is caught in a trap. He can't go on, because he loves you so much, baby. He broadcasts via satellite *Aloha from Hawaii*, singing from the Honolulu International Hotel straight into the living rooms of women everywhere but most of all into the hearts of virgins and their mothers in Guam, Indonesia, the Philippines, South Korea, Australia, and Hong Kong. None of his biographies mention that he ever alighted in Asia after his stint in the Korean War, which he spent in Germany. But years later *Aloha from Hawaii* was bootlegged and smuggled into Colombo, Rangoon, Kandahar, Tehran, Kuala Lumpur, Thimphu. It is Elvis's global smash. It breaks records. It excites Buddhist maidens of the Theravada and Mahayana persuasions alike. Modern Persians, before the revolution, dance to Elvis. Catholics in New Delhi and Christians in Kampuchea, in the silent attitude of prayer, also watch Elvis.

His stopover at the Hong Kong Peninsula, the finest hotel east of the Suez, is disavowed by the fact that Colonel Parker, that control-freak carny, his agent, refused to book him on foreign tours, ever, at all, for reasons still unmentionable. Though the Hong Kong Peninsula Hotel, with its gleam and its gold and its filigree, a corporate wet dream in marble, seems to have much in common with costumed Elvis, the fact is, Elvis hates the banality of hotels. He hates the lonesomeness of traveling. He sings at Vegas only because the women love him. It is love that energizes Elvis. And politeness. Elvis is polite and longs for love. To the benefit of Colonel Parker, he has no wish to disappoint.

The fan magazines show touching photos of the star clutching teddy bears to his chest, *you're oh, oh, oh, my Teddy Beaaar!* Fans keep mailing him teddy bears, and Elvis keeps them. Soon his mansion is filling up with teddy bears, but he does not have the heart to discard them. When he dies, no one knows what to do with them, the mounds of teddy bears. His heartfelt grin in movie magazines is both embarrassed by his sentimentality and aware of its effects. Elvis even in his stills expresses a double consciousness. He is both the woman seduced and the seducer. It is hard in the lyrics to tell him apart from his listener: *You know I can be found, sitting home all alone!* And to the women all shook up, he sings: *My friends say I'm shakin' as wild as a bug. Uhuhuhuuuu.*

All he does is repeat their words.

He says what the hearers want: to be heard.

He is their voice, but also their looking-glass eye, panopticon of their desire.

Sensing the woman on the penthouse floor of the Peninsula waiting for his bucket to fill up, he tries to hurry the spigot by pressing on it, while his feet shake the way they always do, as if he cannot help it (he cannot), and his thighs, in absolute precise rhythm (in his head, Elvis can watch himself moving, a metronome pelvis ticking in his brain), moving just—so!—his thighs moving with the spill of the spigot while the ice slurs, clank, clank, clank, clank, clank, into his ice bucket.

Virginie stares at his shaking back, the man's wavering tassels of white, all in white, like some specular void slowly transforming, a sweating beast. He is filling up a silver bucket, and behind him, dreamily, she waits for her turn as he moves.

When she wakes up, her hand is still on her body, a warmth pervades her in the hotel in Hong Kong, despite the ice. The minute she had left Ludo out there in Pampanga, or Makati, or wherever it was he happened to be after *The Unintended*—the minute she left him, she missed him. In the dream, she does not know if she is coming in the dream or in her hands, and in this way, it seems, the moment of her coming goes on in infinity. Arousal for her is like this. She comes several times in her hands, and she comes several times in her dream, and it is an oddly comforting kind of vertigo, this chain, this superior sleep a woman can have, she thinks, the potential for multiple orgasms suggests that the superior sleep a woman can have lies in the possibility of orgasmic infinity, her eternal arousal, she is moving her hands over her body, her vibrant cunt, the way a vagina kind of buzzes, a tender undulant thing, so alert, so alive. This vagrant pleasure, controlled by her own hands. In the dream, she recognizes she is in a dream. She can feel the dream of her desire and

its consequences reverberating, a concatenation, this infinity—
the way she orgasms, a multiple chain of arousals, and it doesn't
matter anymore whether it's dream or reality; her body is con-
vulsing, warm and powerful and hers, she is depleted and sated,
she shakes to her hands' rhythms, she is replete. She sleeps.

21.

The Photographer at
the Heart of the Script

The photographer at the heart of the script is a woman, of course. Magsalin casts around for her adequate replica. No problem: there are enough white people to go around. The infamous photographer of the Philippine-American War abandons a restrictive, Henry James–type *Washington Square* existence to become bold witness of the turn of her century. She is a beauty with a touching look that her otherwise embarrassingly pampered life fails to obscure. Her name, whether classical allusion, cinematic alias, or personal cryptogram, is still forthcoming—Calliope, or Camille, or Cassandra.

It is 1901.

She is not alone.

The great commercial photographer, Frances Benjamin Johnston, has already scooped the men of her day with her photos of Admiral George Dewey, the victor of Manila sailing leisurely around the world in semi-retirement. Admiral George Dewey is lounging on his battleship *Olympia*, docked in Amsterdam (now on display, a floating historical gem, at Philly Seaport Museum).

In 1898, the USS *Olympia* had fired the salvos at Spain's empty ships in Manila Bay. Frances Benjamin Johnston's photographs of arresting domesticity on a battleship a year after the famed battle are celebrated in *Ladies' Home Journal* and *Cosmopolitan*. The way she tames war for her nation is superb—Admiral George Dewey with his lazy dog Bob, sailors dancing cheek to cheek on deck like foretold Jerome Robbins extras, pristine soldiers in dress whites on pristine white hammocks, and the admiral looking at photographs of himself, with the Victorian photographer in white Chantilly lace by his side.

It is easy to imagine Chiara, reading a library book in the Catskills, *Dewey the Defender* or *Neely's Photographs: Fighting in the Philippines*, stumbling upon the idea of the photographer on the scene of the atrocities in Balangiga. It is the photographer's lens, after all, that astounds the courtroom in the four courts-martial that troubled America in 1902: the trial of General Jacob "Howling Wilderness" Smith; of his lieutenant, the daring Marine, Augustus Littleton "Tony" Waller; of the passionate and voluble witness, Sergeant John Day; and of the water-cure innovator, Major Edwin Glenn (the rest of the men who slaughtered the citizens of Samar are untried).

America is riveted by the scandal, as pictures of the Filipino dead in the coconut fields of Samar are described in smuggled letters to the *New York Herald* and the *Springfield Republican*. They are like bodies in mud dragged to death by a typhoon, landing far away from home.

Propriety bans the pictures' publication, but damage is done.

The pictures have no captions: *Women cradling their naked babies at their breasts. A woman's thighs spread open on a blanket, her baby's head thrust against her vagina. A dead child sprawled in the middle of a road. A naked girl running toward the viewer in a field, her arms outstretched, as if waving. A beheaded, naked body splayed against a bamboo fence. A child's arms spread out on the ground, in the shape of a cross. A woman holding the body of her dead husband, in the pose of the Pietà.* The congressional hearings on the affairs of the Philippine islands, organized in January 1902 in the aftermath of the Samar scandal, hold a moment of silence.

True, the photographer's fame is split.

Senator Albert J. Beveridge, Republican of Indiana, globetrotting imperialist, calls Cassandra a traitor to her class.

She should highlight the Americans who were victims of slaughter, not their enemies who deserve their fate!

She is a vulgar creature not fit to be called citizen, much less woman!

Senator George Frisbie Hoar, Republican of Massachusetts, homegrown anti-imperialist, nemesis of William McKinley and then of his rash successor Theodore Roosevelt, calls her a hero of her time.

Senator Hoar famously accuses his own party's president in the aftermath of the Samar trials: "You have devastated provinces. You have slain uncounted thousands of the people you desire to benefit. You have established reconcentration camps.

Your generals are coming home from their harvest bringing sheaves with them, in the shape of other thousands of sick and wounded and insane to drag out miserable lives, wrecked in body and mind. You make the American flag in the eyes of a numerous people the emblem of sacrilege in Christian churches, and of the burning of human dwellings, and of the horror of the water torture."

Save for a few points of wishful thinking, his words ring:

"Your practical statesmanship has succeeded in converting a people who three years ago were ready to kiss the hem of the garment of the American and to welcome him as a liberator, who thronged after your men when they landed on those islands with benediction and gratitude, into sullen and irreconcilable enemies, possessed of a hatred which centuries can not eradicate."

True that. (At least until 1944, and all is forgotten.)

It is easy for a reader to overlay this calamity with others, in which the notion of arriving as liberators turns out to be a delusion or a lie.

And it would be easy for Chiara to overlay montages of her own childhood with that of her possible heroine: the baby among maids brought out for display at lunch parties on Park Avenue; the birthday girl whose abundance of presents includes her mother's monsoon weeping; objects of her desire in silent parade—rosewood stereographs and magic lanterns and praxinoscopes and stereo pairs from the photographic company with the aptly doubled name, Underwood & Underwood—her souvenir snapshots from hotels around the world—and an antique set of collectible prints captioned "nature scenes": Mount Rushmore, waterfalls, black children, Hawaiian pineapples, Igorot men, cockfights.

Chiara's world can be seen as an easy stand-in, in sepia wash, for nineteenth-century Cassandras. The movie's white-petticoated protagonist clutches the old Brownie camera that is Chiara's prized possession.

The photographer will be one of those creatures beyond her time and yet so clearly of it, beloved of film and epic, with a commanding presence heightened by the backwaters in which she lives and oblivious of the trap in which she exists, that is, her womanhood.

The script, as Magsalin sees it, creates that vexing sense of vertigo in stories within stories within stories that begin too abruptly, in medias res.

Cassandra Chase's presence in Samar is a quandary for the military officers. The enterprise of the Americans on the islands is so precarious, perilous, and uncertain that the burden of the traveler's arrival in wind-driven bancas, rowed by two opportunists, a pair of local teenagers who hand off Cassandra's trunks to the porters with an exaggerated avidity that means she has overpaid them, gives Captain Thomas Connell in Balangiga a premonition of the inadequacy of his new letters of command.

Who has jurisdiction in Samar if a mere slip of a woman in a billowing silk gown completely inappropriate to the weather and her situation flouts General Smith's orders in Tacloban and manages the journey across the strait and down the river anyway on her own steam, with her diplopia and diplomatic seals intact, a spiral of lace in her wake, a wavering tassel of white, complete with trunks full of cameras and Zeiss lenses and glass plates for her demoniacal duplicating photographic prints?

18.

In Punta

In the taxi from Manila Hotel, Chiara reads the email attachment from the translator.

She barely registers Magsalin's pleasantries, how nice it was to meet! etc. She reads online in the cursory way she was never taught at school—in school she had to annotate, then look up words in the *O.E.D.*, then give a synopsis of her incomprehension. School drove her nuts. Slow reading is an art, her teachers kept saying, but their catechism was no insurance against her unraveling. School gave her migraines: teachers kept telling her to expand on her thoughts when she had none that merited expanding. Her brain was a ball of hair in a bath drain, as miserably dense as it was inert. A mess. She did not regret dropping out. True, she more or less went on a drug trip punctuated by luxury tourism and psychiatric disaster. The result was her first movie, *Slouching toward Slovenia*, a study of apathy and melancholia that became an indie sensation, though all she wanted was to portray a certain patch of light on a beach in Ancona, against the Adriatic. Her success was called precocious by some, nepotistic by others, but Chiara understands the stability her enterprise provides—only in making films does she have clarity: there is nothing outside the lens.

Chiara scrolls through the attachment, barely reading the words but taking in without question the insult she is meant to feel—the normal way one reads on the Internet. Libel suits are a hazard of fast reading. She begins typing furiously on her iPad as the taxi careens. After all, Chiara has a right to be angry. After all, she is already a crime statistic in Manila's traffic bulletins. The last few hours of rest at the Manila Hotel have not eased her feeling that the city of Manila wants her dead.

Chiara barely acknowledges the taxicab driver's deep bow as he pockets her tip. Her presence at the front door of Magsalin's home in Punta has the same substance as her online tone: unapologetic, admitting only of intentions relevant to herself.

If Chiara were not so tiny, wide-eyed, looking a bit troubled in her skewed, though still faintly perfumed tank top (you see, the maid catches Chiara's naked expression of distress despite the arrogant blue eyes' barely glancing at her, the servant, who could shut the door on her face), the latecomer would never have been welcomed into Magsalin's home—the home of the three bachelor uncles from Magsalin's maternal line: Nemesio, Exequiel, and Ambrosio, inseparable in their diaspora.

Midnight in Manila is no comfort for strangers. Servants in this section of Manila are justly wary of knocks on the door. Corrupt barangay chairmen harass them for tong, doleful bandits pretend to be someone's long-lost nephew, serial drunks keep mistaking the same dark, shuttered home for their own. And of course, now in this drug-war world of tokhang: toktok-hangyo: knock-knock, plead-plead, or so Magsalin translates the glib coinage of this new regime—the drug-war policeman will knock on your door, and whether you open or do not open, you are doomed.

Chiara does not notice at first that the address Magsalin had scribbled on the bake shop's napkin is a haunted avenue in leafy, cobblestoned disrepair, full of deciduous shadows, aging tenements of purposeless nostalgia amid wild, howling cats, and the occult strains of stupid disco music.

Chiara registers that the location has a disjoint familiarity, like a film set in which she has carefully restored elements of a childhood by dispatching minions to gather her recollections, so that her memory becomes oddly replete, though only reconstructed through the inspired empathy of others. Such is the communality of a film's endeavor that magic of this sort never disconcerts Chiara. Life for Chiara has always been the imminent confabulation of her desires with the world's potential to fulfill them. So while the street and its sounds have an eerie sense of a past coming back to bite her, Chiara also dismisses the eerie feeling. She steps into the foyer of the old mahogany home without even a thank-you to the maid, who against her better judgment hurries away at the director's bidding to fetch the person she demands, Magsalin.

"I DID NOT give you the manuscript in order for you to revise it," Chiara begins without introduction.

"Pleased to see you again, too," says Magsalin. She gestures Chiara to the rocking chair.

"I'm not here for pleasantries."

"You are in someone else's home, Miss Brasi. My uncles, who are still awake and, I am warning you, will soon be out to meet you and make you join the karaoke, would be disappointed if I did not treat you like a guest. Please sit."

Not looking at it, Chiara takes the ancient rocking chair, the one called a butaka, with its grotesquely extended arms, made for birthing. It creaks under her weight, but Chiara does not seem to hear the sound effect, a non sequitur in the night.

Now Magsalin is towering over the director, whose small figure is swallowed up in the enormous length of the antique chair.

"I did not revise the manuscript," begins Magsalin, knowing she must choose her words carefully, "I presented the possibilities of translation. A version, one might say."

"I did not ask for a translation." Chiara looks up at her. "I gave you the manuscript as a courtesy. It is the least I can do for the help you will give me."

"I have not yet offered that help."

"But you will."

"I have a few conditions."

"Co-authorship of my script?" asks Chiara. "Unacceptable. How dare you even imagine."

"You will admit though. My perspective offers àn advantage."

"A translator is not a writer."

"A filmmaker is not infallible."

The chair creaks.

The faint disco sounds are coming nearer.

"How do you know that your perspective does not distort the story?" asks Chiara.

"How do you know that yours has not?"

"No filmmaker would accept such a demand," says Chiara. "You are replacing the story. It's not a version. It's an invasion."

"Oh no. That is not my intention. A mirror, perhaps?" asks Magsalin.

"A double-crossing agent! An occupation!"

As a filmmaker, Magsalin thinks, shouldn't Chiara expect such a reversal?

19.

In the Last Novel by Stéphane Réal

In the last novel by Stéphane Réal, a textual mystery engenders clues that resolve a murder of colonial proportions; that is, a writer dies. He dies in a vaguely political way, in the way in a colonized country only the political seems to have consequence. Otherwise, deaths are too cheap for witness. Does it matter, Magsalin wonders, if one day a world-famous film director disappears in a derelict, tree-laden street in Punta in the Santa Ana district in Manila, to the strains of Elvis Presley singing "Suspicious Minds"?

And if anything happens to her protagonist, who would be to blame?

Part Two. Duel Scripts

Balangiga, Samar

22.

Tristesses

To understand Magsalin, it may be useful to note the allusion to Stéphane Réal. French-Tunisian writer of opaque novels,
or opaque writer of Tunisian-French novels, Réal was a member
of a club of cutups that emerged during the second half of the last
century. They bought typewriter ribbons, wrote notes in cursive,
sometimes cutting out a letter, *e* or *f,* and lived in the banlieues
of Paris instead of those benighted sections of Malate favored by
literary drunks.

Magsalin, succumbing to her fate in a Third World order,
had grown up with a surplus of academic desire. It does not help
that her adolescent streets included Harvard, Cubao, and New
York, Cubao, twin cartographic jokes that, as is often the case in
the Philippines, are also facts. Poststructuralist paganisms, the
homonymic humor of Waray tongue-twisters (which descend,
as always, into scatology), Brazilian novelists, Argentine soccer
players, Indonesian shadow puppets, Afro-Caribbean theorists,
Dutch cheeses, Japanese court fictions, and mythopoeic animals
in obscure Ilocano epics indiscriminately gobbled up her soul. It
is not an uncommon condition, this feeling of being constructed

out of some ambient, floating parts of a worldwide emporium (so glum scholars of the Anthropocene appraise this unsettled, hypertextual state). Typical of her sort in Manila, her passions were global (maybe because her options seemed slim). Her grad-school scholarship to Cornell was almost predictable. Some of her youthful attachments were fetishistic, while others were just symptoms of malnutrition.

She adored the concept of signs, without acknowledging the need to understand it.

As she reads, Magsalin keeps track of her confusions, annotating each mixed-up chapter as she goes, taking out from her bag an actual notebook and a fountain pen, a pale green Esterbrook, bought on eBay. In the notebook, she includes problems of continuity, the ones not explained by hopscotching chapters; issues of anachronism, given the short life-span of the male subject (1940–1977) contrasted against the women, who have superpowers: longevity and dispassion; words repeated as if they had been spilled and reconstituted then placed on another page; a stage set of interchangeable performers with identical names, or maybe doubles or understudies as they enter and exit the stage; an unexplained switch of characters' names in one section; and the problem of lapsed time—in which simultaneous acts of writing are the illusions that sustain a story.

At times, she feels discomfort over matters she knows nothing about, and Magsalin hears rising up in her that quaver that readers have, as if the artist should be holding her hand as she is walked through the story.

But she rides the wave, she checks herself.

A reader does not need to know everything.

How many times has she waded into someone else's history, say the mysteries of lemon soaps and Irish pubs in Dedalus's Dublin, or the Decembrists' plot in Dostoyevsky's *The Devils,* or Gustave Flaubert's Revolution of 1848 in what turns out to be one of her favorite books, *Sentimental Education,* and she would know absolutely nothing about the scenes, the historical background that drives them, the confusing cultural details, all emblematic, she imagines, to the Irish or the Russians or the French, and not really her business—and yet she dives in, to try to figure what it is the writer wishes to tell.

She calls these reader moments the quibbles—when she gets stuck in the faulty notion that everything in a book must be grasped.

Why should readers be spooked about not knowing all the details in a book about the Philippines yet surge forward with resolve in stories about France?

Against her quibbles, she scribbles her Qs, her queries for the author to address later.

ON A BLOG, now deactivated, Magsalin sadly annotates a past paved with sacral relics of bookish bones merged with atrocities of "daily praxis" (a kind of evil, undefined).

I will list here only a partial list of her old Tumblr tristesses:

The retirement of Franco Baresi, sweeper, of A.C. Milan, in

1997 (she used to follow Serie A before the referee scandals and the monopoly of the sport by SkyTV);

Random apostrophes on giant Nestlé Powdered Milk advertising billboards that dominate the ride from Manila's airport;

The death of Wilfrido Nolledo, author of *But for the Lovers*, his Philippine masterpiece reissued too late by Dalkey Archive Press and out of print, of course, in his home country;

Brutal attacks by nice fellow writers at international writing workshops in Iowa, after which she drinks warm Bud Lights with the neoliberal fuckers filled with postcolonial melancholia anyhow;

Readers who declare you cannot truly understand the works of the novelist Jose Rizal if you read him only in translation—a bullshit excuse for not knowing him at all;

Bloggers who keep announcing the end of print books while deploring their extinction;

Finding the mismarked grave of Antonio Gramsci (the map said Giacometti) under the shade of outcasts in the Protestant Cemetery in Rome;

The word *praxis*;

Readers who ask, Why do you always bring up history that no one knows anything about?

Good writers, even white males, who are prematurely dead.

Hirsute, looking practically flammable on his book jackets, the hybrid-continental Réal died, so to speak, in medias script. One imagines the last sight of him was his demonic beard, a fey salt-and-pepper affair, the color of pumice or a crosswise shard of culvert (like those abstract tarred bits lying for months off of Cafe Adriatico, still unswept after the June rains). In the shape of a *scudetto*, the beard, like the Cheshire Cat's smile, is the last to disappear. A number of his works, jottings, diaries, juvenilia, are illuminating, in a haphazard way. Réal's last novel, a mystery, remains a puzzle. It is unfinished.

There is a sense that in her youth, Magsalin, a poor and underfed student from the provinces (Tacloban in Leyte to be exact), would not have minded a ticket from Manila on Air France or Emirates, straight to Nice or Cap d'Antibes, where she would first lie on the beach for a day, the sun being the best antidote to jet lag, then rent a cheap car to traverse horseback-riding campsites and haut corniches through the vals and valses of the middling Midi and on down the horrible French nuclear scenery into the bowels of Paris. She would stop off at Père Lachaise, with the help of the TomTom® App for Finding Dead Writers Who Are Still Members of the Group Blank-Blank-Blank, and she would genuflect before his jar of ashes (or columbarium, as it is called in Wikipedia), in between staring at the not-so-subtle winged sphinx of Oscar Wilde's last riddle and Gertrude Stein's soothing but pebbly grave.

She would love to have helped organize the papers of Stéphane Réal's unfinished mystery or checked out his obsessive annotations of Lady Murasaki (his bedside reading—a surprise, as the Japanese woman of the Heian period has a dreamy expansion opposite to his terse, epigrammatic style); but to be honest, she does not even know the date he died. She had read him a while ago.

First she consults a virtual encyclopedia. She sits before her uncles' clumsy, troglodytic iMac, the one that looks like an alien in the midst of an affecting lobotomy, its sweet bald head kind of droopy. But Magsalin cannot find the exact place and time of Réal's death. She surmises that no reader has minded that void, hence its disappearance online.

1.

The Story She Wishes to Tell, an Abaca Weave, a Warp and Weft of Numbers

The story Magsalin wishes to tell is about loss. Any emblem will do: a French-Tunisian with an unfinished manuscript, an American obsessed with a Filipino war, a filmmaker's possible murder, a wife's sadness. An abaca weave, a warp and weft of numbers, is measured but invisible in the plot. Chapter numbers double up. Puzzle pieces scramble. Points of view will multiply. Allusions, ditto. There will be blood, a kidnapping, or a solution to a crime forgotten by history. That is, Magsalin hopes so.

At her uncles' home, she props her legs up on top of the ancient Betamax machine as she settles down with the manila envelope. Who should she call to help that brat get to Samar? Magsalin is a sucker for anyone interested in the ruins of what she likes to call her home, though the country disavows her affection. Her uncles do not question her reasons for visiting them. However, their silence is off-putting. They welcome her to their rambling house in Punta, amid the reek of the Pasig River, in a section of town where goons sleep on mats with their guns stuck in their flip-flops right next to them on the floor, so that they breathe metal, Johnson's Floor Wax, rubber, and foot ache in their sleep.

Fortunately for Magsalin, her uncles have modern beds, though they prefer their old straw mats on the floor. It is good for their spine, they say, but in truth, Magsalin thinks, at night the return to childhood comforts them. They have deep friendships with petty thieves and drink with police. They are friendly with all the barangay captains from Tutuban to Paco: in the wisdom of gamblers, it's the local chiefs who count. Their wives are in Jordan dry-cleaning the gowns of royalty and in Italy nursing right-wing Catholic buffoons. Her uncles leave Magsalin alone. Theirs is a community of men: tolerant of one another's error, foolhardy, and as ready to corrupt their neighbors as to save their souls. They cherish the material world. Every day they tell her to stay indoors and listen to their well-kept vinyl records of John Denver and Burt Bacharach and, wrapped in mite-bitten plastic from sooty shops along the Avenida, Elvis, of course. Her gifts from Bleecker Street now have prime space on their altars to the seventies. They cook her special breakfasts made from their long-hoarded Spam, and they tell her to watch the noontime shows starring nine-year-old drag queens and twitch-perfect lip-synchers of Mariah Carey and Adele.

Just stay home with us and sing the karaoke, every night after dinner, her uncles tell her, wait for us when we come home from work and relax and take up our microphones and sing.

No, no, no, they say—do not go out. Do not bother to go to Samar.

Why Samar?!

They themselves left their province, Leyte, long ago for Manila—for their jobs on the docks or as guards in the banks or selling at the wet markets. It is an honor to survive in the city's jungle. Everyone leaves places like Leyte and Samar, they repeat, even its governors and mayors, who are supposed to live there. During those first few days, Magsalin sits obedient in her uncles' home watching their TV. She knows it is an affective fallacy to feel the sublime in the exuberant precision of a scrawny kid who can copy Michael Jackson, just so, exhuming the dead singer in an eerie display of late homage—how beautiful is imitation, she thinks, when its vessel breaks the heart.

Her uncles own these faithfully preserved Betamax tapes of bootlegged boxing matches and duets of Dolly Parton and Kenny Rogers. Their home is filled with antiques from the globalization age: Walkmans with Eagles cassettes still in them, a TV with an antenna and no remote, two pre-iPhone Sony videocams, clunky and clunkier. She takes one Betamax tape out from the bottom, a scratched but well-dusted one, the single word *Thrilla* hand-written with care on its spine. She pushes it into the machine. It's a tape of a tape, and for a moment she thinks she hears her mother's voice in the background mocking her three brothers for filming the match they were in fact watching on TV.

Then Magsalin sees the actual TV—the home video zooms out to her mother's living room in the house along San Juanico Strait. She thinks the blur in the video is her mother's hand, clowning around with the lens—she sees a floral housedress moving away, like her mother's. It is odd because Magsalin thinks it should be 1975, the year of the match, but the room has the vulgar look of their later, modernized home in Tacloban—American-style glass jalousies have replaced the capiz-shell windows, and the old grand piano is not in the frame. Then the cameraman has gained control, and abruptly she sees Muhammad Ali in black and white, grainy, young, and unutterably beautiful, holding the length of his arm out toward Joe Frazier's brow, and because the tape starts in the middle of things his outstretched arm toward the smaller man in the opening angle looks like a benediction.

But it is a bruising, killer match. She experiences each punch with a dim sense of herself as a child watching with a crowd in Tacloban at the windows of the appliance store downtown, on Gomez Street, during that time of martial law. Her uncles took her to the sidewalk show. Her mother had banned the bout from the house. On the day they had rewatched this tape and she explained the day to him, Magsalin's husband said he admired her mother for her ethical stance against the dictator's regime.

She had met her husband at one of those drunken grad-school parties, watching World Cup soccer in a cramped, unfurnished place that turned out to be his writing studio—then much later, in nonalcoholic moments, she convinced him to live with her back home.

"You could call it ethical," she told him, "but I think she just did not like the blood."

Her uncles had brought their own footstools to watch the original match in 1975. One uncle carried a kaguran for a chair, an old coconut grater carved to look like the body of a lizard, with its extended amphibian head. She remembered she liked to sit on this kaguran, on the lizard's belly, to watch the traveling movies sponsored by Coca-Cola at the public basketball court. During the fight, Tio Exequiel collected the crowd's bets. He put on a bet for her, for Smokin' Joe, just in case. Everyone was an Ali fan.

Now she realizes this tape must be a telecast from decades later, an anniversary presentation. The tape was a simulacrum of the bout she had seen in 1975: she knows who was with them at this later screening, who was watching the bout from the opposite sofa, with the giant spoon and fork on the wall above his curly-haired brow, grainy, young, and unutterably beautiful. He is revived in the shadows of the frame.

She can delete, if she so wills it.

Erasure, too, is a blessing.

And as she watches the tape, she instead finds herself looking out at the audience for the dead filmmaker and his wife, as if now she and Chiara have this bond of memory.

She watches Joe Frazier go at Ali again, one more time, in one more rope-a-dope. No moment is too small not to have contrasting attentions. The existential condition of sharing the universe every day with strangers hits her as Magsalin watches Ali in Joe Frazier's soon-to-be blinded vision and Frazier is glimpsed from the frame of Ali's not-yet-Parkinsoned arms.

She thinks she sees her—Chiara's mother, Virginie Brasi—updo-ed and uptight, clutching an unlit cigarette in the toxic stadium, so hot in the rising heat that hell would be a relief that morning in Araneta Coliseum. A well-shod woman with a starving look, cigarette in thin hand, staring entranced but also distracted as the camera pans over the tense, fluorescent crowd. It's a traitorous aspect of empathy, Magsalin notes.

The slightest connection suffices.

She turns off the tape before Joe Frazier goes blind.

HER UNCLES THINK her plan to go "cutting," as they call the land trip to Samar, insane.

"No, no, no," says Tio Ambrosio over dinner—air-dried tocino marinaded in Sprite. Its sugary glaze picks a hole in her brain. Every night at her uncles' dinners she eats too much—stuffing herself with luxurious and unhealthy nostalgia.

"Do not go out," Tio Ambrosio repeats—"Do not go to Samar."

"Or why not take a plane? Or even the boat," says Tio Nemesio. "You should take first class and watch the islands in the stream. That is what we are. How can we be wrong? No one in between! And we rely on each other, ah-ahhhh! I always wanted to watch the islands, Mindoro, Cebu, Siquijor, all pass by from the window of a first-class cabin on the MV *Sweet Faith*. Waste of money, but why not?"

"You can make her pay, you know," meditates Tio Exequiel, toothpicking as he rocks on his butaka. "Double the price of the plane ticket and pocket the money! Earn four thousand pesos!"

"No, no, no," says Tio Ambrosio. "Do not go to Samar."

"Yeah," says Tio Nemesio. "Why Samar?!"

"And anyway, do not go cutting trip!" says Tio Exequiel. "My God! You do not know what you are talking about, taking the cutting trip to Samar. Go straight on a boat, not cutting!"

At first, she thinks her uncles speak out of concern for her safety. Maybe it is avuncular habit, or sexism. It has slowly dawned upon her that her uncles voted for the current unspeakably perverse despot. Every night they gravely nod their heads, like wise and worldly Stoics, at the words of their leader, the drug-war-obsessed macho who has vowed to kill every criminal in sight.

"Only addicts are harmed, don't you worry, inday," Tio Ambrosio tells Magsalin as once again they watch more news of the dead bodies after dinner, piling up at the garbage dumps, in the slums, near schoolyards, and on all the monotonous commercial streets of the country—bodies upon bodies. "Are you a criminal? A drug lord?"

"No," she says.

"Then nothing to fear, inday! He is doing it to keep us all safe!" crows Tio Exequiel.

"Bah," says Tio Nemesio, "he is just a bastos—a bastard!"

"True," says Tio Ambrosio, "but he is a bastard who is Bisaya, like us."

Magsalin's uncles keep explaining the country to her as if

she does not know it. They read the news with the sureness of those whose political persuasions lie in their personal relations. She realizes her uncles make her stay home not because they are afraid for her safety—they know enough barangay captains to put a hex on all goons. No, they make her stay home because they believe she is stupid, an alien, having been abroad for too long, though they have nothing against her for that—no, no, they do not question her decision to stay away all these years, even when her mother died, no, no, inday, of course not, we do not question.

We understand, her uncles never say, though she knows what they mean by their polite lack of words.

No one in her family will ever blame her for leaving. The job of a family is to support (though that will not keep them from gossiping).

For her uncles, she realizes, it is as if ever since she left the country for New York City—for nothing! not to send money home but just to "galavant!"—ever since she left she has relinquished her right to her memory of home, and she should not be left to her devices or she will bumble through the nation like a witless tourist who cannot speak its languages, though in fact she code-switches in three of them, puns in five, makes money in two, and dreams in one.

No, no, inday, do not go to Samar! Why Samar?!

But Magsalin also knows that, if she asks, her uncles will call up their crew despite their misgivings about Magsalin's project with that flat-chested blondie who looks like no María Clara.

They will do everything she wants because it is what uncles do.

Magsalin thinks—this is why she has returned home from New York City to work on her book: everyone at home will accommodate her will. It is what families are for.

Magsalin is sobered by the thought. That her life of independence in Manhattan has been, all along, wishful thinking. She believes she is at home in the West Village, treading the streets of Diane Arbus and e. e. cummings and watching comedy shows in the same cavern where Bob Dylan first played. She keeps saying her job fulfills her, having created her own company when she returned to America years after graduate school, finding her niche, as they say, translating credits in the movies or instructions for computer terminals. She dabbles now and then, in fits and starts, in the history that she had studied at Cornell. She watches the seven-hour-long films of Lav Diaz in crumbling mansions on the Lower East Side and imagines that such communion with Third World streets from her distance gives her the cachet that art bestows. She does not go home for her mother's funeral because the prospect of return—the mournful winding road out of metropolitan Manila through the wastes of Luzon into the Bicol peninsula, then on to Samar's powerful desolation and across the strait into Leyte's monotonous green—gives her insomnia. She splurges on a coat from Miu Miu instead.

She has no childhood trauma, she likes to tell her friends—
just a willful desire to be herself, in a way that home does
not provide. The immigrant's tale is also one of agency, you
know, not just misery. That is what she claims in New York.
Instead of returning, through the years, every time she finds
a book about the Philippines, on AbeBooks or Amazon, she
buys it. She searches eBay for old Spanish-galleon doubloons
and American-era war medallions with the words PHILIPPINE
INSURRECTION 1899 circling the rim. Occasionally, academia.edu
tells her an old monograph, say, her commentary on the middle
name Jose Rizal gave to his hero Ibarra, has been uploaded,
and the message gives her a pang. She has an eclectic collection of memorabilia, on the paleology of Butuan, fruit trees of
the archipelago, travels of Midwestern women to Manila in the
years of the Thomasites (1903 to 1935), those prim Protestant
teachers to a wide-eyed Catholic country where the foreigners'
faith failed but their tongue triumphed, and above all, she owns
carefully curated prints from the Library of Congress plus
historical picture books and stereo cards of the war of independence against the Americans.

Lately, the *New York Times* has been sending items to her
inbox three or four times a day. It used to be, reading news items
on a place like the Philippines or reviews of novels by actual Vietnamese or Laotians or other such peoples bombed or invaded by
America was like finding elves in Central Park—the idea of their
centrality in the news was preposterous. But she kept reading the

flurry of articles as body counts rose in the archipelago, and out of this self-inflicted disaster the old colony gained renown, or was at least the target of an outcry, usually bombastic, in the American periodicals that were incurious about how the current times of one included the past of the other, or vice versa. Magsalin was fascinated by the ways her own knowledge gave her insight that was useless, on one hand, but terribly urgent on the other. Before she got the email from Chiara Brasi, her tinkering with a mystery novel was at best a phantom: a haunting.

She tells herself that her decision to return home has everything to do with art, nothing to do with grief. Her husband was gone. Just like that. She had left Tacloban at his death, never to return. Not even for her mother's funeral—a black mark on any child, even if you are not Filipino. She has settled in a new country, borne a new life. Her mother's recent death, by long, lingering breast cancer, does not impel her voyage—no sentiment is attached.

"Do not come home," her mother had said to her on the phone as she lay dying. "I understand. If you feel you cannot do it, inday—do not return."

Magsalin dislikes sentiment—self-pity and regret and remorse and such. What need is there to bare the heart? What is broken is broken. No, her return bears the burdens she prefers. A solution to a writing block takes her to this longed-for place she still calls home.

How will she get that brat to Samar?

HER UNCLES CALL their cousin Guling, an army colonel who will lend them his old-style, new-model Mitsubishi Pajero. The man's old-fashioned in his cars and his sense of command. Guling also calls a pair of privates first class, Edward and Gogoboy, both on duty in Mindoro but happy to return home to Samar for this sudden expedition. Chiara will look upon their military escorts with reasonable trepidation. They look like corner louts in borrowed uniforms, spitting out their phlegm in tandem, one holding an Uzi, the other with a Colt revolver hanging from a holster on his fatigue pants. The Colt man has the smooth yet unhealthy, taxidermic look of a sufferer of diabetes or gout without the funds to treat his ailment. He has no hair. His limbs look swollen. Chiara will stare at the flesh of his ring finger that bloats around his wedding band. Worse, the soldier's name, Gogoboy, will not inspire confidence in his calling.

The other, Edward, has the chiseled cheeks of the malnourished, a recent army draftee, or so it seems, his childish ears sticking out, with the trace of Manila's diesel grime in his earlobes, Chiara notes—that chiaroscuro shading of black dust that bedevils everyone who takes public transportation in Manila. Back at the Manila Hotel, Chiara had kept finding this mysterious grime on her fingertips no matter how many times she washed her hands. Every time she touched her body—the backs of her knees when she sat down to dinner amid the pearled chandeliers, her nape, the curve of her elbow when she reached to slap a mosquito as she crossed poolside—her fingertips kept blackening. In the toilet where Douglas MacArthur had once or twice taken a piss on the country, whenever she blew her nose, the tissue was also smudged with her nostrils' black dust.

"That's what you get for traveling semi-naked all around Metro Manila," Magsalin says, as she watches the filmmaker dust herself off, alighting from her taxicab in the harsh daylight of Punta.

Ladies in their corrugated office uniforms, nunnish taupes and dull beiges, stand by under the pleated roof of the barangay shed, waiting to catch their jeepneys to Makati. The shed is emblazoned with a politician's name: clearly the shed is the afterthought and the name is the point. The maid in the house next door has come out to sweep the dead leaves, tin cans, and cigarette butts from the culvert sunk deep in the Pasig's muddy esteros, like a dinosaur's spine abandoned by the city engineer's office. As the maid sweeps, she stares at Chiara with a candor Magsalin appreciates. She, too, is surprised at Chiara's presence—her promptness, her perfect composure in this unknown place, a city still improbable and fantastical, even to Magsalin.

Chiara is carrying an aubergine and olive duffel bag and clutching her Hermès. Her shades rest on her carefully disheveled hair, and her bronzed look catches light in Private First Class Gogoboy's Ray-Ban sunglasses as he, too, stares from his perch in the Pajero.

"Diesel fumes hide in the body's cavities, you know," says

Magsalin, "in elbows and in the folds of your neck. Those long-sleeved cotton camisas buttoned up to the clavicle are not just affectation. Nor is the dreary umber or brown every working-woman likes to wear, have you noticed, despite the heat: warm colors hide the grime. That is what I discovered when I came here for the university. Everything has a purpose in Manila."

Chiara looks down at her outfit—a camouflage-style safari suit more or less the colors of her tongue, an ocherish thing that she sticks out at Magsalin.

"I got that." Chiara pouts. "I changed for the trip. No need to lecture. So I scrubbed myself all over last night, and sure enough, the soapsuds were black, too."

"Tough," says Magsalin. "But on the way to Samar, don't worry. We will be out in the open country. On the road, we will leave the diesel smoke behind. Won't we, Edward?"

"Usually," says the sorrowful guard, raising his Uzi as if in shy agreement.

Chiara hops into the Pajero, behind Gogoboy, the diabetic driver, who spits out his gum in a practiced way, wrapping it carefully in its silver foil, then he spews out, one last shot, his well-seasoned phlegm, before he revs the engine.

Everyone has his ritual.

Magsalin also notes that Gogoboy has a bandage on his non-driving foot instead of a shoe, but Chiara has already put on her earbuds and adjusted her sunglasses, casting out the morning's eastward glare.

With his look of despondent respect, Edward, the malnourished guard in his baggy fatigues, gestures with his Uzi for Magsalin to get in.

She lifts her duffel bag onto the back seat.

"Ha," says Magsalin, "that's funny. Our bags are identical. Did you also buy it from that shop in Soho that's forever closing out?"

"Come on, Thelma," says Chiara, whose easy acceptance of the presence of armed guards, depressed-looking and diseased and all, belies her preconceptions of the country: no travesty seems to give her introspection—"Road trip! Haven't been on one of those since 1977, when I traveled with my mother in Antibes."

"Geez, Louise," says Magsalin.

But she is suddenly thrilled with this prospect, of traveling on the roads that lead to her old childhood home.

"Geez," Magsalin says, "you're the trip, Louise!"

28.

A Secret, Metastasizing Thing

Magsalin shakes her head at the script. Starting a movie with a voice-over by a society photographer who discovers her soul amid butchery will turn off local viewers. Anti-imperialists are touchy people. And as a trigger warning, the device is risky. In a movie about a Philippine war, why use a nineteenth-century Daisy Buchanan, some socialite photographer who, unlike the truthful shallowness of the *Gatsby* original, will turn out to have a bleeding heart? That idea is so 1970s, when politics mattered, and even the heiress Patty Hearst had a cause. Or that journalist in *Reds*, the Diane Keaton character who nurses the Yankee commie John Reed back to life in the Warren Beatty epic—sure, it is nice to have a woman's voice in a time of war, but does she need to be so—*white?*

Whatever.

It is obvious that the WASP photographer, actually a mutated Ukrainian Jew, is a stand-in for the generic consumer being enticed to know the story.

But that soundtrack—Magsalin hates it.

It sticks in her head.

She heard these songs, including the bovine marginal

declensions—the *wo-ow-wo-ow-wo-ows*—all throughout her childhood.

A sad trick, this pop track.

That the soundtrack for the Philippine-American War is stuffed with bloated late-Elvis, earworms of his crass decay, listened to over and over again—at least, among her mother's generation—will not do.

Why start with Elvis?

Elvis is from her uncles' time.

She marks the script: *scratch scratch scratch scratch*.

Magsalin had never liked the songs, though it surprises her now how all the tunes she thought were absolutely Filipino, like "Are You Lonesome Tonight?"—an annoying kundiman if she ever heard one—turn out to be Elvis.

Except "My Way." "My Way" is Frank. To sing "My Way," you are not allowed to deviate from the Frank-ish phrasings, or you will be shot.

The karaoke murders of "My Way" singers are a badge of honor in some fastidious dives.

But Elvis has this phenomenal stature among local drunks. No matter how anyone mangles his desperate songs, they always bring tears to someone's eyes.

He was inescapable in her childhood, but at the time, Magsalin had no clue. She grew up innocently with her uncles' drinking bouts in Leyte, in which the songs seemed to spring from the bamboo groves, and grown men sang soulful versions of creepy ballads while sopping up bahalina tuba, their local wine. Her uncles in Manila still bring in fresh gallons of this wine from cargo ships that look as if they had known the days of Magellan, and in Manila they translate their provincial guitar fests into insomnia-inducing, mechanical nights of karaoke.

It strikes Magsalin that the congenital link between drunkenness and song in her uncles might be an ancient tumor, a fever of the islands beyond anyone's control, so that Elvis and Frank are daemons, or maybe cancers—forms of visceral necrosis, a genetic malady, and not necrotizing corporations.

She turns the page.

Scratch scratch scratch scratch.

It was a shock when she arrived in America, and she recognized that the culture she had thought was hers to sneer at was, all along, not really. The corny songs were claimed by others. That made her sad. Worse, her own culture, of the fermented coconuts and demented singers, was not visible at first in New York—except maybe in the vagabond diesel from hotdog trucks that gave off the whiff of jeepney smog, but even that missed the necessary attachment of the smell of fishballs.

"Sweet Caroline" was the Boston Red Sox song, not Tio Exequiel's signature karaoke anthem. No one, not even Tio Exequiel's oldest brother, Tio Nemesio, clearly a better tenor, was allowed to sing it. But it was also owned by this humongous sports fandom, an arena of phenomenal passion.

In America, she kept confronting these doubles, cultural

puns—repetitions of details from her homeland that have reverse or disjoint significance in this simultaneous place, as if the parallel universes of Elvises and Neil Diamonds in both the Philippines and America were a dark matter of the cosmos that eludes theorists of the world's design.

That she has Elvis in her bones, a secret, metastasizing thing, just as she has nipa huts and the crazy graphics of jeepney designs, occurred to her as a blow. And once, on a visit to Nashville, when all she heard in this museum she stumbled into—which contained only Elvis's cars—was all Elvis, all day, all the time—as if she were still stuck in some fiesta guitar-strumming session with her uncles, amid palm trees with no way out—the idea struck her—oh gee, what if—

Manila is necrotized in America, too—scar tissue so deeply hidden and traumatized no one needs to know it. One is in the other and the other is in one, she thought, feeling ill in Nashville. Her self overdubbed, multiplied, intercut, and hyperlinked, but which is to be master, she wondered, feeling dizzy, about to fall (she also had too much Kentucky bourbon).

These realizations of *différance* comprise her surrender to her new world of signs.

She does not mourn her dumb recognitions, though she curses the fact that it is her lot to note them.

In short, Magsalin became interested in alternity, to the misfortune of her friends in Queens, who hate to listen to her pontification at their historic ethnic dinners, at which, with exaggerated gestures as they pick up mounds of rice, they like to eat in peace with their hands.

The alter-native.

Magsalin regrets the pun but has no willpower: she does not resist it.

Anyhow, she proclaims to her peers at one of their utensil-deficient dinners as she strokes a mangled piece of pork with her thumb and forefinger—"Everybody is messed up and occupied by others! Even if you are not Filipino! We are all creatures of translation, parallel chapters repeating in a universal void!"

Dead silence amid pigsblood and the dregs of cow marrow.

Then they all go on scraping up dinuguan and bulalo, in clumsy silence, for after all, none of them is any good at being indigenous out in Flushing—they order all the wrong soupy wet things for their monthly pleasure of eating without forks or spoons.

Unquote.

SHE WILL CALL the altered ego—her own version of the heroine Casiana Nacionales—Caz.

Caz Intahan.

Caz Abwat.

Caz Alanan.

Caz Angkot.

Caz Saysayan.

Caz Inungalingan.

In the script, Caz is clutching an envelope, a thick manuscript, at the start of the film. In Caz's overture, there will be no voice-over, no soundtrack, no song lyrics. The montage of the pampered wife in Chantilly lace, in glitter, in lace and lamé, in Vegas, in Manila, in the south of France, freezes and dissolves. Caz will be a schoolteacher in Giporlos, Samar, or maybe Oras, Bicol, or better still, a doubling site—Sorsogon, Sorsogon, or Bulacan, Bulacan. She is a slight, brown woman the color of her rocking chair—a butaka of soft fruitwood that cracks in dry weather. The awkward man, deliverer of the packet, does not take the chair offered to him. To himself, he calls her by that name.

The Intended.

Rocking by itself the chair already looks haunted. The messenger watches her agitation. Caz is trying to hide it, her tears.

1.

By the Time They Pass Oras

By the time they pass Oras and Sorsogon, in Bicol, Chiara has slept through the eternity of traffic down Quezon province and Camarines and even the city of Legazpi, by which she could have glimpsed the perfect cone, preternatural landmark for old galleons arriving from Acapulco, that receding volcanic view, the beauty of Mayon that resists trivialization even as it makes of this hinterland a tourist trap. But she is asleep, and by the time they are passing the Bicol region, Chiara has lost the sense of intimacy, embarrassing to be sure because she knows it is unwarranted, that she had felt when she first entered the Pajero.

The car looks like a bank vault on wheels, tinted, over-air-conditioned, and enormous, but maybe it is the accouterments, the two soldiers, one in combat fatigues (echoing her safari suit), the other in casual wear, who offer her the jolt of nostalgia. One is fat and the other thin, a specious duo of contrasts. For Chiara their gazes in the mirror give her back this recall, the way for her as a child everything was reflected through cameras and strobe lights: and through the sunny refractions of the tropical sets she observed the many sweating men lugging electric posts and exotic furniture specially carved for *The Unintended*'s colossal dinner scenes. A whole country of men doing her father's bidding, with a dignified intensity no one questioned. What were they like when they returned home? Edward, the boy with the Uzi, looks like he is twelve. She imagines Edward seeking his position in a city where his lost, provincial status gives him this stiff-backed solitude, he and his Uzi upright behind her in the mirror of the Pajero. What is the condition of a soldier? To be far from home.

For a stretch on the road, Chiara keeps feeling like a child, the way her safety used to be given over to armored vehicles and helicopters at hand and paid interpreters amid a palm jungle. At any point, she thinks, she will come across a classroom of Chinese toddlers and not be surprised that she recognizes each one of them, her classmates in the forest—a dream. In this way she has déjà vu feelings when she wakes up amid the farms of the Bicol peninsula—the sight of chickens sleeping in trim triangular thatches, a poultry bivouac of pup tents all in a row in Barangay Lovey-Dovey; the indifferent gaze of the carabao that nevertheless looks up and stares straight at her; the schoolchildren walking on dust roads who, no matter which town they're in, wave at the passing tinted car in excitement, as if a Hollywood star were in it, which happens to be true in this case, but still.

Even the food at the stops—the buko juice she is offered straight from the awkward orb of the newly hacked bowl of a coconut shell, the stained red eggs, the rice cakes flaked with cheese—has the slippery texture of memory's sap. Each stop has its own delicacy, the leaf-wrapped cakes and the peanut brittles and the local versions of biscotti, and this effulgent sensation, as she takes in the peddlers of straw fans and woven slippers and breathes in the familiar, dry whiff of abaca baskets, drives her into sleep. For such a famous filmmaker, Chiara's snoring, with its slight gleam of spittle, is mundane.

Magsalin knows she keeps giving the trip her lapsed child-hood glimpses. The old farm roads used to be rutted and endless, with wild camote and malunggay and guava trees in sight, and anahaw mats of unhusked rice grains spread out right on the roadway's shoulder, prey to dust and pebbles. Everyone used to wave at the buses when they passed, as if each passenger vehicle were some thrilling distraction from a vast boredom, so that Magsalin always felt she was leaving something behind, her sig-nificance, as she moved away from the waving children toward her destination.

But now this track down Luzon's southern expanse has lost its dust lanes. The cutting trip to Samar, a journey of stops and splices, now glides through national roads with impersonal numbers and generic names, like C-4 or SLEX, and the road's distance from the familiar farms and the inland rivers with the washerwomen and the kids who bathed for pleasure, not for coins, the highway now wracked by posters for whitening creams and Western jeans, measures once again for Magsalin the distance in time. Private First Class Gogoboy tells them they can rest in Legazpi City, if they wish, but if they keep going, he says, they will be in Samar by dusk. Such is the power of these twenty-first-century roads: her old childhood sense of an endless voyage is foreshortened, as in a fast-forward spell, and before she can dream up Chiara's next perfidy or accident, the Pajero has reached the island's southernmost edge, Matnog on the butt end of Luzon, and the Ro-Ro is waiting to take them to Samar, so Private First Class Gogoboy announces.

"Ro-Ro?" Chiara murmurs, not quite awake.

"You know, like ro-ro-row your boat, gently down the stream!" says Magsalin though she has no idea, too, why Gogoboy calls the vessels Ro-Ro. She imagines it is another pun, maybe a historical one. "You know Filipinos were taught YMCA camping songs by Thomasites, American teachers, in the beginning of the 1900s. The teaching of English was part of the articles of war under McKinley. First, soldiers were made to do it. Then paid emigrants in Victorian clothes. Clever form of pacification. Very smart. It stuck, you know. Camp songs are the backbone of my education. I learned the song 'Row, Row, Row Your Boat' in nursery school. I sang in English before I wrote in Waray. Actually, I never learned to write in Waray."

"And I sang your anthem in Tagalog before I spoke my own country's pledge of allegiance."

"Oh, yeah," remembers Magsalin, "I heard you singing that on YouTube."

"It was my mom who filmed me. I still know the words. *Bayang magiling, perlas ng sinungaling!*"

The two guards are gawking at the foreign passenger.

Edward, the malnourished one, claps.

"Good voice! Good job!"

"Hehehe!" says Private First Class Gogoboy, plucking lint off of his bandaged foot as he whistles: "Beri gud!"

"But you have the wrong words," says Magsalin. "The word is magiliw, not magiling."

"What does that mean," asks Chiara.

"Giling means grind—I mean, magiling sounds obscene. But magiliw means loved: oh beloved country, the song is saying. Oh country I love."

"So Barangay Lovey-Dovey is magiliw."

"And the word is not sinungaling. It is silanganan. That means east, or orient. Pearl of the Orient. Sinungaling means lies."

"Oops, my bad," says Chiara.

"I mean, you sang, *Obscene country, Land of lies*."

"I could have sworn that was what my teacher taught me."

"That is also likely," says Magsalin. "Everyone's a joker. Anyway, don't worry about it. No one ever gets that song right."

The vessel, MV *Blanket*, arrives into the pier belching smoke from its behind like a dragon in reverse.

"That ship looks like no gentle thing," says Chiara.

Private First Class Gogoboy pipes up, "Ro-Ro, ma'am, it means Roll-on, Roll-off. See? Trucks and buses roll on and roll off from the ship! It is very modern. It can take ten Philtranco buses or twenty Pajeros in one trip!"

"Funny name for a boat," says Chiara. "MV *Blanket.*"

"It is the youngest child of Michael Jackson," volunteers Edward. "It is the smallest Ro-Ro among the Speedy-Cat Lines. Too bad we did not get MV *Prince Michael*. That one is usually the biggest and the best!"

23.

Cassandra Chase's Presence in Samar

Cassandra Chase's presence in Samar is a quandary for the military officers. Their enterprise on the islands is so precarious, perilous, and uncertain that the burden of her unexpected arrival in wind-driven bancas, rowed by two opportunists, a pair of local teenagers who hand off Cassandra's trunks to the porters with an exaggerated avidity that means she has overpaid them, gives the officers in Balangiga a premonition of the inadequacy of their letters of command.

Who has jurisdiction if a mere slip of a woman in a billowing silk gown completely inappropriate to the weather and her situation flouts the general's orders in Tacloban and manages the journey across the strait and down the river anyway on her own steam, with her diplopia and diplomatic immunity intact, a spiral of lace in her wake, a wavering tassel of white, complete with trunks full of cameras and Zeiss lenses and glass plates for her demoniacal, duplicitous photographic prints?

On the other hand, the men of Company C enjoy watching their captain squirm. He's a greenhorn, this Captain Connell, a fancy-pants Easterner from New York. He is not one, of them.

Most of the men are farmers' sons, cow milkers, cheese genies, and cornhuskers eased off their lands by the brutalities of the market, the shifting economic priorities of their experimental republic. William Jennings Bryan, Democrat of the Corn Belt, imagines he is their voice. But they have no idea who the hell William Jennings Bryan is. For one thing, their mail is delayed. The mail's tardiness is driving the men of Company C insane. The Americans in Balangiga are at war in the Philippines for no reason they can express, but what they feel is powerful enough.

They are homesick.

Homesickness makes them mad.

Stories of dementia among the americanos are legendary.

A set of filmic wipes follows, showing hairy scenes of cinematic lunatics, mostly stolen from B movies by Samuel Fuller.

Americano mucho malo, chant the Filipinos.

And quite right, that.

Americano mucho enfermo—that is also the case.

Thoughts of home eat the soldiers up like the soothing rot of cavities. Some men, conspicuously losing their wits, disappear in the jungle, abandoned to the mercies of local witchcraft. The famous black soldier, Fagen, is up in the jungles of Mount Arayat, defected to the insurrectos. Damned traitor will get his, but who can blame him? The tropics have the mystifying effect of making memory insufferable. Seward Scheetherly wakes up thinking it is Christmas in Schenectady. Seward Scheetherly runs amok, howling in the rain toward Balangiga river, screaming *Hark the herald angels siiiing*. What the fuck do harking angels have to do with shooting up cassava patches on Balangiga's riverbank? His Colt revolver scares the washerwomen, who are slapping the army's scratchy felt blankets against the rocks.

Meyer the bugler and Randles the sergeant chase Scheetherly to the riverbank. Markley the orderly and Irish the corporal of the guard follow. Bumpus takes up the rear, smoking a cigarette. It takes four men to wrest away the Colt, wrap the howling Christmas caroler in a pup tent, and tie him up in abaca rope. It is September. Fiesta is near. So say the locals. Scheetherly looks like a pig ready for basting, and the washerwomen, still slapping things on the rocks, emphasizing their vigorous notion of hygiene, this time on the sheets, cannot help it.

They giggle.

Randles leaps, raising a fist at them. Irish, though, is quick. He drags Randles away from the washerwomen. The girls are backing away from Randles, a sweating, red-faced man with an adolescent simplicity whose one sign of maturity is the handlebar mustache curling in halves like two sides of a sharpened machete, both sides ridiculous. The girls are backing into the water, leaving the army's sheets afloat and lifting their lacy patadyongs as if protecting their clothes from the mud—though their thin cotton camisas are already wet from their exertions, sudsy and foamed and revealing their limbs. They tuck their bunched, bubbling skirts between their glistening thighs, mutely watching as Scheetherly sings.

Glory to the newborn kiiiiing!

Teenage Meyer, the smooth-chinned bugler, smirks at the soapy, gleaming girls.

Soon all you can see of Scheetherly are his raving eyes.

The last time Scheetherly had gone nuts, they had found him obsessively swimming in figure eights in the river, for hours on end, unable to stop.

Randles wants to take him to the hospital in Tacloban, but it is Bumpus, the lieutenant, who gets the job. Everyone loves Bumpus, he gets whatever he wants. Even the local chief of police, who keeps beating Bumpus at chess, has a soft spot. Captain Connell, you can tell, is a pushover. Bumpus went to Harvard. Connell did not. Bumpus's parents are big shots in Boston. They are friends with the senior senator of Massachusetts, Senator George Frisbie Hoar of anti-imperialist fame. (Sadly, this exalted connection will not save Bumpus, soon to be hacked to death in his sleep.) Tall, lanky, golden-haired, and young as the lot of them, Bumpus has the feral charm of a black sheep. Drinks the locals under the table, so survivors remember. A Brahmin of bahalina tuba, claims a local historian always ready to wax lyrical over his homegrown wine. Valeriano Abanador, Balangiga's chief of police, the most educated man in town after the parish priest, acts as if he merely tolerates that madcap Bumpus, but every day anyhow Abanador, known among locals and americanos alike as the Chief, invites him to his hut near the water, where the two play chess and discuss arcane military arts.

At reveille, as Meyer the bugler walks back toward his post, Scheetherly is seeing reindeer, wise men, and snow. Griswold the surgeon shakes his head over Scheetherly's sad shape. Bumpus takes the deranged Scheetherly on the boat to the big camp across the water, to Tacloban. Bumpus keeps his secret to himself, so as not to arouse the miserable men: Padre Donato the priest has said to Bumpus that in Tacloban he will find a surprise—the soldiers' long-lost mail.

For the arrival of Cassandra on the boat has buried the soldiers' hopes—they have been dreaming for months of the mail steamer, but instead they get this silken pest in a canoe, a woman with no business being a photographer, a vulgar job unfit for women. In fact, she has no business having a job at all.

She is also rich, as you can tell by her inability to see them, these desolate men standing in the mud and the carabao grass. Certain types of ladies have no reason to acknowledge they coexist with people like them, the soldiers in Balangiga, even though they meet on the other side of the world sharing a common unease, the unease of aliens. The men fail to catch Cassandra's brief expression of distress, as she blushes at the ragged sight of the company she is to keep. They see instead the arrogant blue eyes barely glancing at them, the men of Company C, America's military servants—disheveled, smelly, and demented. Still, the soldiers look across the riverbank with a hopeful air, gazing at Lieutenant Bumpus and his insane cargo in the distance.

But beyond Bumpus's disappearing boat, there is no mail boat, no other boat in sight.

The men's feelings of longing, of being adrift in an infernal solitude, dislocated from family, crazed by distance, heighten with the descent and portage of each steamer trunk and clothes chest and clanking camera and hatbox after hatbox disembarking from the imperious Cassandra's bancas—one by one the baggage of extravagant displacement mocks the men's sense of being marooned in this hellhole, this humpbacked paradise that is Samar.

In addition, everyone at some point or another has had lingering pernicious malaria, or filariasis, or syphilis, or dengue hemorrhagic fever, and other wastes that go on for years.

The men stare at their fearless leader, that pink-faced boy in the old-fashioned mohair collar who makes their lives wretched.

Captain Thomas W. Connell, all of twenty-six years old, barely out of his West Point grays, watches Cassandra's stance of self-sufficiency around the bancas. She has that smug look of completion and command that irritated him when he first saw her at a dance, at General Jakey Smith's huts in Tacloban, one of those upper-class civilian soirees that offer reprieves to Connell as surreal as the war. To some he was a catch, but it was clear that to her, he was just some cog in a wheel.

An imperialist's stooge, she pointed out.

—I beg your pardon, he said, wanting to smack her but keeping his hand on his chin, as if reflective.

And she proceeded to lecture him, asking him if he had ever heard of the speeches and writings of that editorializing mountebank, that despicable radical Mark Twain—which he hadn't, he explained, as he was off fighting a war.

The violence of his sense of injustice before this woman kept his lips tightly pressed. And at the dance he had that feeling of incompetence, of unstable consequence that still rules over him in passing moments of civilian life.

—Well, you should read his essay, "To a Person Sitting in Darkness," captain, she had advised, with that earnestness that to him added to the unseemliness of a woman's thoughts, her passion confirming she had too hastily subscribed to them—It was a sensation in *North American Review*! Every American should read it: he is like Hamlet, he is our own Shakespeare: Twain holds a mirror up to our nature!

—Ouch, snorted that busybody Bumpus, passing by—I had no idea of the darkness in which we sit, here in this sunny paradise, Tacloban.

But Bumpus was nothing if not a charmer, and he eased the captain aside at Jakey Smith's salon, teasing the woman as he approached.

—But if you dislike this war so much, what are you doing here with us? grinned Bumpus.

—You need an observer, she said, touching the young red-faced lieutenant on his epaulet with her lace fan.

Clearly Bumpus's blond good looks gave his equally

disagreeable views a pass in this shapely harridan's eyes. And called upon to return to her friends, a bunch of sweltering Filipinos in three-piece suits—*americanas,* they called their uncomfortable wear, without irony—she bowed to them both, giving her farewell with that nasal turn on the word *gentlemen* that Captain Connell recognized: he had once lived among the striving classes in Manhattan. Her voice was the mark of her stature and of his diminution, he with his accent of a nobody from Buffalo, from the wilds of upstate New York, a town as beastly in her mind as its name.

So Connell thought.

That morning on the riverbank in Balangiga, the captain has the pursed look of a parish priest that even the parish priest does not have. Padre Donato waves and smiles at the elaborately dressed señorita with her phalanx of glass and mirrors as if he, the token brown man in the scene, is playing the role of the good cop in this tribunal by the banks, while the soldiers and their captain, watching the incidental woman's progress along the talahib path, after the mad adventure with Scheetherly, are the evil ones out to get her.

Cassandra goes straight for the parish priest.

In the first stereo card of this encounter, Padre Donato looks like a dwarf in scale, an elfin miniature amid vertical, unsmiling shades. But even all by himself, the padre looks like a badly drawn, joyful comic of himself. His pate is flat, like the hammerhead shadows that darken the archipelago's waters, so that the children call their squashed-looking priest Butanding while he pats them on their heads anyhow. Padre Donato is a short, fat bundle in a surplice, a happy sack of juvenile *carne*, piglet or veal, wrapped in a soutane.

The captain, on the other hand, is a superfluously moody figure in a dress shirt so neat it looks fake, art-designed against the palms (so it is, with the prop master studying military manuals and historical costume books of American wars, from the Civil War to the Sioux plains to the Battle of Manila Bay in 1898). Captain Coño, the locals call the head of the garrison, though they claim not to understand the translation of his name. Connell has the rigid posture of a man pretending he doesn't sweat, though he must be dying in his woolen shirt. His furry collar itches. He has summer's white cotton dress in his quarters, but he won't wear new clothes out of delicacy. Some of his men still wear the blue rags they wore in May to fight the bantamweight Boxers of China. Oh these forgotten men of the Military Order of the Carabao! Not only minds but clothes have gone amok in the hurly-burly of the sea crossings, from Hawaii to Manila to Pekin, all the dirty little wars that are now sadly America's burden, though it need not be so, for invasion is only optional. The captain has not known a woman since their departure from Manila. But just in case, he keeps his clothes tidy.

In the stereo cards, the captain does look as if he has a stick up his ass.

Connell's expression gives nothing away.

On the other hand, Padre Donato's smiling Buddha face shines from the coconut oil streaming down his groomed hair and beneath his outlandish broad-brimmed straw hat, the kind no priest on the island wears (priest hats are wool, imported from Singapore). This priest in a peasant hat raises red flags to the knowing, none of whom includes the Americans. Padre Donato always has a hilot nearby to massage his temples and the small of his back, his solar plexus being a particular health concern, astrologically. The hilot, a peaceable charlatan, may be seen lounging under a coconut tree, shading his eyes with a peaked hat, the triangular kind seen in Vietnam War movies in bird's-eye-view before all the rice-planting peasants die.

Cassandra looks the priest in the eye and shakes his hand as if he were the leader of the isle, exclaiming:

—Padre Donato, so good to see you again! You will get your picture taken today for me to send to New York, ha? You promise?

—Ah, anything for you, Señorita Cassandra, Miss United States of the Americanos! Promise!

29.

The Intended

"He left it behind. We thought you might want it, since you are the letter's intended." He speaks in a foreigner's English, softly. Caz will not place it. She will not remember him, his voice, or his words.

He gestures. His voice lacks confidence. He feels unbalanced. "It is your name," he points. "On the envelope."

"Thank you," she says, her mouth visibly shaking, and he is afraid. She stands at an angle away from him in her living room, half facing the dark. But he can see, the way her mouth opens in a cry, a crumpled anguish that has no sound, that she is deep in a place that has no entry anyhow, she is all alone in it, and it is a mistake to be a witness. He feels his neck growing warm, his brow and the back of his head and the parts of his body—that had been cold when he entered these rooms weathered by the habagat—feeling suddenly hollow, febrile. He feels it suddenly, the heat, beads down his cheek.

She stands there, her arms wrapped around the manila envelope tied in rubber bands, her body bent over it in a bow. She does not touch the other package, the paper bag. Her posture does not invite consolation. He moves backward, as if about to leave, when she speaks.

"You were there?" she asks. "You saw him—?"

The messenger is at the door and turns toward her in the darkness.

He speaks slowly, as if his words need measuring, as if he, too, is sorry to reveal it.

"No, ma'am."

Oh, her mouth says, another crumpling, a silence.

"No, ma'am. No one is there."

"So no one heard," she whispers. "Who if he cried would hear him. No one saw. Can that be true?"

"Pardon, ma'am?"

"Can that be true—there was no observer?"

The messenger stands still for a moment, as if trying to understand her question, as if needing a translation. The man's thoughts on the matter of the film director's death have been muddled, a burden of incomprehension new to him, a weight of horror and guilt and anger and sorrow. Mostly sorrow.

He had witnessed her departure from the set months before, but the gossip on their breakup was hushed. It had taken him a few days to get her address, here in her new place by the Pasig, in Manila. Freddo made him do it. And he had only done it, he thought, because although the man was not of his country, the messenger felt he was of the director's clan. The family of film. Even she, for a while, had been a part of it. They say the man was a genius. He, the messenger, was only a carpenter. He did not know him. He was surprised once when the man spoke to him in his own language, Farsi.

He had learned it, the director had explained, in Denmark, where he had lived for a time in Christiania, he said, neighbor to a family of Persian immigrants.

The man was also a foul-mouthed genius, the carpenter had discovered. He could curse like a devil in Farsi.

But now that the messenger is here, at her home, he wonders at the futility of it.

The director was gone. Just like that.

His lips quiver.

"Yes, ma'am," he says. "It is true. There is no one. No one is at home. There is no observer."

He uses the present tense as Filipinos do—he has been too long in these islands.

"You know it does not exist," she mutters.

"Pardon?"

He feels dumb. He keeps saying stupid words, as if his English is half forgotten.

"It does not exist," she repeats, looking at nothing. "The world does not exist without an observer."

Now I am alone.

The messenger shuts the door behind him. He feels the cold beads drip down his cheek. He does not understand if it is a river of sweat or tears.

1.

MV *Blanket*

MV *Blanket* powers toward Allen, Samar.

Magsalin has followed Chiara up the deck of the ferry, watching the woman's high-heeled strap sandals as she climbs. This is a professional. Not a hair out of place, not a speck on her camouflage-print safari-style Louis Vuitton suit. She perfectly intuits the measure of the stairway's steps, ascending without waste of space or spiky heel dangling in the air.

"Oh my God," screams Chiara up on the top deck. "What is that!"

Passing all of them by, eating up the expanse of their ocean view, is a giant head of the Virgin Mary.

The statue's two eyes stare past them like enormous Sohoton caves.

The gargoyle, a gigantic white shadow, would perturb the most rational agnostic.

"It is the Virgin Mary," says Magsalin.

"The Statue of the Risen Christ!" explains Edward. "A masterpiece of the Samar artisans. See. It usually floats on the water. An engineering feat!"

"Oh," says Chiara, "it is—usually fantastic."

For a moment, their thoughts pass, until the entire dream, in slow motion, moves on toward Catbalogan.

"I guess it is like that scene in Fellini—*E la nave va*—a film unjustly neglected by critics," Chiara says, regaining her high-heeled poise, the habagat's torpid air on the ship's deck making no impression on her sharp suit."My dad made me watch it. There's this huge ship that blocks the town's view of the water, sitting there, when the movie begins. It gives you claustrophobia. You feel you're going blind—there's too much mystery. Your entire left sight line of what should be water is erased by the ship. That movie made me phobic. Since then I've been scared of huge, unnecessarily bloated things, like air mattresses, or blimps. And Jeff Koons sculptures. And that thing. That Virgin Mary."

"Lots of people are turned off by Jeff Koons sculptures. I don't know about the Virgin Mary," says Magsalin. "That is a pretty dramatic effect of one film. My favorite scene in *La nave va* is when the journalist interviews the Grand Duke about the dead opera singer, and the entire scene is a quarrel over the translation of 'edge of the mountain' versus 'mouth of the mountain.' So funny."

"I knew you'd say that," says Chiara. "But yeah, I like that scene. That is my favorite Fellini."

"It's the one about the funeral of an artist, isn't it? The ship is on its way to blow the artist's ashes out to sea."

"And what kind of a name is Allen?" Chiara says.

"Why are you changing the subject?"

"Who is that town, Allen, Samar, named after?"

"Whom," says Magsalin.

"That's not nice."

"Sorry," says Magsalin. "I was raised by a grammar Nazi. Come to think of it, my mom was probably trained by one of those American Thomasite teachers. An entire colonial school system for fifty years mainly training people to be the police of English grammar. Not the best formula for educating a nation."

"So who is that town named after?"

"Woody," says Magsalin, "You know the movie *Bananas*? In the early days, when TV was just starting, commercial TV in Manila had no live programming, and the TV stations just borrowed films from the foreign embassies. I used to watch *Take the Money and Run* and *Bananas* every day for months, over and over again. I thought all movies were about madcap existentialism and comic revolutionary plots. That town is named after the guy who made *Bananas*. You know, where Woody Allen dresses up like Fidel Castro and drives out a dictator also dressed like Fidel Castro."

"My favorite scene in *Bananas* is when the South American translator translates the words in English of Woody Allen into English," says Chiara. "So funny. Turns out the translator is insane, just escaped from a lunatic asylum, and there's a chase scene of his doctors trying to catch the crazy translator with a butterfly net."

"Hey, that's my favorite scene, too," says Magsalin.

"I know," says Chiara. "I think I need a butterfly net. So really, who is the town named after?"

"Guy named Henry T. Allen. Some American who probably gave the water cure to a bunch of rebels, and so of course he gets a town named after him. He was really good at getting his amigos, the Filipinos, to turn into US Army scouts. He organized the Philippine Constabulary—which is what Marcos also called his martial-law goons—the PC—history in this case seems to be mainly just kind of an extended epilogue. The policing and counterinsurgency in this country are all inherited from the genius of Henry T. Allen. The tortures and killings by the police have a long history—extrajudicial is kind of traditional. But Henry Allen outdid himself. Eventually, his brand of bureaucratic genius killed three million Filipinos, mostly civilians, by 1913. Counterinsurgency broke the Philippine revolution. And hunger, of course, as the Americans starved out the guerrillas by burning rice and farmlands and farm animals, killing the carabaos and such."

"I prefer your *Bananas* story."

"Everyone does. But it *is* true, though—I did watch *Take the Money and Run* and Vittorio De Sica's *Sunflower*, with Sophia Loren, over and over again. In the seventies, when I was a kid. The TV stations in the provinces were taken over by the dictator's men, with no live programming for months. Later I understood. In emergency situations, the stations reverted back to old habits.

Some joker from the Ministry of Public Information probably had long overdue rentals from Thomas Jefferson Cultural Center, or the British Council, and just slotted them in. Old habits die hard."

24.

Days of the Habagat

And the priest crosses himself with a dramatic reach across his shoulders and a pious coupling of his palms, bowing toward the lady.

The impression he gives is that he is a bit of a dolt.

Nevertheless, that afternoon Cassandra Chase takes pictures of him for Hudson Valley Stereographic Company, the Tru-Vision arm of Underwood & Underwood, budding conglomerate of the budding century. Padre Donato will keep his pose as Cassandra gathers more extras, the soldiers and the laborers and the washer-women and the town officials, deaf and dumb Kapitan Abayan with shy Balais, his mild-mannered vice-mayor with the classical name, Andronico, in a composition she holds in her head, lifted from battle scenes in Paolo Uccello or mystical groupings of onlookers in lives of the saints.

Cassandra loves hodgepodge, mixing knight and animal, soldier and martyr. Especially she is struck by those Italian pictures about peripheral scenes in dramatic moments, such as the sleeping guards at the Resurrection of Christ or the bunch of chatty town burghers who do not notice the centurions in the background, torturing a man wearing a crown of thorns. She keeps adjusting, but her groups are never quite right. She switches the smooth-faced bugler, who is too tall, for the sullen laborer, who is too lean. She spies the Chief and the surgeon ambling beneath the palm fronds, and she waits for them.

What she aims for is awkwardness in symmetry, an aesthetic principle and uneasy weight as she travels through the islands. The idea might be good for the Renaissance, but who knows if it works in postcard-size 3-D. Sometimes, she frets, the effect she produces is just of forlorn, too crowded congregations who have come together in a palm jungle without rhyme or reason, squinting at the sun.

As the nineteenth century turns a corner, imagining itself into perspective, the wonders of stereopsis have taken hold. The illusion of depth is a fetish. The rosewood stereograph, also known as the Holmes viewer, is a precursor of such toys as the twentieth-century Baby Boomer's View-Master, with its seven-pair color reels showing pictures of Popeye eating spinach in six moves, or the Seven Wonders of the World, or the adventures of animated mice—one pair of frames at a time in seven circular 3-D clicks. But instead of a fourteen-picture disc, the product of Cassandra's rectangular art—the Holmes viewer's stereo card, 3½ by 7—is an elegant, sepia-toned twofer.

Griswold the surgeon is walking along with the Chief to pose for the New York lady just arrived in their swamps. He is a fan of her machine. A propos of her charms, he confesses how he

carries with him from Albany to Honolulu to Manila his trea-
sured stereo cards of doubled tourist shots of the Grand Canyon,
Niagara Falls, the Tuscaloosa Pig Festival, pineapple gardens
of their new possession Hawaii, and the wild horse passes of
Yosemite Park. In fact, the sets of cards had given Griswold, a
doctor with a placid practice in Plattsburgh, New York, his itch
for adventure. First, he had signed up to be a surgeon in Cuba.
Instead, he was assigned to Niantic, a stone's throw from his
birthplace in Connecticut. He tried again, and he advanced a few
yards, to Fort Warren. Finally, he scored, sailing first to San Francisco, California, on his way to the Philippines. It was not Cuba,
but goddamn, it was war.

In Balangiga, Griswold the surgeon keeps his Holmes viewer
in its original box at night, a velvet-lined crypt, right by his bedside. His stereo cards are meager but much perused.

None have survived.

Griswold the surgeon is explaining the history of the Holmes
viewer to Valeriano Abanador, the police chief in charge of the
town since the Spanish days and an eager listener of foreigners'
tales since time immemorial, that is, for three eternal years,
including this endless revolution, first against Spain, then against
America. No idiot wants to be chief in these conflicting times.
These days of amigo warfare are not good for the Chief's bowels.
Amigo by day, revolutionary by night. The man did not drop out
of San Juan de Letran de Manila just to come home to this. It
gives him diarrhea. The burden of a chief of police is to live at

cross-purposes with dual bosses, the demands of the invader and the loyalties of the insurrectionist, and constantly the Chief feels a pain in the pit of his stomach, no matter what he does.

But Valeriano Abanador, the Chief, takes up his burden, a man of duty. He turns his face to the doctor. A philosophical man of leisure who once led a desultory life until his goddamned people made him chief of police, Abanador speaks four languages (plus posturing Latin for special effects)—to wit, Spanish, Waray, Tagalog, and English, the last with a note of doubt, a speculative hesitancy. He is just learning it. His halting words often end in a raised, questioning pitch. This endears him to his audience, who becomes talkative and gains confidence in his inarticulate presence. In this way, the officers of Balangiga take pity on the bumbling chief in this sorry town, including him in general remarks whenever he is in their hearing, and the Chief's good humor coupled with his bad English lull the men into never questioning how it is that he understands everything they say while they have no clue what he is saying to everyone else.

1.

Settling Finally onto Samar

What is she doing anyway, Magsalin asks herself, as the Pajero rattles down the plank, roll-on, roll-off, settling finally onto Samar, and Chiara rolls down her window to the unexpected sea air.

Magsalin remembers no coastal road. The way to Balangiga used to be an inland trail on pocked paths without pavements. Even she is unsettled by the beauty of this novelty, the ocean vista on the road to Eastern Samar.

"Beach resorts," says Private First Class Gogoboy. "It is now full of beach resorts on the way to Balangiga. So now we have the beautiful road by the sea. The Maharlika Highway. Marabut, Full of Haven, Tubabao, Calico-an. Surfer dudes, GI Joes, German nudie people. They love Eastern Samar! The hitchhikers and the money-honey tourists."

"Wow," says Magsalin, "back to business after the super-typhoon, too."

"Yes, yes," mourns Edward, the boy with the Uzi, "all this, along Maharlika Highway, was usually destroyed after the super-typhoon Yolanda."

"Haiyan!" says Private First Class Gogoboy, explaining to Chiara, "what you call our typhoon—Haiyan!"

"Yes, yes," says Edward, "all the houses gone. Even the coconuts—look. Kalbo. You know, bald. Like Gogoboy! The coconuts—they are usually destroyed after the typhoon Haiyan. But not so many dead because the Balangiga people— they usually evacuated, yes they did. They know where to go up in the hills."

"But the money-honey, they are back in business," says Private First Class Gogoboy. "The beach resorts—they advertise the cultural paradise, the natural resources—and the money-honey tourists, they come."

"And the New People's Army, who used to have the run of the hills?" asks Magsalin.

"They are now just directing the illegal logging in the forests."

"The Philippine Army and the communist rebels in Samar," explains Magsalin to Chiara, "have been going at it for decades. No love lost between them."

"Surely privates first class Gogoboy and Edward have reasons for thinking badly of their enemy," says Chiara.

"Everyone has reasons."

Whom does she wish to impress? Why turn the image so she looks not at herself but awry, through a lens not her own? Why follow Chiara through her private labyrinth when her own reasons for return give her nausea?

The humidity on the deck of MV *Blanket* has turned into a

salty, swampy breeze on land, and momentarily, before the air conditioning revs, Magsalin feels her armpits turning into some sort of soup, though the feeling of heat in the wind gives her that pleasurable inertia of summer vacation. Chiara, on the other hand, leans back like a model for *Vogue*, and the folds of her silken suit are arrayed with casual art about her limbs.

Does the woman not sweat?

25.

The Ordinary Miracle of Stereopsis

A stereo card is slipped into a wire stand on the stereograph's rosewood slide, says Griswold the surgeon as they walk among the palms—this flat piece of wood jutting from the lens of the Holmes viewer. It is our nature, Chief, you see, that the ability to see depth is a trick of the mind. Depth is only an impression, a mathematical calculus! says Griswold, trained in eye, ear, nose, and throat diseases in Bellevue Medical College of New York City. He has a generous spirit, especially for sharing his knowledge, which goes on and on. He even carries around his teaching implements. Our vision is imperfect, only surmise. A disparity exists between the sight observed by the right eye and by the left. Notice. In order to see correctly, the mind must compute. Oh do not misunderstand, Chief. Not like a machine. Our mind *imagines*. That is how we see. Through illusion. But look here, try this. See. Move it until—

Aha!

In the Holmes viewer, the calculation of the illusion of depth is manual, not just mental. Your hand *adjusts* the two-picture stereo card on the slide to create the ordinary miracle of stereopsis, that is, our everyday way of seeing with our two imperfect eyes.

With one mechanical flick, here, a flat photographic world in doubled mirror images, there, turns into three dimensions, see! *Voila!*

The miracle that is sight!

The flat world is round again.

Ojo! interjects the chief of police, looking into the stereoscope the doctor carries: *Eyyyyeee—! Can see! A coconut!*

Yes, you can, the doctor exclaims. You can see! You have a new eye.

A very American—what is the word—trick? says the Chief, placing the instrument carefully back in the doctor's hands.

Yes. It is a very American invention, nods Griswold: We have manufactured how to see the world.

Ah, but doctor, grins the Chief, knocking his knuckles against his head, but I can see that coconut with own eyes already—I can see that coconut with my own coconut!

And he keeps knocking at his skull, grinning.

Sure, you can, says Griswold the surgeon, but I do not think you are getting my point.

I get it, says the Chief, you have the coconut in the picture and the coconut in Balangiga—you americanos, you just want all of the coconuts!

A mania for reality took hold among hobbyists in Griswold's late nineteenth century. Photography is only one of the means that makes possible the fantasy of Tru-Vision. (A historical survey unfolds on the screen in a sequence of irised stills, silent-movie style.) William McKinley's world has a firm lease on the dream. Stereo cards of McKinley himself are sold everywhere, and he had the distinction of becoming the first celluloid president, through the graces of Thomas Edison. In the moving film by Edison's company, McKinley has a look of banality that suits him. In Griswold's Holmes viewer, he is distractingly plump, with a cadaverous gaze. You look into the intimate, tender frame of the stereoscope, and his eyes' emptiness pops out, as if his sad future were already upon him, the assassin's gun pointed at his vacant eyes.

Citizens are eager to buy the spoils from William McKinley's war. Stereo cards of serene views of the ruined battleship *Maine* by Guantanamo Bay, of Admiral Dewey on the deck of *Olympia* after his victory in Manila, of soldiers advancing on Havana, riders up San Juan Hill; picture books bearing titles with resonant pronouns, such as *Our Islands and Their People*; and albums of naval ships en route from San Francisco to Hawaii to Guam, another novel possession. Of course, also the postcard sunsets of Manila Bay, along with infantrymen amid cogon grass in Tondo, and above all, the grainy brown dead in bamboo trenches all around Luzon. Every stereo card is a propaganda coup. (Theodore Roosevelt, that interfering assistant secretary, is especially proud of the pictures of *his* Navy.)

Tru-Vision, Stereoscopy, Praxino Pictures, Panorama Moving Effects, Keystone View Company. Underwood & Underwood, Cassandra Chase's employer, is one of the prime capitalists of the new venture. The word movie has yet to be invented, though

Thomas Edison's minions come up with an exciting word, *kinetoscopy*! Sadly, unlike his other geeky coinages, *gramophone* and such, that word will not take. The world is in such a state of wild invention that the names of things are still in flux. The dream of the peripatetic photographer Cassandra joins with the curiosity of her sedentary consumer to line the pockets of the seers, the bright men of Wall Street.

Chiara's assistant prop makers, troops of Irishwomen with mops of hair in botanical, secondary colors, mint, tangerine, and grape—a summer fad—report to Chiara the many places they find scattered snapshots from Underwood & Underwood—eBay and other auction sites. At Strand Book Store in Manhattan, an enterprising intern, Fionnuala of the nationalistic, lime-green hair, finds stereo cards stacked in neat boxes in the Rare Book Room on the third floor. The men of Company C of the Ninth US Infantry Division in 1901, of the historic Manchu Regiment, survive in the troublingly mirrored images. One by one, she picks through the pile. Fionnuala the intern thinks (after all she is a woman with her own revolutionary history, being from the west of Ireland) that the cards multiply unnecessarily the error of the men's position in Samar.

In a stereo card of that day before the massacre, done at morning on the riverbank, Padre Donato T. Guimbaolibot, formerly priest of Guiuan, now of Balangiga, is the only one smiling. It is possible to view his clownish presence—the bowing toward the white woman is a bit excessive and not becoming of his actual sentiments, soon to be revealed—as par for the course in a war movie with amateur extras, as the stereo card fades into the film's action. Viewers might pass over the details of his moving figure as trite, comic prelude for our modern times— the calm before calamity that audiences of generic action scenes have now learned to expect (though even Shakespeare had such expositions). Plus, butanding is not a hammerhead; it's a whale shark (the young interns, checking only the Internet for local terms, and to be honest, mainly skimming Images and Videos, keep getting variable results). Historians of Balangiga, in fact, describe Padre Donato as "noble," "tall," and "revered." Magsalin is uncomfortable with ahistorical humor in movies, sensing that it inscribes an unnecessary gap between commerce and art. It is said that tall and noble Padre Donato, tortured by Americans after the affair of Balangiga, retires to his hometown, Guiuan, with post-traumatic stress disorder (or *na-stre-stress hiya,* the citizens of Guiuan report): his heart rate changes whenever he meets a white man.

But she has to admit that some of her own revisions—the coconut oil in the priest's hair, the holy hilot waiting to massage his temples—seem like mere remnants from some beach vacation, details lifted from visits to island spas. The peaked straw hat that the charlatan masseur wears is a costume-design flaw, Cambodian, not Filipino, secondhand relics from other movies about a war yet to happen in a different, also misbegotten place.

1.

On the Way to Balangiga

On the way to Balangiga, Private First Class Gogoboy stops at a beach resort. Six porters in red trousers and katipunero hats—with their straw brims turned over to show the insignia of the revolutionaries, embroidered also in red—appear, all studiously barefoot and bearing scabbards for their absent bolo knives. They rush to grab the luggage. They stare nonplussed at the guests' sparse, identical cargo, the pair of green and purple leather bags.

"But I thought we were supposed to go straight to Balangiga." Magsalin asks, "What are you doing, Gogoboy? We don't stop here."

Edward looks sideways at Private First Class Gogoboy.

"For lunch, ma'am," says Gogoboy. "This is always the place for lunch before going to Balangiga!"

Magsalin remembers how the buses that drove toward San Juanico Strait always chose the same rest stops, and the idea of trying a different eatery instead of the carinderia shown to you by the driver was anathema. No one ever thought of trying an alternate shop. It was like a mafia of luncheonettes dotted that highway.

Magsalin waits for Chiara to move, but Chiara does not, so Magsalin sighs and gives the tip to the two porters who won the bags.

"But wait," says Magsalin, "how will we know whose bag is which? They are exactly the same. Let me put a tag on my bag."

But the porters have already gone ahead.

"Before it used to be they usually carry knives. But the tourists complain," explains Edward. "So now the porters, they usually now only wear the hats."

"KKK?" Chiara asks, her first sign of alarm.

"I know, it's weird," says Magsalin. "Their hats have the initials of the secret society—the katipuneros who won the revolution against Spain, but lost to their frenemy, the United States."

"Kataas-taasang, Kagalang-galangang Katipunan ng mga Anak ng Bayan!" Edward raises his fist. "Sulong, insurrecto!"

And he fake-kicks the last porter, a mere boy, about Edward's size, still waiting for a tip though he has no bag to carry.

The boy bends his elbow, pretending to take out the illusive knife from his empty scabbard.

Edward taps his Uzi.

Edward wins.

The boy lopes back to the cabins, holding on to his paper-thin hat.

Their rest cabins are airy, stand-alone huts with a view of the plaza on one hand, with its statue of the hero, and the beach on the other. Magsalin realizes the abnormal configuration once she sees the water. The beach has invaded the poblacion, the town proper. No self-respecting town has a plaza without a church nearby and the principal houses, the priest's kumbento included, within the sound of the bells. A beach resort right next to the town plaza, without church or bells, destabilizes Magsalin's compass.

This town lacks gravity.

But as she leaves the hut to take the path to the open-air restaurant at the end of the plaza, she understands her error. It is a fake plaza: the statue in its center is not of the hero, the traveling poet in his European cloak. It is a cement whale shark, a standup butanding. Even the flag on the pole is a trompe-l'oeil: the yellow sun in the middle is a fried egg on a tapsilog. The waitresses in their striped outfits, camisa, pañuelo, and patadyong skirt with the same checkered décor as the tablecloths, greet them posed like tinikling dancers without the required sticks on the ground snapping at their feet. The ring and middle fingers of each of the maidens' hands are stuck together in glued grace, in constant motion, making winding figure eights about the dancers' earlobes as if warning of a buzzing Chiara and Magsalin cannot hear.

As she passes through the restaurant's puka-shell entryway, Magsalin notes that the women are in fact skipping to the authentic kuracha beat of the karaoke in the background. An old man dressed in contemporary Philippine clothing, a Lakers jersey and a Miami Heat cap, has a microphone in his hand, ready to sing "Horse with No Name." The pleasure of being amid the random kitsch of the country's props animates Chiara. She is hungry, and she eats up the pork liempo, lechon kawali, dinuguan, crispy pata, chicharon, and all other matters of pig, along with the cookies shaped like guns and roses, also pork-full—of lard.

But all Magsalin wants is saging na saba—the kind of plantain her mother first boiled then simmered in a block of molasses.

"Bimboy!" Private First Class Gogoboy whistles to the youngest porter. "Sab-a!"

Sure enough, the treat comes to the table: a display of kalamay-encrusted fingerlings arranged around the plate like petals, a corolla of carbs.

Edward watches intently as Chiara takes a bite.

"Do you usually have that viand," Edward asks, "in your country?"

"Ba-yand magiliw!" Gogoboy sings. "Edward—ba-yand is meat! That is dessert!"

Chiara eats up an entire fingerling of sugared banana.

"No," she says, "this viand has no translation in my country. There is no translation for saging na saba."

"Like malunggay," says Edward with satisfaction, "only the Philippines usually has malunggay and saba."

Private First Class Gogoboy spits on the restaurant's dirt ground.

"Pweh," he says to Edward, "that is a stupid reason not to take the construction job in Saudi!"

"What?" asks Magsalin.

"He will not go," says Gogoboy, "because only the Philippines, he says, has malunggay and saba!"

"Usually," says Chiara.

"You could probably get malunggay in Saudi," says Magsalin. "It is called moringa, a miracle herb."

"No, ma'am," Edward vigorously shakes his head, "only the Philippines usually has malunggay. I cannot live in a country without malunggay."

Magsalin gives Edward a high five.

"Aprub!" she says.

"Me, too, I approve!" says Chiara, "stick to your principles!"

Edward's smile is shy but proud.

"It is not my principles, ma'am," he says, "It is usually my stomach."

Private First Class Gogoboy nods.

"He is a delicate—that one," he explains, "always having gastro-enteritis!"

26.

Padre Donato Feels the Heat

Padre Donato, who rarely sweats in his soutane, feels the heat in a way he has never done before. He has always welcomed the days of the habagat. When he was a boy, the gales released him from summer's suffocations and the boredoms of Lent (a deathless monotony that turned the weak-willed against God)—he'd lie in wait for the cool winds, oddly welcoming, unlike the June monsoons. The habagat, westerly winds that gently ruffle the seas now graze the lady's petticoats. The gusts reveal the sea-gray lace billowing under Cassandra's skirts. The gangrened soldiers ogle the skirts, the womanly sight freeing, for the moment, clouds of pent desire hanging over the americanos of Balangiga.

Even the priest pities them, these smelly Gullivers with their devouring eyes.

It is clear from the close-up of Captain Connell that he is completely aware of the lady's windy disarray, but Cassandra passes him by after the exchange with the padre and cuts him from her vision, just like that.

As she passes, the captain stares at the river, at the ripples scalloping the surface against the low-tide mud. He notes a tadpole, or is it a sea slug, that vile tripang, trying to make an impression in the slime, a quick, wriggling shape just barely visible, bubbling up then burrowing away from sight. A plop, a nonentity. He feels an obstruction in his throat and tries to clear it.

At the strangled sound coming from the americano, the priest assumes a pose of gravity. The priest spits in solidarity with the captain's gurgling, as if his thoughtful saliva were settling a theological quibble beginning in the captain's throat and his meditative spit were thus giving the pair summative consequence in the awkward moment before the lady.

In this scenario, a lady clearly holds some aces.

The captain does not stir. This filthy islander habit of public expelling, no matter how holy, disgusts Connell, and the priest's salvo hits a spot on the captain's well-shined shoes. But Connell is hoarding the phlegm in his own throat. Bouts of acid reflux have been troubling him ever since he and his men hit the island—since August 11, to be exact. He keeps his thoughts and phlegm to himself as he stares at the bubbles in the mud.

The captain is a meticulous diarist, and he will later note even the saliva, the stain on his leather boot, the furtive pests in the mud. When his notebook is recovered, miraculously untainted by the copious squibs of movie-ish blood, the effect of his minute descriptions is destabilizing, the way reality seems, in retrospect, not really credible.

Cassandra gestures to the porters, and they proceed to her

adoptive home, a grass-hut shelter owned by the family Nacionales out in the forest beyond the farms. Cassandra, a literary
woman, like many of her home-schooled class, considers it a symbolical name, Nacionales, worthy of the country's noble hopes.

Cassandra's romantic imagination, fired by Tennyson, "Loch-
invar," and George Gordon, Lord Byron, especially his death
by revolution though not his life by amorous indiscretion, casts
upon everything, but especially names, an emblematic mystery.
How is she to know that in 1849 the official, random distribu-
tion of villagers' surnames is the colonizers' tactic against their
pet peeve: tax evasion? But Casiana Nacionales, a trader Cassandra had met in her riverboat rides around the Visayas, has
an intriguing boldness that anyhow would make her memorable,
no matter her name. Cassandra would love to study the wildlife
and customs of her town, she had said to the trader Casiana,
relating that she, Cassandra, had also been to Panay, Cebu, even
Siquijor (a deliciously creepy place, full of aswang—powerful,
shape-shifting women who wander at night and are partly dead;
Cassandra notes in her diary—the phantoms are likely actual
women deranged from their miscarriages).

She wants to see everything in the islands, she says to Casiana
the trader, including all the exciting but also the most boring
parts.

—Then you must come to Balangiga, Casiana Nacionales says
(she is such a joker)—We will bore you to death!

Captain Connell has the power to detain Cassandra Chase,

command her to remain within the military detachment and not live among the farmers, beyond the poblacion, the town proper.

But what would be the reason for Cassandra's arrest? For fraternizing with the locals?

Morale among American soldiers is so low opinion is divided even over punishment for desertion. Soldiers have gone AWOL and returned with baskets of mangoes to no one's great regret. And he knows her answer will cut him down to size. She had sent the military garrison her letters of commendation in advance, an official one from the governor, that fat Judge Taft, and a cordial message from a family friend, a much-creased note, now obsolete, signed *Assistant Secretary of the Navy Theodore Roosevelt.* She knows him from Oyster Bay. Salvos of privilege precede her arrival, and all the captain can do is accept it, her presence. He watches as the bearers of her goods march, one of them his own servant, the young Francisco, past his men who are already feeling the queasy residue of their finale with that mad Scheetherly by the riverbank.

Right on schedule, their stomachs are rumbling.

The americanos have occupied Balangiga town's entire plaza, including the kumbento, the church compound (it is the only building made of stone), for forty-eight days. Sullen hands are counting. Five hundred seventy-six livid chickens; two thousand twelve prime fingers of saba; fifty-three buko per day, two thousand five hundred forty-four silot in all wrangled direct from the prickly palms and hacked in two for their silvery juice, every goddamned morning for seventy-four insatiable men (only a few follow regulations and stick to the US Army ration of canned goods, though the records state otherwise).

And that's only breakfast.

All around the islands, the wilderness of Samar included, the foreigners' appetites empty the pigsties, cash out the camote crop, hike the price of sugar. The americanos used to delight the *comerciantes*, women like Casiana, who came in rowboats along the riverine trail to Balangiga selling pearls, Chinese slippers, rice cakes, coconut wine, fans, and straw mats. With the arrival of the garrison, the selling has stopped, but the devouring has not.

The soldiers have come to cut the supply of goods to rebels who must be hiding out beyond the storm-battered coconut trees. The laborers, the able men of the town, are now hacking down those trees, which have just recovered from the great typhoon, on orders from the captain.

The soldiers agree that the sweet saba, the boiled banana, which the locals cut fresh from the plantain trees, tastes nothing like its fleshy counterpart, Idaho potatoes. And the damned strings of that banana starch keep clinging to the teeth, like Iowa's summer corn way past its season. Buko juice gives them acid reflux. Guavas are killing their insides, curdling their fragile gastric juices and churning their slushy shit into shitty grit. And is it their imagination, or do the coconuts of the buko man, Dong Canillas, begin rotting in their bellies even before the men start sipping their juice in the beastly sun? And that local delicacy, the sea slug, that vile tripang, is no gastronomic treat—it's a nasty trick. Malunggay soup, the people's universal panacea, is no cure. Reaping the rewards of Samar, they agree, is no picnic. Those straw goods—mats, flutes, fans—are as flimsy and useless as the women traders' thin, gauzy blouses (about which nonetheless they have recurring dreams). The traveling wine, welcome as it is, lingers, a tannic toxin, on their tongues. It creates a fuzzy residue viscous as the islanders' cloggy spit, fit for ungrateful swine, not men.

And yet they keep taking it, the islands' produce.

After all, what are they in power for?

Following Cassandra in her wake, the men leave the red herring of her arrival to return to their breakfast in the open air. They imagine they hear mad Scheetherly in the distance, but it is only the tolling of the bells. The bells of Balangiga ring for ritual matins as the men march back from their morning adventure by the river—a comforting sound anyway for those like Captain Connell, a devout Catholic who discovers kinship with the strangers when he arrives on their islands. The joke is on him. His own servant, a ten-year-old orphan, chants uncannily the names of Mary, *virgo veneranda, rosa mystica*, as he stitches chevrons on the captain's shirts. Even surnames sound like pious sermons: San Juan Bautista, Angeles de los Santos. Connell came to civilize the barbarians only to discover that they share his Roman, rosary-loving God.

And it is no surprise, this early in the morning, for the men to see the Chief, Valeriano Abanador, strolling about for his chats with the officers—Connell, then Bumpus, now Griswold. The Chief is so skinny and dark that in the pictures one first mistakes him for a shadow. In one of the pictures, he looks directly at the camera, standing with his arms crossed among the men of Company C—their sullen amigo, beanpole mascot of their will. The soldiers march beside his too casual stride, this useless busybody and absent-minded mediator between the captain and the locals.

The locals, the Chief has been warning them, have been grumbling over the captain's orders—to dig up their camote, cut their malunggay, chop down the palms that screen the sentries' view of rebel marauders on the beach, and worst of all, burn their rice! There are rumblings about destroying their own trees that have just sprouted again after the terrible storm of 1897, *nga maugo!* And yet, the Chief reports, despite these complaints, the locals will obey, of course, the captain's orders. Except for burning the rice. Over their dead body. But otherwise, the men of Balangiga will follow.

He, the Chief, will see to that, siempre. That is his job.

The soldiers know that it is the captain's threat of curtailing the coming fiesta that keeps the people in line, not Abanador's work ethic.

The Chief, though pleasant enough, is ineffective.

The Chief was up early today for the melee with Scheetherly with that maddening alertness he does not display for his actual duties, such as corralling the laborers Captain Connell needs to clean up the town before the inspector general arrives from Tacloban. Or for keeping the peace during cockfights. Or for separating the maidens from the men. Brawls that arise over the presence of comely women who keep appearing all around town, bearing laundry and water jars on their heads, never break the Chief's deep siesta. If locals gang up on a soldier, such as on the hapless sergeant, Prank Vitrine, God bless his wandering soul (though one day he will return, predicts the Chief), the Chief strolls along after his nap to tell the captain the same thing.

It is always the americano's fault.

The women are simply going about their business, the Chief cannot stop them from husking rice, plucking chickens, drying their budo, their salted fish, carrying their bamboo water containers to the river, and feeding pigs while wearing their skimpy clothes that they have been wearing since the Jesuits came to catechize the islands in 1581! The Chief knows his island history, and if you have enough time, he will tell you all about it. My God, señores, we have been living in peace in our underclothes for generations. You foreigners are molesting the town's fair women, and you are blaming it on the women's outfits! *Jesus Maria!* Not even the Spaniards, who molested women in the name of God, were so foolish in their logic.

And why would you not, anyhow, the Chief says philosophically, his quite tanned character giving nobility to the film's enterprise, and the actor who plays him must have the gravitas of James Earl Jones plus the wisdom of Bruce Lee—the worst thing about going to war, the Chief says, is you still have a penis, but you don't get a medal if you keep it in your pants, though you should! You should get a medal, the Chief exclaims, for purity. Purity is a brave man's last stand!

Upon this, the Chief and the captain wholeheartedly agree. The captain listens to the Chief because he is the only one who responds to his schoolbook Spanish. The Chief breaks the news of the americanos' stupidity with that shrug of his shoulders, the way he gestures when the lieutenant Bumpus takes a pawn or when an opponent in the art of arnis grazes him with a bamboo spear before he knocks the dumb man to his knees.

He has been telling the captain no one in town believes anyway in the innocence of that soldier Prick, for instance, the adjutant once seen going toward Giporlos with Casiana Nacionales—so the captain need not make an example of the man's disappearance as a sign of the treachery of the Filipino people, our *sin verguenza* style of friendship! Sure, sometimes Casiana returns from trading, arriving with the boats of alimango from Basey and the baskets of gaway from Guiuan, at the same time that sightings of the disappeared Prick crop up along her trade routes, but her rumored aiding of his desertion is no clue to Prick's pure intentions the day he took that long walk in the forest. He was a man of reflection, unlike you, I must say, captain—curious about the world around him, that Prick. Into whose snare he was caught that he did not reappear is Prick's own business—oh, yes, it is better to believe that red man Prick went nuts, not AWOL, deserting the benevolence of your kind, but that is your own look-out!—oh, and do not come crying to us about the madness that has come over your soldiers in our jungles—no one asked you to come!

His name's Frick, the captain says, not Prick. Benton Frick. And he came back with his own stories to tell. He did not desert. He was tricked.

Sure, sure, that Prick was tricked, says the Chief. And then there is the case of Prank Vitrine.

Frank, the captain says. His name is Frank Breton. And you better give us back his lame-ass body, or you will be sorry.

It is clear that the captain is unconcerned about the fate of Prank. Everyone knows he will turn up after some orgasmic time, with Casiana or Paciana, who cares; and he will be summarily punished, for sure, but who can blame him?

Sure, sure, Prank Vitrine, says the Chief. He is a good man, pobrecito, that americano, that sad lubberboy, that Prank.

In these conferences with the captain, whether discussing the fate of the eighty-two laborers jailed by the captain for three days now or pointing out the virtues of the martial art of arnis, that is, whether discussing matters of import or impulse, the Chief always has a slightly rueful look, conveying facts as if they are beyond his ability to understand them.

Valeriano Abanador, the Chief, keeps getting tangled in his crisscross of tongues, Spanish and English, mangling both, so that the captain often gives the Chief's unyielding sentiments the benefit of the doubt, filling in the blanks of his words. And the man has this curious way of stressing his vowels and then mistaking his fricatives for labials and vice versa, so that you cannot tell if he is saying "penis" or "finish," or truly meaning "prick" for "Frick," or not. It is said that in the early hours of their acquaintance, the Chief had spoken Spanish well enough with the captain, who floridly answered in coin, for he had learned it for Cuba and was delighted to display his knowledge. Only for the captain to be disappointed, as the days wore on to a month, then almost two, that the Chief was in fact as clumsy with Spanish as he was bumbling in his new acquisition, English, which is no surprise, thinks the captain: he pities the fool.

One thing the Chief is good at is arnis, the ancient martial art with bamboo sticks that fascinates the soldiers, and it has become a pastime, before sundown, to watch the Chief demonstrate his skills. This is his true talent, the soldiers agree as they relax in the town plaza. They have converted the plaza into a sprawling bivouac of tents, copper kettles, and a long trestle table in the middle. They clear it for his afternoon demonstrations, post siesta.

It is clear that ensuring the town's adherence to military principles and policies is not the chief virtue of the Chief. This is his true talent—to wield batons of bamboo in dizzying configurations, with slight movements of his wrists or jerks of his elbow landing blows on a target of feathers, almost killing but at the last minute saving someone's pet rooster, or with a withering slash surprising a blameless bugle out of Meyer's grasp. Woeful as a man of security, at best defensive at chess, earnest but unconvincing in conversation, the Chief is a changed man at arnis—bold, precise, and calculating. He should be in a circus, the soldiers agree.

And you would be good in a stew, the Chief responds. Hehe. You know, he cackles, slapping them on the back after his exhibitions—because you all look so guapo, like San Lorenzo Martir, our good-looking patron saint, the deacon of Rome! *Turn me over, I am done!* That is what he said to the Romans while they boiled him in a pot!

From afar, Padre Donato watches the Chief with Griswold the surgeon, trudging up just now from the commotion on the riverbank. Griswold is talking and gesturing, then waves his hand goodbye toward the bright-eyed Chief with a weariness that, in any case, will soon be laid to rest.

Padre Donato, feeling the hoped-for wind of the habagat yet weighted somehow—by its indirection, its unruly coming?—walks behind, watching the soldiers march toward their mess. His fat flesh, beads of coconut oil running down his chubby cheeks, cradles sweat in his collarbone, and in this way his body's greasy monsoon keeps dribbling down his breast.

As the ominous music rises, with some subtle, off-putting disco notes—he and the audience know soon enough what is to come.

30.

Days of the Dead

She had clutched the envelope given by the shy messenger, but she had never opened it.

The Intended.

True. The message from the director was for her.

A joke between them—a bond.

Though in her view he was no Kurtz: all he wanted was to finish his film.

Caz is surprised at the attendance.

There is no body, just this blasphemy, his inexplicable remains in a jar, a bowl of ashes that mocks his actual mortal substance, this foreign form of dying—as if some obscene power had turned him into what repulsed him, an indifferently presented dish.

She thinks—but how everyone is at his wake. Now they come. A critic who had mocked his ambition. His childhood friend from North Fork, Long Island, a man named Horn, or Hearne, who decided to travel last minute, coupling the funeral with a tropical vacation. A tired-looking actor, now bearing only a fleeting resemblance to his past onscreen good looks. A drunkard whom the director had known at the height of the man's fame.

The mansion in Magallanes is too much for one man's needs, she used to tell him, but he was oblivious to his environment, living with just a change of clothes, his soccer shorts and rugby shirts, when he found himself alone. It always seemed too vast, beginning with the entresuelo, a hall of Persian rugs and gilt mirrors, and this gloomy sala, with its mahogany decor, that always looked underfurnished, though it was full of entire living room sets straight from Silahis Antiques, a room dwarfed by that crazy fixture, the disco ball, that loomed like a sore, crystal eye over everyone, living and dead.

But now there are enough people milling about the driftwood rooms to make their sudden appearance, all of these creatures crawling out of the woodwork, a rebuke. There is no risk in respecting the dead.

Now they come.

When his movie was in peril, his funds drying up, and his producers threatening to pull out, he had passed time by telling her stories about his friends, his childhood in New York, his love for a polar bear, the first animal ever to be given Prozac. Really—Prozac?, she said. He had lived a varied life. He had been to Ezra Pound's castle in Italy and read through the poet's posthumous texts (Pound cursed in three languages; but in all modesty, the director said, he spoke seven; his mimicry is not a talent, he dismissed, just a genetic aberration, though his childish gift for tongues took him far). His austere and mortal advisor at Harvard, Anna della Terza of the poetic name and cowboy boots, believed he would be a scholar, like her. But the castle was full of crosses, he said, crossing himself, and Pound's daughter, a Countess, was still a fascist so many years after the war. He couldn't get out of that creepy place fast enough. He grew up bourgeois, he said, which explains why he liked anarchists. A vagabond post-college, though with letters of introduction in his pocket (that was the protocol then), he had hitched rides through the Riviera and felt this constant ascetic urge to shed material things, so that street urchins found themselves playing boules in his oversize jerseys, all along the Alpes-Maritimes. (His secret shame, known only to her, was that he recalled a shirt he wished he had kept, his black varsity letter, for his soccer team, with the crimson H—a frivolous wish that made him blush.) He had taught, later with hindsight's regret, the horrors of Edgar Allan Poe to sad-eyed boys already allied to death, out in a place called Walbrook Junction in the inner city of Baltimore. He'd hung out with hippies in Christiania, Denmark, and had gone skinny-dipping on the peninsula of the Greek Orthodox monastery of Mount Athos. The monks came to arrest him, but his look of malnutrition saved him, he said, he had not eaten for days, boat-hiking in the Aegean Sea, and instead the monks offered him bread and wine. Sounds like a Jesus parable to me, Caz ribbed him. Nudeness is next to godliness, he said. He had led a picaresque life of improvised adventure.

But at the time, he did not really impress his investors.

And now it is as if all of his stories were just preludes to this final act, each one a code encrypting his sorrowful mystery. As if each adventure were not a moment in itself, vulnerable to an alternate choice. Ecstatic, not fatal. Now it is as if the conclusions were linear and ordained, leading to this end, and everything else is only cumulating retrospective. A story foretold. This falseness begotten by chronology: the way recent events—this form of death, suicide—camouflage his life's truth.

It makes everything else he has done suspect, giving everything shade.

It's such crock, she thinks, how death distorts him.

He will never again be seen for who he was.

At least as she remembers him.

But who was he, she wonders.

A restless hunter, she thinks. With a monstrous vitality. Looking for something.

A locked-room puzzle.

One of his favorite plotters, Edgar Allan Poe, had invented the terrible geometry of very physical, almost cinematic ways of disappearing: each crevice and cranny in a deteriorating mansion could be a clue, however unforeseen.

Uh-huh, Caz said to him—I'm an English major. I know those stories. No need to explain them to me.

But despite the detail in the cases that fantastic writer produced, he said, there are no signs of intrusion either at ingresses or exits—no discernible clues for why the victim dies.

Such stories, Caz told him, have a name. They are called locked-room puzzles.

Hah. That's a great title for a movie, he said.

Thank you, said Caz.

But you have to make it, he said.

I'm not writing a movie.

But you should, he said.

Sometimes, she thought, though she loved him, Ludo sounded like a man whose world had relevance only to him—and he made things up that he had no business designing.

Poe's solitary delight, Ludo went on, was to astound the reader by deliberately withholding the clues.

But she had loved those moments when he went off on a tangent, explaining in detail a problem about his fictions, as if she could in any way help him. It was his deep absorption in his own plots, which were always in flux, that drew her to him. For Ludo, all ideas had alternate endings. After talking to him, she would return to her home as if she, too, were on the verge of transformation, like his stories. The unstable nature of the filmmaker's art paradoxically gave her a sense of fulfillment—as if, similarly unfinished, she had license to make of her own life whatever she wished.

Caz thinks: those stories had fooled her all along, the complicated inventions of his favorite writer, Edgar Allan Poe.

The locked-room puzzle, the terribly physical configuration that undergirds the horror of Poe's mastery, the intricate construction of a mystery tale so carefully mapped, a graduate thesis Ludo had forewritten with footnoted remarks that he had foisted on a nice professor, John Duble, a schizophrenic poet at Johns Hopkins—Poe's annotated, indexed, geometric constructions might be, after all, mainly metaphysical.

A room no one enters, a final solitude.

A philosophical horror.

What the fuck, Ludo.

Will we never stop thinking about why you died?

Is your goddamned death your final, fucking, goddamned locked-room puzzle?

She sits there scowling before the funeral guests.

Ludo's absurd plots about obscure wars in irrelevant lands gain resonance in the telling of his friends' sketchy scenarios, now that the gaps have a haunting message with the inventor gone. Everyone speaks in whispers, the way disappearance becomes the story when to her it is his presence—his vibrant magical presence—that is missed.

Caz wants to kill everyone else, all of his friends who have outlived him. She imagines herself training her eye on all of them, these chattering, random guests, shooting them all with his old goddamned Colt .45.

It is possible they feel the same about her.

They nod their heads at the brown woman as if not knowing how to pay respects to the one he did not marry yet came to his wake. It is said they had quarreled, an amicable parting nonetheless, as he had intentions of returning home, to the Catskill Mountains in New York. There were his wife and child, after all, traveling somewhere around the world—though they did not bother to come. So his friends, in muddled respect, throw her a bone of their avidity, a glance hurriedly cast.

The wife—that is, her lawyer—had sent her regrets. Someone explains she is somewhere, in the hill towns of Le Marche, or was it the perched villages of the Riviera—anyway, incommunicado, with their curly-haired child, all wrapped up in Igorot scarves.

No one speaks to her, the brown one, the mistress.

The Filipinos are already at the mah-jongg tables, stacking the noisy tiles. The extras, American soldiers from a naval base, and their newfound friends, gaffers just in from the abandoned location in Giporlos, are smoking as usual like kaingin in the corners, wide-eyed as they stare at the stars. Smog from the pig roast mixes with the smell of weed. On the director's desk in his studio by the sala are his note cards for the movie that had almost lost financing. Vases full of red roses fill the rooms. Frail, falling petals rustle on a manila envelope, on scattered photo cards on his abandoned desk. The mahogany rooms now smell of pork, pot, and roses. The cinematographer at loose ends, an Italian, stares at a hand-drawn trail traced in pencil and tacked on a wall. Who knows what it is for? Is it of Catbalogan or the Catskills? Is it of Hanoi? Hong Kong? Is it a railroad in central Massachusetts or a river path in Sohoton? The loudmouth critic from New York, a member of the aborted press junket, wanders into the dead man's studio. The two men confer, and though one speaks little English and the other is drunk, a consensus arises.

Without a legend, no one will tell where that unfinished trail goes.

31.

The Trail

The trail from Basey up to Sohoton Caves is an ancient track. At first it seems nothing could be mystical about Sohoton because the guano of the bats has created an off-putting addendum to its fame, and so kids in the outlying towns call it a shithole and strangers in the wild hold their noses, as if the defensive gesture might dispel its stench. Mangroves, if men were wise, would bury the mystic caves in their deserved obscurity, making them unreachable at least by water, except that locals by decades have whittled off the wood of the mangroves to feed the cheap mandibles of the Chinese lumber mills that keep churning out half-assed plywood from the earth's nonrenewable boon.

In 1901, Ludo reads, hacking the inland trail from Balangiga to Catbalogan, from Catarman to Sohoton, is the goal of the American soldiers left to fend for themselves in Samar. Linking paths all across the island, they will surprise the damn damn damn insurrectos in their own land. Telegraphy will kill the freedom fighters. Modernity is the people's assassin. At the very least, countersurveillance will thwart their diabolical revolutionary traps.

It is true that the American survivors of the Filipino breakfast ambush killing the captain Connell, the lieutenant Bumpus,
the doctor Griswold, and forty-five of their men, all while eating
oatmeal and saging na saba, with the cook Walls dumped into his
pot, just like San Lorenzo, their patron saint, *turn me over, I am
done!*, while the sergeant Randles was stabbed by the buko man
Dong Canillas with the knife used to split the coconut open for
Randles's morning buko juice—it is true that in the aftermath,
these survivors of blood in Balangiga ended up with the mission
of patching up Samar with telegraph wires. Ludo reads about this
in a racist book, true, but unfortunately it is still in circulation.

In the wilds of Samar as they worked, the survivors saw bolo
knives and sundang, assassins and insurrectos not just in every
tree but rustling in their very bones, paranoia lodged in their
maw, and hatred, amorphous and powerful, stuck in their ruined
guts. The revenues of fear and a quotient of woe—subdivided
by vengeance, self-pity, and madness—are deposited in the surviving Americans' nerves. They hear the voices of their dead in
the immense, whispering woods. The comrades who in death
squealed like chickens, the farm boys from Idaho who died like
pigs, the absurd captain, still in his starched underclothes, hacked
to death like a dog.

Even for the fresh soldiers, from F Company in Tacloban,
come later to man the garrison, the mayhem they did not
witness will unhinge them. Their own shadows spook them,
and their sleep gives no rest. But most of all, the Americans

will see their enemies everywhere: in the faces of the porters who carry their mess, in the sounds of the lizards mocking their mission, *gecko, fuck you, get out,* in their carriers' slouching shoulders bent over all the soldiers' worldly baggage, tents, canned goods, worn out shoes—they see their imminent deaths in the dark eyes of the helpers, the porters they call googoos and ladrones—who forage in the forests for the American soldiers' food but won't look them in the eye. Who want them dead. Who want them dead.

And the soldiers will kill them, kill them, kill them.

And in this way, the American soldiers burn Samar—from September to December in 1901.

Ludo keeps seeing the laborers who died—the camote farmer whose wife miscarried from her rape; the family men who stand by while their puny homes are overtaken with war's impunity; the chief of police who loped about as if with a sense of humor, whereas his sense of duty equally possessed despair, and the Chief smote himself in his own wrist, as he tried to figure out what was to be done for his town, Balangiga; and the women in the shadows, whom his movie has yet to name.

Puring Canillas of the beetle brows, Marga Balasbas of the fat cheeks, Delilah Acidre of the sarcastic hips.

The actresses, still to be cast, will haunt the movie—alive one day, then gone.

His twin sympathies, for the murderer and the massacred, are grist for the mill, Caz tells him.

It's just a job, Caz says—don't think you can change the world. You are only making movies—don't kid yourself.

But history is a weight any white man carries into his home in Makati, with its weird disco ball and gold-leaf balustrade.

It's for the fact he works so hard, Caz thinks, that she loves being with Ludo. The recognition that an artist is after all just a worker—a laborer—makes her love him more.

In addition, there is the daily sight of those toys, an ugly troll and a Potato Head eye, untouched on the marble floor.

True, his personal life is also a mess.

What leads him to his unguarded moment with an ancient Colt .45, from 1908, in the empty rooms of his mansion in Magallanes Village? Caz would like to imagine this crippling empathy, his point of no return once he finished the story, or a terrifying multiplication of states in time, or maybe, just an ordinary unlucky shift in his mood, a residue of his love and pity for a world of compulsive set designers and playful child actors and itinerant carpenters and skeptical locals, these lovely people.

Not a unitary, disfiguring delusion closing in on his mind.

She would like to imagine him at work, doing what he loved.

But why should that kill him?

The dull, heavy gun is so antiquated, symbolical even, that for a moment the coroner says he has an eerie feeling in that mansion in Magallanes, falling back to the age when the death of a white man in the city was a monumental act and not, as these bloody facts in his medical report suggest—just a sick case, with a godless end.

Fuck you.

So help me God, the coroner ends his story as he signs the guestbook at the wake.

A scientist trained by Jesuits, he lifts the pen and crosses himself, unprofessionally.

Caz wants to grab it and stab him with his goddamned Bic ballpoint pen.

But she keeps her hands crossed before her, smiling at the guest.

The day after the wake, as Caz attempts to write down her thoughts, even she knows that what she is saying is bullshit.

She is beset by fallacies arising from her own desire.

Hagiographical décor, windows of truth without a ledge, hopes grounded on partial knowledge.

For the survivor of suicide, everything is possible and nothing is true.

A locked-room puzzle.

His end is shocking because it is so unlike him, say the news reporters who had once noted his exuberance for living— even the way he ate, gorging on his spaghetti alle vongole, so described an interviewer in *Time*, was a sight "as if the sensory claim of mere victuals were a matter for enlightenment." His manner of death gives pause, produces hopeful delusions in both friends and strangers. Communists—the Urban Sparrows of the New People's Army—intruded on the foreign filmmaker, one Manila tabloid screams. It was the dictator's own men, bunglers out for vulgar cash, because they could, say political philosophers, pretending to be in the know.

But it is an immaculate room in which he is found.

The pious coroner ad-libs: there were no invaders but flies.

And one obsene dead cockroach, like an upturned boat with frail masts.

She understands that if she allows herself to dwell on it—the ambiguity will kill her. Unlike the haunted men in the house of Usher, for her no ghost comes back to explain the tale.

A jumble of numbered note cards in a rubber-banded package, a sketchy map, an unfinished script, a trip not taken.

A plot about a crime of history that no single vision can redeem.

All of the clues are viable, none hold weight. Postcards with twin pictures, spilling out of their plastic cases. An unmailed gift in a box covered in pale blue whorls, with its signed card.

Death had no observer.

It is only later that she will discern the cunning of surviving. She will focus on small things. His amusing mimicry that could retell the *Odyssey* in different voices, the way he could talk forever about sundry matters to the banca pilot until the sun set and she knew their journey will therefore never be made, his perfect Waray accent when he spoke Tagalog, saying *puydi* for *puede*, he was such a mimic, his way of cackling over her trilingual puns, Waray, Tagalog, and English, as if they were original, the terrible grunts he made in bed, at which she never had the heart to laugh.

Memory was her focus.

Knowing is beside the point.

But that is a thought she articulates only years later, with the benefit of distraction. There will even be an afternoon when, sitting at the university, a writer with two books to her name and a third, a mystery, on its way, she will mention his name in passing, as if practicing, and strangely her voice will have no recoil, and a scholar will say how selfish it is for anyone to die that way, with a six-year-old child to boot, and she, Caz, will note the critic's understandable but mistaken view; that is how her pain is renewed in the moment, but it does not diminish the tenderness she will feel. She knows, despite the cliché, time is not the healer. Her pain lasts, debilitates, but (at least at that moment) it will not kill.

In the meantime, she keeps packing. Income tax returns. Books with slips of paper falling out. Index cards slipping from loose envelopes. A stash of library books he thought he would have time to return.

1.

Across the Strait

"Over there," Magsalin says, pointing across the strait.

There was nothing to see, Chiara notes, but the expanse of water and the faint line in the distance of what must be coconut trees—what else?

"My mother lived over there, in the province across us, by the water, in barrio Nula-Tula, near SOS Children's Village. My playmates were the orphans. I think my mother liked the comfort of groups," Magsalin says, "her high school students, the orphanage where she volunteered, her mah-jongg crowd. She was a busy woman, always among friends. And strangers. I think she lived a full life."

"You are still in mourning," says Chiara. "Is that why you came with me to Samar?"

"You think I have no wish to help you?"

"No," says Chiara, "I know you don't."

"But let me tell you, I don't want you dead," says Magsalin.

"No, you do not. But your reasons for keeping me alive remain obscure."

They are strolling along the beach after lunch.

"You know, Chiara, that it is all a trick of the eye," says Magsalin. "This whole place is only made to look like a town. That flagpole, the statue, the hollow hut with the hilot in his muu-muu outfit, the fake arnis fighting competition—just tired old beach resort come-ons."

"Like a film set," says Chiara approvingly. "But that basketball rim is real. And the free-throw markings on the cement court. The hibiscus blossoms."

"Gumamela," says Magsalin.

"The gumamela blossoms. The mosquitoes. That gun."

"What gun?"

"On that man, out by the beach."

"You have a good eye," says Magsalin.

"It's my job to observe," says Chiara.

"Are you sure you want to keep going on to Balangiga today?" asks Magsalin. "We can stop here awhile."

"I want to keep going."

"I think the driver, Gogoboy, is tired. I think he has an illness. Charcot foot disease. It comes from diabetes."

"How do you know?"

"Research. For a mystery novel."

"Right."

"Actually, I asked him. It's sad. He will lose his job if he amputates his foot."

"I guess a lame soldier is—"

"Pretty lame."

"You're right, it's sad," says Chiara. "But if we get to Balangiga today, wouldn't that be better for all of us, including Gogoboy? He can rest while we work."

"You know you can stay as long as you want in Balangiga. I need to leave you there a few days while I get to my mother's home."

"You're leaving me?"

"I have contacted people to help you—historians and scholars. They are waiting for you in Balangiga. They're very good—they will give you everything you need. I will meet you in Basey or Catbalogan, on your way back to Manila."

"But you're my translator."

"Chiara, everyone there will speak English."

"But you said your mother is dead."

"She's in a graveyard, you know. I can still visit her graveyard."

"But why be in such a hurry to get there now when you waited all these months?"

Magsalin stops as they reach the edge, facing a man pissing into the water against the limestone rocks, holding his gun with his free hand.

"You really know how to hit where it hurts," Magsalin says.

"I am sorry," says Chiara. And for a moment there, Magsalin believes her. "But it's my job to observe."

27.

Noon

The breeze of the habagat provides a false sop against Balangiga's heat. In addition, the kumbento's location against an inland river gives the men of Company C a daily noontime reprieve. You have to be nuts to get up at the height of day to trudge toward the water. Siesta, according to Filipinos, meets the rational demands of the islands' weather. The laborers about town are released every morning from their jail to hack at trellises and random fruit trees—hemp-wrapped jackfruit that look like ugly, swaddled infants; fragrant fruits with the texture of sand, called chicos; and that prickly fruit that always looks deformed, with buboes, the atis, and when you scrape its insides, it is like everything else in this island, deceptive. Atis looks demonic but tastes like Eden. It is the custard of paradise. The men look sullen in the blinding swelter, but everyone on the island looks put-out anyhow.

Randles the sergeant hates this part of his job, babysitting docile mutes in the wilderness.

These prisoners look harmless enough, as agile with bolo knives as the chief of police with his sticks—and under his eye, the men at their hacking are energetic and careless, nimble and inept, but Randles does not give a fuck. Randles the sergeant would regret what had got him here if this shithole offered him the refuge to remember. His butt is full of maggots and his prick has a rash. Pimples rot his face. His pale pink flesh is eating him alive. His limbs look swollen. Sometimes the sores appear in his nostrils, sometimes around his balls. His fingers look like baobabs, pustular skin swelling about his death's-head rings like botanical knobs around his infested scars. This is his reward for his courage in China (consisting of guarding the Temples of the Gates of Heaven of the Empire of the Sun, another skull-numbing job)—the diseases of the whores of Tientsin, Pekin, or maybe Nagasaki, who knows—this unrelieved sensation. Every orifice in his body is corrupt. It does not matter that the rashes also occurred in Indiana, before the wars, and in Fort Warren, before the trenches. Memory anyhow is no aid to his wounds.

His short-lived days in Malacañang Palace were his only solace: for some reason, his squad's station at the mansion in Manila had calmed his crotch, when for two days he had guarded Fighting Fred Funston's meek prisoner, the tiny, shocked general of the bandits—his insurgent person already divested of all signs of revolution (many souvenirs—medals, combs, and spoons—had already been looted by Fighting Fred's men, so Randles's only spoil was one of the man's sorry, blood-spewn spittoons). As he had stared at the miniature martyr, General Aguinaldo of the Palanan jungles, Randles could only think he looked like a Chinese doll he had once seen abandoned in a yard in Taku. Those two days against Manila's river, the Pasig, had soothed Randles, as if the chilly air that swathed the inert captive were an omen of his own sufferings' finality, though Griswold the surgeon says his body's sense of reprieve is just his imagination. At no season in Manila is the air ever "chilly."

It does no good to wash every day (these neatnik people here love their baths, which they take shamelessly in the open air like babies). Any form of cleansing makes his scabs tingle, opening up fresh pains. Rot from his dried pus sticks to his clothes. It embarrasses him to give his underpants to the women, washer-women are all gossips anyway, and in private Randles washes his clothes himself. Still, to his mind, a smell of rat, sewage, and humid blood always clings to his breeches. But when he falls into this pit of self-pity, he must remember that he came here across the stupid seas to save these sons of bitches. He is a vessel of God. Though what that preaching woman in a uniform, that captain-slash-pastor Tommy Connell, knows about his dumb-fuck soul, he could care less. Cocksucking cunt. Pardon my Chinese. Captain Connell coddles the natives. Laws against touching the women, laws against drinking the wine. *Beware of fraternizing with the locals*—what the hell was a good fuck anyway but god-damned benevolent assimilation? Randles starts giggling to himself, lifting one hand to his handlebar mustache to keep it in its greased place, his eyes smarting as involuntarily his hand feels up his pants.

Fucking prick.

It hurts.

He giggles so much he is shaking, his woolen body a blue blur in the steaming sun.

This squalid man who looks like a walking mop with bald patches—kalbo nga sip-hid nga yawa nga naglalalakat-lakat, *waray didto waray dinhi*! She hates having to go near him—she thinks clumps of skin might fall off him if she merely breathes by him, and then his putrid flesh might rain upon the air, like the ash of kaingin. Some parts of his face look like the crinkled skin of roasted pigs—the popped, crunchy parts with bubbled fat. The children call him Calavera nga Layaw—Corpse at Large. That's no wonder, but to be honest, he looks worse.

Kalooyi: have pity on us, Frank used to say.

And once upon a time she did.

It annoys Casiana Nacionales that Frank's voice muddies things up.

He'd repeat her words and say them, like yawa, and bugas, just so she might laugh. Her words in his mouth had a childish joy. She had never disliked his people, she said to him, until you actually showed up. But isn't it good, Frank said, we are teaching you English, we are putting up the telegraph wires?

The better to tell us what to do, the better to spy on why we do it, she said.

She told him—

There are consequences to your desires that you will regret, no matter how much you imagine your evils are unintended.

That's deep, he said.

She sighs, thinking of Prank Vitrine, as the Chief calls him—her lubberboy. He's not a bad man, just an unconscious one.

Casiana Nacionales prefers her venom pure, like the water she carries to her father. She had always been the fierce one as a child—though maybe that is no distinction among the Nacionales clan. Even the Chief, when he has doubts now about the tactics, consults her. She looks down at the rosary against her neck. She must remember to list the details of the breakfast operation for the Chief one more time—the keys that will be stolen, the bells that must be rung, the costumes men should wear. Wait for her signal with the rosary beads. A good number of men must go for the barracks. A good number must go for the mess hall. But the best men must go for the officers, the captain, the lieutenant, the surgeon—they all need to die.

Count them, count them, count your men, she keeps telling the Chief.

You need to have enough. Get more. Call in laborers from the other towns. Explain it to the captain—he needs more workers to sweep up his camp. And when the captain refuses, keep pretending you don't know what the hell he's talking about, you're good at that, then go on and do it anyway—that is always a good trick.

The officers are the key—leave them for the best of your men. With the head gone, the Americans lose their spirit, and our people will leave no one alive. She keeps repeating the plan. Sometimes the Chief forgets the details. But in truth, he is soft-hearted. For instance, Bumpus, that alcoholic, the Chief says—he's so nice. He likes Bumpus because the Chief can beat him at chess. And the doctor, the Chief says, is a good man who just likes to talk. He's a harmless chatterbox. Susmaria, Casiana thinks—men have the hearts of babies if you do not keep them in line.

So she keeps repeating the details to the Chief.

The women must be told so they can escape ahead of time. The pigs must be sacrificed. The fiesta strategy must not be suspected—anyway, easy to indulge these drunkard americanos in their gluttonous ways. Lastly: disguise your men. The americanos will be suspicious if they see no women at mass in the morning! I will make sure the wives leave their skirts behind!

So many things to think about, and the Chief, that chess nut, is her lone confidant. The mayor Kapitan Abayan is still pretending to be deaf and dumb with too much conviction and just keeps petting his chickens when she goes near. Even the priest looks a bit distracted when she gives him the lowdown, though he was in on the idea from the start. He's threatening to leave when the going gets tough, but that's a man of the church for you.

And so it is up to them, the women.

Casiana hates having to carry the heavy tubes of water up to the plaza, where the town used to hold the fiesta dances and now the americanos have taken up the space. She wishes she could just scrape this occupation away and all these men like the snot of silot across a cracked coconut. Or like the sins from her chest—the way Padre Donato says she should just wipe her bloody, sinful thoughts away with prayer.

Her father is in their prisons. For being a man, for having two hands that can work, that can hack at his land. Two jails that fit a dozen, but with eighty-two men packed in. Every morning, when they are released from their massed misery, she looks out for her father. He has those wide cheeks, which stretch even wider when he smiles. His smile before the americanos came used to be so broad, it reached his sun-scorched ears.

He has lost it.

Sometimes she does not recognize her father, looking like all the others, skinny, grave, and beaten. He has worked so hard on his lands that his rice fields once stretched to the edge of the forest, almost to Giporlos.

The captain had commanded him to burn his granary.

"A blasphemy against God!"

Benito Nacionales refused.

Susmariosep, Casiana crossed herself at the mere shadow of the expression of the thought.

Burn the rice.

What kind of a devil, demonio nga yawa nga iya iroy, commands the unmentionable act, then goes to church the next day?

She saw them take her father, hands tied behind his back.

She saw them carrying their water containers and their hemp ropes for their cure. They spread out his arms and his legs, they tie him up on their contraption, a metal crucifix, they put a stick in his mouth and a gauze cloth over his face.

They pour water over the thin cloth mouth, the stick cracks his jaw open as he cries.

His mouth full of their oaths and his eyes wide open.

His belly will bloat, he will drown in his tears.

This water is no cure, it is a curse.

Captain Coño, she said.

Let him go. I will do it.

The smell of the smoke was so strange and unknown to the people of Balangiga that the women came out from their huts, looking about for its source, its scent. They gazed out toward the edge of the forest, to the granary of the family Nacionales.

The strange scent of burning trailed the riverbanks down Balangiga, toward San Roque, out by Guiuan and Giporlos. The news spread through their noses, this sweet and terrible smell, this news that was not benevolent, the news of burning rice.

And the smog and the scent billowed over Balangiga as Casiana burned.

Burned it, burned it, burned it, burned the rice.

And though it was not yet Angelus, people stopped in their tracks as they hacked at wood, set the table for their absent men, fed their pigs. They stopped, crossed themselves, and mumbled the prayer.

It sounded like insurrection.

What kind of a devil burns the rice?

And after she did it, she watched her friend the red man Frick and Markley, the orderly, bear her father away from his ordeal in Samar, from their bamboo buckets and their water cure.

In this noon heat, she watches her father take his bolo knife from the sentry. Benito Nacionales accepts his own farm tools from the American arsenal of confiscated weapons without complaint. He will never be the same. All day, for weeks, laborers hack at the grass, clean up the yards, make fences, cut down palm trees against the beach.

For what?

So insurrectos will be visible if they attack. So insurrectos will starve because they will not have rice. Damn damn damn the insurrectos. It occurred to Casiana, who had always believed it a mere story, a separate thing, this revolution that was a plot beyond their lives, it meant nothing to her—

But that's it, she thought. That is who we are.

Insurrectos.

That is how she explained it to the women.

We are the insurrectos.

There is no one else to do it but us.

How strange it is to understand finally who she is.

Insurrecto.

And they agreed.

And why is this goddamned man's hands always up his dick?

When the laborers stop to rest, Randles watches the women

come out from the huts to offer their men their merienda. No day is proper without the mid-day snack—coconut pastries, brown jellies in banana leaves, caramelized custards that attract flies, rice cakes with their melting carabao cheese. The men drop their knives and eat with their hands. Casiana watches Puring Canillas waft the bibingka about the twitching lips of Mister Sergeant Bigote, Calavera nga Layaw. It is like another facial organ, Randles's mustache, a stiff limb with involuntary moves. Delilah Acidre has an almost visible rump, hitching her basket of salukara up her thigh. No sergeant can resist Delilah, and she used to always have her husband, Ambrosio, right where she wanted him—but what good is that now that he has been in jail since August, working for the americanos around the outhouses? Tasing carries her nigo of morón around—the chocolate delicacies—with her husband, the mayor Kapitan Abayan, nowhere in sight, deaf and dumb out among his chickens. Marga Balasbas, a bandehado of rambutan balanced on her head, smiles at Randles, Corpse at Large—sweets for the sweets one, she practices her English, winking as Casiana trudges by.

Randles wants all of it, he has the urge to just grab all the cakes—jams of purple yam and lightly crusted rice treats with the soft fillings and flat egg-white pancakes lathered in lard and served with dark sugar. He would stuff all of them up his nostrils and then down his pants, warming his dick, if he could. The scent of roasted coconut meat—the smell of the Philippines—he wants to devour it, keep all the home cooking to himself. Randles cannot account for this phantom hunger, the way nothing soothes him, this burning itch up his flesh.

As always, the women keep carrying their straw plates to the sentry. It is their custom to share their food. Randles is aware of his stench and their immodesty. Their eyes laugh at him when he refuses. He is glaring at the spot between their breasts and the cakes. They are teases who cannot take no for an answer. Flirts. And the next time they offer him a rice bun, he moves his hand from his crotch to grab his Krag.

The women draw back.

He is on duty. He cannot fraternize with the locals.

Anyway, to them he is just a dirty bastard. Who smells of sweat and blood of lice.

But Dolores Abanador and Felisa Catalogo have already come and gone from the Sibley jails. Their sons, Exequiel and Nemesio, lie asleep, their depression having reached an advanced narcoleptic stage. The boys, when they are out at work, at the captain's orders, look like wraiths sleepwalking amid the talahib, as they cut the grass and hack even more trees from phantasmal groves. For their malaise, they are confined to jail, even for the hour of merienda. Dolores Abanador and Felisa Catalogo bring bamboo water carriers to Nemesio and Exequiel. Thirst is a complication in the heat. And the boys swiftly take the women's bamboo tubes into the Sibleys. The last sight of them is their hands, outstretched to take their mothers' goods.

The shift to birds'-eye view is instructive, as the high-angle frame can catch the entirety of the crowd scene—the way, in the nosebleed seats in the opera, one has a sense of omniscience as the small, antlike human figures go about their tragedy on the stage. The choreography of the women's actions becomes clear. One sees from this angle how the dance of the flirtatious Delilah around Sergeant Randles deflects the sight from the glinting knives hidden in the bamboo water tubes that the mothers give to the sleepy boys, and the chatter of the trio, Puring, Delilah, and Marga, distributing their sweetmeats and whispering in their men's ears, are cover for the men to know their attack positions at the coming fiesta, to hear the coded instructions for the women's plot of cross-dressing revolution—a susurrus of sopranos that indicates subversion must be at hand.

Plotted by the insurrectos—the whispering, smiling women of Balangiga.

Operatic heroines of coordinated gestures and can-can kicks, while Mister Sergeant Bigote, Randles the Corpse at Large, Calavera nga Layaw, sentry of the americanos, stands in place amid the swirling skirts and clutches his dick, the dumb fuck at the center of the moveable parts of this crowd scene—a man of misery, who witnesses all and sees none.

Randles watches the old men, the ones so useless they do not need to be jailed, coming out from their midday stupor to pile leaves into heaps for the afternoon kaingin. Everyone greets each other as if there is no tomorrow. Just a few days ago, the old men had been jammed together in the two stinky Sibley jails, smelling

each other's armpits and asses and unable to stand up or kneel—
the captain had made them all familiar enough with each other,
until he released the infirm and whiplashed the strong.

Backslaps, handclasping, ringing voices. The old sluggards
are all roused out of their homes. After siesta it's a goddamned
reunion of the sloths. Then the screaming of the pigs. A
150-year-old man, Mr. Methuselah of Samar, P.I., carrying a
pole and a rope, reminds Randles—the man's aged hand is as
limp and creased as the curled hemp in his grasp—hey, Joe, it
is fiesta tomorrow!

Hey, Joe, it's the feast of San Lorenzo Martir, the patron saint!

My name is Gustav, not Joe, Randles thinks, but his mouth
sores hurt, and he is silent.

The Chief, that easygoing bum, had asked the captain to give
all the workers a reprieve, just for the holy day.

Oh yeah. Big deal, you woolly mammoth, thinks Randles.

First siesta then fiesta, your cycle of life.

And this is the life of Randles—a Hoosier from the Wabash
jaded at age twenty-four, sold by his father at nine to work in
the mills around Muncie, whose own war of independence is
to become a soldier in the US Army and, first, kill the ghost-
dancing Indians in the Dakota plains and beat up the strikers
on the Pullman rails, then, second, sign up for Cuba in 1898,
without ever once seeing a map. His first sight of the open sea
is on the deck of the ship *Zealandia*, which takes him from
Honolulu to Guam and, third, Manila Bay (not to mention,

fourth, a detour to China)—and here he is, fifth, stuck in Bal-angiga, where the sounds of dying pigs are the only echo of his miserable childhood, and he has the urge to squeal, in unison with the familiar pigs, from the sudden, acrid flaring in his fucked-up dick.

1.

Not Even Her Mother's Phone Call

Not even her mother's phone call had moved her to return home, though Magsalin could imagine how terrible it must have been for her mother, a vain woman like everyone else (not just vainglorious Warays), to be losing her hair, her eyebrows, her fingernails' sheen, not to mention her peace of mind, and Magsalin heard with clarity and dread the toxic language of her mother's cocktail of Taxotere plus Cytoxan, a precise pharmacology that her mother, a word nerd, repeated in full like the Greek names of rhetorical devices that she liked to teach to her students in Tacloban. Magsalin had looked up the words, Taxotere and Cytoxan, and she noted the side effects. Apart from stress-induced alopecia, there were neuropathy, GERD (gastroesophageal reflux disease), and depression.

But still, Magsalin told her mother: I cannot go home.

"Do not come home," her mother had said on the phone as she lay dying. "If you feel you cannot do it, inday—do not return."

28.

What She Wants Is the Sense of a Ghost

"How dare you," he hears the words as if from his dream.

It is in Randles's language, nasal, a monotone, but English, though the sounds occur in pieces, unarranged. He puts his hand back on his gun. He smells her fragrance—a mix of river breeze and roses—before he turns around to see.

"How dare you imprison the Filipinos and cram them in tents like animals and then put them to labor without informing them of their crime? Do you know of the writ of habeas corpus? You know the writ is not suspended in these islands, Mister Sergeant. I insist on seeing your captain."

Randles is confused—but relieved, too, that her object of contempt is not his groin, his dirty hand.

In close-up the woman is framed in the camera at first out of focus, a reddish scarf (not really suggesting the blood to come) accenting her pallor, cheekbones checkered by the shadows of the tall fronds in her line of vision (chosen by the obsessive-compulsive art director, Freddo from Gubbio, Italy), mouth slightly open and only slowly appearing, so that the sense of flesh, of moist ripe fullness, is delayed, and fringes of hair on her brow are tossed as if carelessly, though the dresser has gelled them just so, to appear at first in sensual abstraction, like commas in the wind.

The director says that what she wants in this shot is a sense of a ghost rising from a river, a whitish impression that at first seems like sea foam, or maybe the shadow of a despondent creature moving in figure eights in a man-made pond, or a fluttering flag of surrender.

But of course it turns out to be Cassandra's flesh. Her whiteness establishes the frame.

It's hard to do white like that and get contrast, grumbles Freddo from Gubbio, who do you think I am, God? But he does it anyway, using dry ice and some fog machines (but to be honest, in the end he makes it all look as he wishes it to look—like the mystical air of damp spring mornings on his native Monte Pennino, near Perugia).

In the next, a dolly shot as Cassandra strides toward the man, Cassandra Chase's stance, hand on her hip, has an imperial look next to the pathetic soldier. A reversal of perspective. He with his red, pimpled face and the absurd mustache that punctuates his youth, in dissolve, and she with her magnificent, though careless, beauty, in focus. Maybe it is her posture—slightly slouched, though not quite awkward—that makes her seem unaware of her power, as if she is costumed in voluminous Victorian lace only from a sense of decorum that weighs upon her.

Her look of command, of a woman complete and whole in the frame, now occupies the scene.

"I demand to see your Captain Connell—Sergeant—?"

She looks down upon him, at his sleeve.

Up close, Cassandra Chase is taller by a full head.

He looks down at himself and is conscious that his chevron is tatted on his faded blue kersey cloth in uneven cross-stitches. He feels what he is—a syphilitic drudge who does not even have the strength to sew his patch back on with a steady hand.

"Sergeant Randles," he says, then adds uncertainly, "ma'am."

"And why can't you just accept their midday snacks, Sergeant Randles? What's the harm in eating a bibingka? Why should every second of your presence in these islands be a humiliation of its people?"

"I am on duty, ma'am. Miss. It is not my job to fraternize with the natives. And—sorry for the inconvenience. It is not your right to question the regulations of the United States Army, the commander of these islands. Miss Cassandra. I mean, Madame. Ma'am. Miss."

"Oh, hush. The US military governor is now under civilian authority, and a civilian, Governor Will Taft, commands these islands. Your General Elwell Otis is out. So is your lousy Arthur MacArthur, slashing and burning to kingdom come, who told him he was Mister General Sherman of the Central Luzon plains! Or didn't you know? The War Department is no longer in charge."

Randles's eyes widen.

"Excuse my blasphemous words," she says, "but it is so."

She sighs.

"I suspect you do not get the news here in Balangiga."

"No, ma'am. The mail ship is six weeks late."

"So you don't know that President McKinley—? Ah, never mind."

"Ma'am, we have received no mail from home since we left Tong-ku harbor, in China."

"Well, then. Get me the captain, and I will give him a bulletin straight from New York."

"Ma'am, to be honest, we would prefer our news from our families instead."

Cassandra laughs.

Should the blur around her eyes suggest sympathy? Choose the cut that does not sound condescending, or only pitying.

"Don't worry about that, sergeant," she says, her voice changing, but not unkind. She taps him on his threadbare patch. Her fingernail further unravels his skimpy insignia. "Your mail is arriving from Tacloban with Lieutenant Bumpus. I can promise you that."

1.

The Sea Is Memory

And here she is, with only the San Juanico Strait between her and return. The sea is memory. It is mesmerizing. Its beauty is intolerable. What it buries is vaster than what it reveals. Every so often you get a glimpse of what you forget, or you wade in and something snags you, a broken shell or a sea urchin the fishermen missed. She hates jellyfish stings; she hates the water's surprises. But she is an island girl: she loves the water. He used to laugh at the way she wore full body armor just to float on the waves. Swim cap, goggles, wet-suit shorts, flippers. There. A memory of him. She watches the waves, it rides the surf, it is gone. No waves speak with the same voice, though they share the same elements and motion, the regular beating of the surf, their rippling heaves.

The porters lug the bags out toward the Pajero.

"Bye," Magsalin waves at Chiara, who already sits with her notebook in the front seat.

The porter tosses a bag into the back.

"Bye," says Chiara from the Pajero.

The car has turned the corner toward Maharlika Highway, on the way to Balangiga, when Magsalin pats her duffel.

Magsalin realizes it is not hers.

Their bags are switched.

She tries to wave Chiara back, but the filmmaker is scribbling notes in the Pajero, head bent toward her script.

32.

The Monstrous Idol

It was not Ludo but the art director from Gubbio who had come knocking on her door. He was thinking of a model for the monstrous idol that was to dominate the set of the village. A gigantic Madonna of the Orient, an enormous gargoyle that would float on the lagoon. He was thinking of the murals of Umbria, the flat-faced Pieros of his hometown. The madonnas of Piero della Francesca, for some reason, look Asiatic to him, like dozing bodhisattvas that he had once seen carved in Dunhuang during an Italian tour through Marco Polo's China—contemplative goddesses, eerily serene.

One of the Italians, a gaffer, had seen her with the children, who had run from their teacher at the sound of the military drums during a morning lesson. At first, with a break in her heart, Caz had believed her brother Francisco had found her, and he will make her leave town, for good, before he attacks it, his own village.

But it is only those deviants, the cameramen.

When she reaches her giggling charges, they shout—ma'am, the circus, the circus is in town!

Caz has tried to avoid the moviemakers, on this point agreeing with her brother: this wastrel spending to fulfill one man's vision is a crime. Francisco goes on and on about its imperialist stink, bla bla bla, these escapist hatches of neocolonial cinema that cloud even his peasant soldiers' dreams.

Caz thinks—his teach-ins must be the worst, once Francisco gets to cultural criticism.

The cast of hundreds had invaded one day in August. In the blinding heat of the noon sun, they work. In their khakis and jeans, their vests with pockets for their cigarettes and lenses, the carpenters with their crates and the masons in their lug-soled shoes, with their transistors, hairdressers, electricians, cookware, condoms, and penicillin, and a whole village of genuine orphans ready for their slaughter rented from the SOS Children's Village across the bridge, from barrio Nula-Tula in Tacloban. They are a phalanx, a battalion, an army, a war; and they hire their own enemies and drag along their own dead. They have guns, ammunition, trucks. They have cranes with moving cameras, and a caravan of jeepneys filled only with canisters of film. They eat mangoes with their hands and speak through walkie-talkies. They love to ride the bancas, commandeering the riverbanks. They work like dogs at all hours, odd and off, and even when they rest it is strenuous, swimming miles down the river, hiking through the mangrove swamps, talking, talking, talking, talking about their film.

Caz and the townspeople wait for the signs. Donato, the

cockpit boss, bets on the skinny one to go first, the hyperactive druggie, a long-haired actor who attempts to climb the coconut trees the way Valeriano the tuba maker does—with his bare feet. The demented man whoops on the way up, hollering a Christmas song, *hark the herald angels siiiing!*, all the way up while cameras roll, though the crew is on break. A few grips, their heads wrapped in T-shirt cloth completely covering their faces except for their orificial totems, which reek a sweet soporific fume, start clapping, puffing on their weed—the smell of their weed is the most prominent feature about them.

The kids tug at Caz's skirt, Ma'am, ma'am. Their hands gesture toward the sky.

When the invaders had first arrived, Caz made a point of never passing by them, taking the interior route instead to her home. She takes the long talahib path to her father's inn by the lagoon that embraces the caves with their ancient stalagmites like tonsils hanging from the depths of a halimaw's jaws. She grew up slipping and sliding on mossy ledges while her dad led tourists through stalactite caverns he could draw in his sleep. She is ashamed of her neighbors—the way everyone has given in. It is true that her hometown had always been a damned tourist attraction, even during the Spanish time, because of the natural creepiness of its caves, her childhood haunts, a marvel of limestone sculptures and supernatural bats. The famed revolutionary battle that drums up local visitors and some ghosts of war during its anniversary is remembered only at the annual reenactments on makeshift stages that local teenagers pelt with tiny guavas, if they stick around to watch their history at all.

Her father had not been the worst of the tour operators, but he was close. His inn had catered to the thrill seekers—Germans and Japanese and nudist Dutchmen sunbathing on rocky banks after emerging from the advertised, spooky caves. Then they came complaining to her father that the experience was nowhere near the orgasm his brochures had described. Her brother had hated their family's business. He told his father that he was just a dumb comprador who collaborated with the enemy, those lazy beach bums, not quite the running dogs of capitalism, but obscene enough. Her father—whose open, generous, yet poker face was excellent for a tour operator, so used to the haggling of the trekkers but never budging from his price—just raised his hands, letting Francisco go on, his broad smile reaching ear to sun-scorched ear. He had those wide cheeks, which stretched even wider when he smiled, but he would not budge even for his son. Still, he always let Francisco do whatever he wanted. And so Francisco did, leaving her to take charge of the house, though it was she who had straight As at school and won the scholarship to the university. All the time she was at college, she felt guilty for being away.

Her father would have kicked himself—to have died before this bounty arrived, these moviemakers raining dollars on the town.

Caz returned from the university when their father died. She had grown up hating her hometown, its unbearable picturesque stasis, the cursed beauty of its waterfalls and coves; but with her father gone, she found herself unable to leave her home. She had no wish to go back to the city. She, too, like Francisco, had joined the rallies, the midnight raids on Malacañang palace, or at least the palaces's gates at Mendiola, where they taunted the dictator—which was as far as the students could go. But she was tired of marching. She was tired of being angry. At the president, at the generals, at the constabulary soldiers who hunted the farmers and the students, the workers and the rebels, at her brother for making her feel guilty for not joining him in his cause, up there in the mountains. The whole world was falling apart, in Uganda, in Nicaragua, in Biafra, in Iran—what does her marching do but infect the streets with her useless despair? When the time is ripe to bomb the palace, call me, she told Francisco—but before that, leave me alone.

Caz keeps to herself in the forest, closing the inn's frontage, leaving its privileged, direct path to the caves unweeded, living behind her childish garden of dense anahaw, gumamela, and bougainvillea, watering the orchids, listening to the radio, reading novels, planting root crops. She bores herself to tears.

The Catholic school refuses her application. She laughs at the excuses of the principal, her own uncle, who makes noises about the terrible consequences of the acts of her brother Francisco bla bla bla. He's doing it for your country, she reminds him. Her uncle shuts his door in her face. Fine, she says, I'll teach the Chinese. So she works at the school for Chinese toddlers. She becomes a fixture in town, with her red bandana and self-sufficient look, which people take, correctly, for arrogance. Caz does not care. One drunk from the next town, which does not speak their language, mistakes her lonely figure for a chance at passing romance, and for his pains he gets the barrel of an ancient revolver, rusty but impressive, stuck in his stupid face.

The white woman, a thin, nervous lady in a silken suit, anxious and immaculate, arrives with her blonde, curly-haired child in September, and with no effort the golden-haired girl fits in with the group. It's the child's capacity for joy that is charming. Granted, she has a charmed life. All the toddlers love Chiara because she looks like the Santo Niño, they say, the Holy Child. They love to make her sing their imperfectly memorized songs— "Abakada," "Bayang Magiliw," "Bahay Kubo," et cetera. The children are fascinated, they stare with amazed silence, whenever they hear Chiara speak the songs in Tagalog, as if their speech were a miracle in her mouth. They make her do it again and again. The toddlers are demanding. Chiara does it with gusto. The child takes in the world.

Language is witchcraft, a transformation. Chiara's childish mnemonic talent, her ability to mimic, is uncanny, though she wishes she could remember when she used to speak those words. If there had been no video of her singing "Lupang Hinirang," taped by her mother, Chiara would have no memory of her life with the Chinese toddlers. The script uses passing sights of street games to provide local detail. Chiara learns bulangkoy, a kind of soccer, a game of the feet, but with a metal washer, not a ball. She freezes like an expert at Statue Dance, a contest with music, and learns not to giggle when the music stops because when she does, all the kids fall over, screaming with laughter, and then they can't play the game. She plays tumba lata, throwing a slipper with deadly aim at a makeshift target, a Carnation condensada can or a rectangle of Spam.

Good eye, Chiara yells whenever she makes a hit.

They let her win all the games, and even that seems natural.

Good eye, the kids yell, guday! Guday-puday! the kids rhyme.

She loves the sound of the words, the way things sound more lyrical in Waray.

For Chiara, everything is a thrill—plastik bubble, a kind of balloon candy she is not allowed to swallow but she does anyway (it tastes like snot); kropek crackers, a taste pretending to be shrimp; her favorite cookie, roscas, shaped like a gun. Chiara plays guns with the kids, clutching the fat trigger of the roscas cookie, which is like an Italian biscotto but humongous, with the crumbly barrel pointed like a finger, a cookie of guilt, at everything she sees. Bang, bang, bang. Insurrectos! I'm a juramentados, can't you see!

And the kids giggle in Chiara's wake, eager to please her. They let Chiara play the villain, while they play dead.

What these scenes wish to do, says the script, is capture it— that time she was six when she felt absolutely loved.

Chiara vanishes just as suddenly as she arrives.

Caz has no way to console the kids. Now when Caz takes the children on field trips—to watch hermit crabs shrug off their homes, or to make watercolor sunsets—the kids look out for the return of the changeling child, imagining they see her strange curls in the forests, one of the disappearing duende. But she does not return, nor does her nervous mother.

That day, the children are in the grove to gather leaves to make palm-frond pipes—slim shards of primeval design. But the primitive white man in his underpants shinnying up the coconut tree is more interesting than the dumb reeds Caz wants them to make.

Who can blame them? The filmmakers are a trip.

Her next-door neighbor, the barangay captain Donato, also cockpit operator, is striking it rich providing bloody cockfights in his sabong for the big spenders. Cures for San Miguel beer hangovers, mosquito repellents, advice about the bats: everyone has a niche. Women dream of pink, blue-eyed babies, scions of the GIs all over the place. They're extras, Caz wants to tell the women—layabouts they must have picked up in Olongapo and Angeles, without a cent to their name. But who is she to call anyone a fool? Tell us about your brother Francisco, Delilah the fruit seller says, and we'll give up on the GIs. Francisco is setting up a business in Cebu, Caz retorts. Right, says Delilah, flashing her rump—and the nice people around, his New People's Army, they can kiss my butt! Criminals! Communists!

As the script notes, the setting is a Third World dictatorship, propped up by American guns.

Even the town mayor, Kapitan Abayan, has given up his con-
crete home to live in a makeshift hut (made originally for his
maids) while the film is on location. The mayor is making ten
times more than he gets on pork barrel from Manila, Donato
spits: Sonomagun! Children are learning English from the Italians—*buona notte, fanculo, tagliatelle.*

Her charges squeal and shriek and beg to stay, then they settle
down to watch the show. Caz sits and waits it out, resigned to
one more spectacle, the moving picture of her hometown.

Ma'am, ma'am, the kids tug at Caz's skirt. Their hands gesture
toward the sky.

Sure enough, the long-haired man—drug-addled, drunk,
self-medicated into joy, with a suspicious itch up his ass—waves
his triumphant arms on top of the coconut tree. Not waving, but
flailing. Filipinos sit in the shade—watching from the shadows
of their homes, or from the shade of balete trees, from wide-
brimmed hats after siesta—smiling and gracious and counting on
their fingers the minutes before he falls.

Usa, duha, tulo.

Smug bets among the knowing. Pigafetta, Magellan's scribe,
had counted their ancient numbers in his traveler's alphabet, but
at the time no one had any use for his erudition.

The actor is grunting now, grasping at the coconut balls, then
the not so feathery fronds, the smooth trunk—and when he slides
from the tree, then falls, it is the Filipinos' turn to clap.

Upat, lima, unom.

One down, too many more to go.

Valeriano the tuba maker feels bad, that is clear; he gets right up to the top of the trunk, up in the sky, an acrobat, cuts down a few silot and, in lightning movements, on earth, hacks at a young coconut for its juice and offers it to the fallen man, all in a trice.

It is not a hard fall, just a stupid one.

The actor looks dazed, the juice dribbling down his mouth.

He faints.

The camera crew, the hairdressers, the caterers, the makeup men, all gather around, giving the actor even less air to breathe. At this instant Caz notices the gaunt, curly-haired figure in cheap pants made entirely of patched-up rice sacks. He is wearing a blue and yellow rugby shirt and rubber slippers, the ones she still calls ismagol, though the boholano smugglers who used to sell them have long set up a stable business in town. His brow is his best feature, after his eyes: it remained smooth, so delicately sculpted, like a baby's, as if it had just been formed, shaped like the half of a heart—that is, until they turned it, his cheek, one day, and as she stared at his dead body in the funeral home, at that angle she flinched: he was unrecognizable.

The man's lofty hair is a fantastic, gnarly bird's nest hovering fairly a foot above his slightly hunched frame. He has this habitual stooped pose of attention. His curls stick up in the air, unwashed. He looks like a life-size figure of one of his daughter's toys, a Danish troll.

The world parts for him.

Ludo is gawky, leaning forward, one foot ahead, as if about to fall. All eyes are on him. His broken glasses, bandaged with tape at the sides, enlarge his glare. He cares for art, sex, and food in that order, and has no use for minor details, like shoes or matching clothes. His wife had always thought his inner life was well adjusted, but on location his exterior was a shambles.

He has just arrived on the scene—too late to watch the denouement, the coconut tree catastrophe. The mongering men scamper away.

His hand on his waist, elbow poised as if eternally cradling a megaphone (his studied pose—he knows the uses of authority), he berates the crowd, then bends toward the man on the ground.

The Filipinos, grinning among themselves, shake their heads as the crew disperses.

Another one bites the dust.

Donato says: I knew it. Give me five, Frank.

Betron, a loser on the countdown, gives him exactly five silver pesos from his rigged-up piggy bank, a gasoline canister cut in half. Others rush up to the crew with their woven anahaw, fanning the loiterers. Some offer drinks: twenty pesos each, criminally overpriced. Another offers a man a ceramic pig, its head bobbing for no good reason.

Caz notes the strangely mixed responses of her town—skepticism and compassion, mercantilism and pity, mercy with laughter to spare. People watch, with toothpicks and toddlers, waiting for the wild gago to die, but just in case they will offer him bahalina tuba if he rises. Their attitude toward bad fortune is the same as toward good: a slightly removed sense of being, as if their bond with the material world is at best a borrowed thing, a trap. It's a group that has long survived mainly through luck—their God-given waters and natural caves have provided them historical concessions. Random waves of war, disease, typhoons ruin them, oh well—life is chance. Their existential lucidity makes them extra observant (though their narrow conclusions attest to their hermetic world).

They are clear-eyed, philosophical, and ruthless.

Just as they expected, the white people have been falling like flies—fevered, hallucinating, emaciated from their labor. Kapitan Abayan, the mayor who has leased his rambling Spanish-era house to the director for an astronomical thirty thousand pesos per month, one thousand pesos a day, wonders aloud at the americanos' ways. No Filipino worth his brains would be out in the sun when shadows grow short. Even chickens have the sense to retire, looking for a nipa roof. Benton Frick, the hilot with sad eyes, hums an old harana, fanning himself to sleep. Dogs lie like dead in the shade, and the townspeople, ancient logicians of immobility, follow suit. Whereas these millionaires shuttle about at the height of noon like mad chickens, always screaming Action, Action, when nature demands inaction.

Idiots.

Seward, you prick, get up!

As if at the sound of the director's stern voice, the longhaired man moves. Caz watches it all happen—a miracle—the scruffy actor gets up, first onto his knees, and then he starts tap-dancing before the director, singing: Ta-da! *Hark the herald angels siiiing!*

Caz resists the urge to applaud. What she understands is that the director of a movie commands the world's will, and when he says so, the dead are resurrected.

In that pose, with her mouth open in surprise, red bandana fluttering, cheekbones checkered by the shadows of planted fronds, framed in the sun's haze, almost like a puzzle, Freddo the art director from Gubbio captures Caz with his tiny Rollei, an extra camera he keeps in his pocket, just in case. Like everyone else on the set, he is a workaholic, alert to the technical solutions chance provides.

29.

Stereovision

Her camera is the size of her largest hatbox, carried by the young Francisco, the captain's ten-year-old servant, the orphan. The photographic lenses are borne separately by solemn adolescents awed by their charge, and they walk the way their fathers carry San Lorenzo Martir's carromata in the town's yearly fiesta parade, following an invisible line in lockstep. Her porters carry her goods around as she wanders the town, eyes alert to its possible compositions. Both aesthetic and pathetic fallacies cloud her judgment. She does not notice the lack of toddlers or their mothers in the dirt yard. The only women are a few old cooks with those staunch peasant calves and bowed heads and her young friend from her last visit, Casiana Nacionales, the lively trader and church lector, now also her hostess. Cassandra notices the numerous pigs out for slaughter—who could not?—but it is, after all, the day before fiesta, so Casiana tells her.

Bisperas han patron.

Cassandra Chase has no calendar on her, Butler's *Lives of the Saints*, or the Catholic missal, to check the feast day of the patron, Saint Lawrence of Rome—San Lorenzo Martir—a date that falls in August, not September 28. So fate escapes her vision.

She notices instead the tranquility of the suffering workers in the heat. What strikes her in her tours about the country is that everything is heartbreaking and yet, she thinks, art-designed. This is cruel. The laborers who look like medieval martyrs (she cannot help her art-damaged perception) are exactly like the suffering figures of supernatural calm that she had studied in the churches and museums during her Grand Tour of Florence, Venice, and Rome. On one hand, she would prefer that the horror she witnesses throughout these islands be only what it is—a gross injustice. But even the burning of the towns in Central Luzon, by a man she would call Lucifer if she had a pulpit, even the terrible flames of the mahogany forests in Arthur MacArthur's scorched Luzon were a technical problem of vanishing perspective.

How to focus given her distance, sitting as she did on the veranda of the itinerant governor-general's home?

For a month or so she had volunteered to take pictures of the islands as Governor William H. Taft made his inspections of the subdued towns.

Her camera's eye was a curse.

—But your position is worse, don't you think, asked Casiana Nacionales the trader, that time she met her in Giporlos.

—What do you mean, asked Cassandra.

—Surely your position as the governor's guest, going along

with his masquerade of peace, is a worse thing than your eye for art?

Something burned in the photographer at the impudence of the woman, but she kept quiet—after all, Cassandra was only a guest in her country.

Cassandra swings her parasol against the talahib path, following the carriers toward the plaza.

When she was a teenager traveling through Italy, her favorite pictures had been the gruesome ones. Her secret, growing up amid the world of glass traders and hemp speculators in New York, was that she bore a sense of horror that the world around her mocked—she was coddled from birth, showered with toys after all; but she felt this wound, a subliminal perception without root or reason.

And she found her interior illness strangely externalized in Catholic Italy.

Disemboweled Saint Erasmus with his pancreas in a jar. All the luminous torsos of so many Saint Sebastians. She wanted to examine each of these grotesques, limbs pierced with arrows and art, mutilated and comforting. Saints with their intestines strewn about their bodies, their gross guts looking like the things called rosaries that they held in their hands, flies feasting on their lips (she notes how Casiana Nacionales wears her rosary, like a noose at her throat). Above all, she had loved *The Crucifixion and Apotheosis of the Ten Thousand Martyrs of Mount Ararat*, a painting she had dutifully described in her notebook during her tour of the Accademia in Venice.

—I wish I could show you my sketches, Casiana, she had said to the young trader in Giporlos—but it is in the trunks I left with my father's friends, in Malacañang.

—It would be a pleasure, polite Casiana answered, but please excuse as I need to boil the rice.

The bodies of ten thousand Roman soldier-converts hung naked from cypresses, leafless olive trees, rocks winding through a Calvary of bodies, all of which build to the vertiginous shape of their city, Venice. The morbid multiplication mirrors the infinite faith the painter hoped to reproduce, and in no other painting is this principle of divinity so well cataloged. The painter's realism eternizes a fantastic trope—the hysteria of holiness. One body dangling from two forking branches is a calculated study of the cross, a vision both mechanical and awesome: a triumph of technique and symbolism, emotion and science. The golden age of perception, so the caption in her guidebook says. She is grateful for her travels—

And she glances back at the carriers with her bags, marching past Casiana's hut in Giporlos. Even at this distance, she can see Casiana standing in the doorway like a Saint Elizabeth, waiting for the Christ, in her pañuelo and striped, jewel-toned skirt— haloed in the doorway, bowing over her ancient pot.

Still Life with Rice and Rosary, she could call it.

Sometimes, true, in the process of photography she feels transformed.

Her family considers her its black sheep, though her parents mail her checks to ensure the propriety of their name as at first she traveled with the governor-general through northern Luzon, then Bicol, then Cebu. The prim and proper Midwesterner, Helen Taft, in her journal of her trips of state, called their urbane companion "an eccentric woman no more foolish than Alice [Roosevelt]—and polite, for a New Yorker." Cassandra still believes in property rights, good manners, and wearing the correct silks. She is no wild thing, no, not a Diane Arbus, not even a Frances Benjamin Johnston, who was vulgar in that she sought fame through her art.

She had felt agitated on her return to New York after Venice, the dull visits to old dowagers on Washington Square, the dances with the profiteering traders of her father's world, who made money from dressing up troops in Cuba or speculating on Manila hemp. Her own father did glass and rope. When she took to photography, it was a shock to her peers but no surprise. Beset with unease but possessing no self-doubt worth mentioning, she did what she pleased. In this way, women especially found her repellent, but in a way that haunted them. Letters and diary entries by socialites of the time attest to the troubling memory of meeting her, that strange woman, that vagabond, that artist, Cassandra Chase.

The American soldiers of Balangiga do hold the attraction of being shitfaced and obscene, like Renaissance goons about Golgotha. Cassandra takes her job seriously, designing the photos of troops benevolently assimilating in the tropics for the patriotic reasons that make wartime commerce so attractive. Anyhow, they are also the beasts carrying the white man's burden, is not that right, she thinks as she walks the talahib path, Kipling being still widely quoted in 1901, and again and again she will make the soldiers pose for the edification of her nation.

Padre Donato is once again waiting for Cassandra in the plaza, his faithful masseur fanning him with anahaw. Cassandra positions him and then some laborers, this time against the backdrop of the church. The bells of Balangiga will be at the center, creating perspective. Then she includes soldiers arrived from bathing in the river. Plus her new friend, Sergeant Randles, who scowls authentically at Cassandra Chase as if because hidden she cannot see him (her head is obscured by the dark pall of her huge camera).

The group, in hindsight, is bizarre—the male prisoners with their spiritual look, rosaries around their wrists; their wives with their square laborers' chins veiled to the mouth in stiff katcha, shy, muslin scarves, with their thick ankles and masculine calves hidden in wildly striped skirts, the satiny, semiprecious colors being the pious women's single nod to lurid passion (though all will wash out in black and white); Americans in Victorian forms of beach undress beside venereal Randles in full US Army gear, including the Colt in his belt and the Krag with its bayonet; Walls, the cook, who, in a spontaneous yet artful touch, carries a wooden spatula, whittled flat for making salukara pancakes—a local tool that he wields like the icon of a proud guild—and last but not least, the luckless Prank Vitrine, he of the woodland escapade, recently jailed for going AWOL but back in business as sergeant at arms.

Prank Vitrine is caught in the camera looking off to the left, his profile brooding, staring at Casiana Nacionales (she is in the movie, though not in the picture). The hilot lounges in a heap nearby, picking his teeth with a stalk of grass. In the middle of the bivouac, like a shiny, displaced fish, Padre Donato's oily face smiles broadly for Señorita Cassandra, Miss United States of the Americanos—a sunny day in Balangiga, bisperas han patron, the day of vespers for the Americans, captured for posterity and later sold, in New York souvenir shops, for two cents.

1.

She Rides along the
Coast toward a Historic

She has more armed guards than she has luggage. She has a sense of purpose even Magsalin admires. She rides along the coast toward a historic place and, by simply stepping on its soil, she will accomplish her duty. An homage to the dead, but not only for her benefit. Films, after all, have a sociality not even the most narcissistic can subvert. They require the possibility of observers. Thus consumers are significant to her story. For an inland, riverine town, this coastal road is invigorating. So much of this journey seems to be a start. Holiday goers pass by in a rented vehicle toward the surfers' beach, advertised also on a store, then there is a truckload of rice sacks and pigs. A child sucking on a lollipop on the back of her father's motorcycle waves cheerfully at the tinted Pajero. She has a frilled dress, a book bag, and curly hair. Chiara waves back, but that is so dangerous, to put your kid on a motorbike on the highway without a helmet. The father shouts at the kid to hold tight (Chiara thinks). Chiara holds on to the door handle as the Pajero jolts at the sound of the shots. Two policemen on motorcycles, riding in tandem, rev past them. First it is a goat that appears on the road, then a pig. The Pajero twists and turns out of the way of the corpses. Then it stops.

"What are you doing, Gogoboy? We don't stop here," says Chiara.

For a moment, she is afraid.

She will not believe what she will witness.

She hears but does not see the men behind them, also on motorbikes, pulling alongside the Pajero. There is an inconsiderate lapse between vision and hearing that angers Chiara, as if injustice lies in this syncope, or some sound mixer were off duty. She keeps feeling sensory gaps, the tape keeps being advanced to the wrong moments, so that the bad cuts have the effect of miscommunicating the scene's pathos. The sounds of the motorcycles before them are already erased, unheard, and there is no wailing at the sight of the bodies. Her gaping mouth is silent. It is no pig or goat.

It is the mangled length of a father and child.

The father lies face down on the asphalt road, his slim Suzuki motorbike still upholding a spinning wheel, and his arm thrown out. It had reached out to the child before its fall. The child's blood darkens the highway. Chiara does not understand why there is so much blood. At the father's chest, soaking his white T-shirt. On his child's curly head, oozing onto her frilled dress. Her book bag has the odd shape of Chiara's old pet Misay, a furry cat, lying flat on its back. It, too, is soaked. The daughter lies next to her father, her face sideways and her hand above her, suspended. Splayed, as on a cross or as if she is about to wave. Her posture is one of motion though she is absolutely still. Her small, pink mouth is open, and Chiara cannot tell if the stain on the tongue is the child's blood, or is it the color of the lollipop. The lollipop is steeped in blood. The blood keeps seeping away from their bodies, a hyperbolic dark shadow, an excessive notation of their fall that soon will encompass all—palms, jungle, nation, ocean. Gogoboy's bandaged foot is now stained by the spreading blood. Edward's combat boots and the butt of his Uzi have a trace of blood, as the two men kibitz by the road with the policemen. It is a contagion that will soon touch the entire road, the ooze radiating outward beyond the bodies, as of an awkward halo drawn too wide. For a moment it seems to Chiara that an enveloping sea of blood has contaminated even the sunlight's rays, a dark glistening that overflows her vision. How did Edward and Gogoboy jump out of the Pajero so fast? The spatial and temporal logic is jerky. Then she sees Edward moving onto the side of the road.

What is he doing?

He is vomiting out his guts.

He is always having gastroenteritis.

Only the policemen have squeaky-clean attire, practiced as they are in treading upon blood.

And where did these policemen come from?

Chiara tests her voice, a gargling sound, and she feels stupid in her short shorts.

She gets out of the Pajero.

She is glad that her platform shoes make her taller than everyone else.

She stands outside a pool of blood. It drains crosswise toward the palm trees on the shoulder of the road, toward vomit and grass.

"What is going on?"

"Ma'am," says Edward, with his forlorn air, his face now a sickly shade of mourning, "police, o. They will usually check your bag."

"What?"

"They are usually here to check your bag."

"What are you talking about?

"Sorry, ma'am, it is the police," says Private First Class Gogoboy, approaching them. "They say they want to check your bag."

"Ma'am, good afternoon," says a stocky policeman, practically a midget, his brow reaching her non-cleavage. Like Gogoboy, he has a bandaged limb—his hand. He holds up the shredded bandage of his arm as if to say, sorry, I cannot do the honors of shaking your hand, I am a diabetic, I have a Charcot hand, pardon me, then he continues, "It is reported by the man at the resort about your bag."

"What man? What is reported?"

"I told him, ma'am," says Edward mournfully, "you are photographer usually come to take pictures of the statues of the historical massacre in Balangiga. He is not listening."

"The security at the resort. He reported about your bag."

"Mister policeman, sir," says Chiara, "your job is to deal with—with this scene. Oh my God, this blood! Why is there so much blood?"

She backs away in her platform sandals. But it is too late. Her sandals are touched with the blood pooling on the bodies, on the leaves, on the vehicles, on the trees, on the sun.

The blood of the child in a frilled dress.

The other policeman, in aviator glasses that obscure his eyes and both of his cheeks, so that he looks like a walking Ray-Ban without a face, walks over to the Pajero, wading through the blood.

He is just full of it.

"What are you doing?"

He pulls out her duffel bag from the back of the Pajero.

"What are you doing? Gogoboy, take my bag away from him."

"Ma'am, they are the police."

"But aren't you the army?"

"But we are off duty."

"What the hell? What's the use of having armed guards if you just let bandits open up my bags with impunity? Edward, this is the time to use your stupid Uzi."

But no one follows the director's orders.

"Ma'am, what is this?"

The faceless policeman with the aviator glasses has ripped open the bag.

Triumphantly, he shows them all a square pale blue box.

He takes it out of the green and purple duffel and hands it to his crippled partner, who gently shakes the box.

Everyone stares at the square box, decorated with pale blue whorls, that the stocky one handles with his free, unbandaged hand.

"What is that?" says Chiara. "Who put that in my bag?"

The policeman lifts the cover off the pale blue box, and he extracts a plastic bag full of gray dust, the plastic bag limp in his wounded hand.

"Aha," says the effaced policeman, his sunglasses in victory slipping almost to his chin, "just as it is reported. Shabu!"

"What?"

"Drugs, ma'am," mourns Edward, shaking his head. "You have drugs in your bag."

"See," says the policeman with the bandaged hand, "it is even marked on the box: S.A.V. Must be a new chemical, they are now making all new kinds of shabu."

"What the hell is shabu?"

"What is it called in America?" Private First Class Gogoboy asks the policemen. "Fentanyl?"

"No. Meth," says the bandaged policeman, the one who seems to be in charge, "meth crystal. Also known as cracks."

Chiara laughs. "Are you out of your mind? That is not crack. That is the wrong texture. Meth is fine and bright, like powder. That is gray and pebbly, like coral beach sand!"

Now everyone is staring at Chiara.

"I am sorry, ma'am, you are under arrest," says the stocky one with the bandaged arm, "for transporting shabu to Samar."

"So you will arrest me for trumped-up drug possession, you will put me in jail instead of investigating which of your motorbike-riding colleagues killed this child right in front of our eyes? My God! Someone killed a child. We saw that shooter riding in tandem behind the driver on the motorbike, just like yours! I bet he was one of you. So you will hide your colleagues' crime by arresting a foreigner, a bystander? You're criminals. You're bandits."

"No one is seeing a motorcycle riding in tandem. Did you boys see a riding in tandem?"

And the faceless man in aviator glasses turns to Edward and Private First Class Gogoboy.

"The father is a drug addict, that is usually for sure," grieves Edward. "That is usually the reason why they die."

"Usually?" says Chiara. "Will you stop saying *usually*, Edward? You are driving me nuts! You know very well that is not the reason why people die. These policemen are usually the reason for these deaths!"

"Now it is you who are saying *usually*, ma'am," mourns Edward.

"But you have shabu in your bag, ma'am!" the stocky policeman declares. He points to the bag in his open, unhurt palm. He puts it back in the box and shakes the box before Chiara. "That is right in front of the eyes!"

"That is not shabu, you idiots!"

And now they all turn to see who has come upon them.

"Cut! Cut! Cut!"

It is Magsalin in a pedicab bearing a duffel bag and her rage.

She leaps out, hands Chiara the bag she carries, and snatches the pale blue box from the policeman's arms.

Magsalin cradles the box against her body.

Magsalin, holding the box and staring straight out at the father and child, has begun to weep.

She cannot help it.

She is wailing.

It is a monsoon wind that will never stop.

It is a perplexingly rational sight to see the image of a woman bending in sorrow before the scene of carnage on the road, silhouetted against the morning light, swaying and wailing before the bystanders, the soldiers and goons and the foreigner on the periphery—though in truth she is wailing for a box instead of for the dead that lie before her eyes.

No one moves, frozen in this game of Statue Dance, listening to Magsalin.

"Ah," says Chiara, "just as I thought. I knew it. I've been trying to piece it all together. Those are his remains. You have been carrying them around with you from Tacloban to Manila to New York and back. You carried it with you in Cubao. You carried it with you on the ferry to Allen. It has been your mission on the road to Samar. You are carrying your husband's body, whom you hope to bury with your mother across the strait, in Tacloban."

Chiara mentally notes problems of film, even of costume design: how did a pedicab get here so quickly? Why is she, Chiara, wearing short shorts? Who gave her platform shoes? Why will justice never happen? Who in their right mind would mistake cremains for crack? And will Magsalin ever just mourn, without plots and stories and gestures that distance sorrow?

"Yes," Magsalin says. "This is my husband's body. I left the country when he died."

"It was too painful to remember."

"Yes."

"You could not return home even as your mother lay dying."

"Yes."

"So you began writing a mystery story instead, parceling out your pain into your characters' lives. Is his name Stéphane, by any chance?"

"No. His name is Stig. Though it's true—people always ended up calling him Steve. Even my mom. His name was Stig Alyosha Virkelig. He was a writer. He was in the middle of writing a novel when he died. It is unfinished."

30.

Vespers

Bisperas han patron is the busiest day of a town's year. At vespers the day before the patron saint's feast, everything must be cleaned—the yard of litter, the head of lice, the kangkong of dirt, the fish of guts, the chicken of feathers, the goat and pig of hair and tusk, and the soul of sin. People do not wait until Angelus to go to confession, and Padre Donato hurries away after kissing Cassandra Chase on both cheeks, *beso-beso*, in the European way. He is in a hurry, clasping his hands in prayer as he runs, his speed implying the sanctity of his chores.

He never reappears in Balangiga.

In time with the Confiteor, animals outside the convent begin to die.

Fiesta is an ominous day for pigs, chickens, and goats, but especially pigs. The massacre of lechon, roast suckling swine, starts bisperas han patron. Guests in their finery should not see the unshaven carcasses, and it is profane on the day of the patron saint to listen to them die.

Cassandra is writing down the above details of fiesta customs for her captions, embellishing with a traveler's fancy. It's not a rule, for instance, that pigs are slaughtered the day before: you want pigfat fresh, since the best fat is liquid, not solid. Pigs, truth be told, are just as often slaughtered under homes the actual day of fiesta, and guests could care less if they hear the pigs squeal as long as the product is crunchy. Cassandra writes with devotion about the islanders' faith. The errors in Cassandra's captions will be translated into five languages, Spanish, Italian, German, Russian, and French, arrayed in italics on the cardboard back of the stereo card.

The pig in her second picture is vertical on a bamboo pole, all alone, nothing to denote scale, so at first glance you mistake it with its pointy ears for a flayed bat. She takes another view of it, with its legs tucked and the gaping void of its robbed and bloody flanks, slit clean to its muzzle, bereft of intestines and organs, the black hole staring at you in abstract design until the figural point of the portrait takes shape, a beautifully basted, still heaving carcass, tied with art in Manila twine. Her best is the one where the pig is slit at its belly, and the laborer, in the pose of Saint Anthony the Hermit, patron of pigs and skin diseases, has just begun the basting act, hemp and knife held aloft. Her sharp camera catches these odd, singular details—the flattened, wet gristle, the plaited, entwining rope, the glittering knife. She has studied the history of Western art. The details appear like those emblematic non sequiturs in Old Master paintings, in which the skull at Jerome's feet implies a meditative life, and a pomegranate, rolling toward the viewer from a basket, offers resurrection.

33.

The Portrait

Caz sits before Freddo, the art director from Gubbio. Despite herself, she loves his stories. Italians and Filipinos are twins, he says; they are separated at birth. Your roscas, made of lard and anise, is a biscotto. Your lechon, the roast pig, is the first cousin of porchetta. You know porchetta? She knows he does it to make her feel at ease. Caz shakes her head, smiling. There—keep that smile. The Madonna of Monterchi has a smile like that, head down, please, yes: she looks shy, but do not be deceived. The Madonna is his only Virgin who undoes her clothes to share the secret of her body, swaddled in her soft under-linen—Piero's Madonna gives you a little peek—it's just her inner clothing, don't worry, it is very tame, after all it is still only the Renaissance—so divine is her domestic gesture the angels around her applaud. It is Piero della Francesca's homage to his mother. It is, of course, a gesture toward himself: he is the child in the swollen belly of the lady of Monterchi being applauded by all the pretty pastel-colored angels. Or maybe the madonna is really thinking of porchetta, and the anise and the fennel to season the meat, waiting to be done posing so she can go to the market and eat her fill of pig.

Eh? Don't worry, we will be done soon. It is lunch.

How can you so patently distort a portrait you obviously adore?

Caz grins. Her teeth show.

Uh. Please stop, he says. No smiling like that now.

She can see that Freddo loves Piero della Francesca the way boys adore their marbles, their jar of jolens—glassine suns, vermilion tears, and cerulean moons. But Caz understands that Freddo's photos of her will be models for the sculpture of a terrible idol of the village Tommy Connell of Company C razes to the ground in Samar—the opposite of love.

The Madonna Freddo loves is the monster he is making.

It is Balangiga that Tommy Connell witnesses, but it is his fantasy that will be slain. A hallucination and a hoax, this wild tribe of island devils, and perhaps also a matter of opium—but none will be the wiser. Everyone in the movie will die.

She has seen the green-haired a.d. Fionnuala and her crew already practicing the scene of carnage with the orphans from SOS Village, imported from across the strait, from Nula-Tula in Tacloban. They have played dead for hours, lying along the riverbanks, in the talahib, in the muddy crevices of the winding trek to the caves, the batter of their blood stuck on their cheeks and limbs when they get back up to play their games—bulangkoy, jolens, tumba lata, Statue Dance. The baby ghouls are a bizarre sight though they have settled well enough in the forest. They hung around for days for their single scene, then played with the Chinese toddlers in their off hours.

Caz had watched these children, with their gashed skulls and battered eyes and hair matted with blood and mud, dancing and laughing in a circle as one boy with no brains, a rigged sop of organs dangling down the back of his neck, sang out—*Stay-choo!*

And the kids in the circle froze.

It was part of their game, Statue Dance, recess between the scenes.

But this eerie, frozen stance was also their pose in the forest as they lay down dead, with their mothers, their chickens, their brothers and their sisters and their household goods in the long scene of despair that would be their claim to fame.

It was odd to see them upright in the poses of their dying: cracked blood on their matted cheeks as they stood still.

When the people of her town first saw the scene of the massed dead children, Caz could see they were finally impressed. Their professional kibitzer's calm was shaken. It took days to film the children: the idea of the single shot was to pile body upon body, legs and pigs and babies and carabaos and grass and goats, in a long pan of destruction in which the morbid multiplication would mirror the infinite spiral of historic slaughter, mimicking the exhaustive horror history has already cataloged. The scene would eternize a trope. The a.d. Fionnuala made one particularly nimble child, Estrella, climb up onto a tree, dangling from two forking branches, as if a storm had cast her there, her arms splayed, as on a cross. It was not clear if little Estrella was proud or petrified, but she was good at it. It was uncanny. The child had the capacity to be absolutely still. Caz had watched the villagers watch the scene of the children, the scene of the massacre of the reconcentrated villagers of Samar in 1901, and she thought how strange it was to see it dawning upon them, as they stood motionless, hands upon their open mouths, not even stirring to strike at the flies or berate the Chinese toddlers, that this was their history unfolding before their eyes.

Filipinos will slaughter forty-eight Americans, then Americans will slaughter thirty thousand Filipinos. Tit for tat. The ruinous hallucinogenic idol, a symbol, a giant windmill toppled by the maddened Tommy Connell, is a mirage, but it wreaks havoc enough. The toppling dissolve that dominates the screen, the nightmare of Tommy Connell, is the face of Caz mimicking the Madonna of Monterchi, mother of the precocious genius Piero della Francesca (born 1415) who dreamed into legend his own gentle birth.

With these guys, thinks Caz, everything always ends in self-portrait.

She grips the seat of the raised stool, with a feeling she is toppling over—and at that point she meets him again, in the eye.

Ludo is only passing, but the gaze is enough.

A PENIS IS funny. At rest it has the look of a raised scab, an overlay of rotted fish, or wrinkled flesh, thin-skinned. It is sad. If you wave your fingers above it, not even touching, it will follow like a headless puppet. It has a mind of its own, but no brain. Even the penis of an internationally famous movie director salutes you like a sad private. Caz takes it in with a witchlike cackle because it pleases her to fake it. Acting allows her to be herself, to be pleased. She wishes to be an idol, a monster, a madonna, a stranger. She likes this pleasure of being the mistress, the anonymity of one who does not ask the questions or need to weep when she is alone. She loves the freedom of not needing to know who he is, though she loves his stories. Her father is dead. Her brother is in love with his endless war. She is an orphan. She screams with pleasure.

Caz soaps routinely, without thinking—the inside of thighs, then shins, calves, and ankles. What is it about him that she misses? She cannot even recall moments of her anger, why she had left. She left because it kept raining while the movie was on location. She left because he had everything to do, a movie, while she had the sight of monsoon destruction in her fern and anahaw garden. She left because she wished she had something to do, like the seamstresses, the pot sellers, the cameramen in his movie. So many months later she can call her recall nothing—not nostalgia, not memory, not even sorrow. She has no words, they hold emptiness. Her friends at university, the ones who were not ashamed of her affair, say, it is normal: of course, she is numb. But in one sense, she does not miss Ludo, not the entirety of him, not his presence as a person, a human being walking, his loves and fears and ambition. It is hard to keep him alive in her head. As if he were an exercise in memory, and not its point.

The figure of the loved one in his wholeness escapes her.

It was she who had left him. But the minute she left, she missed him.

Her brother Francisco had visited—don't you dare preach to me how to live my life, she told him, but he preached to her anyway.

It's a movie, Francisco, not a passion play of your impossible angst and self-righteousness, she told him.

They are orphans, Caz, he said. Not figments of his egotism and self-regard. How could he do that to children? Make those children replay tragedies they cannot soothe or erase for themselves? Children who are already haunted by grief—who knows what they have already witnessed, being so abandoned?

Has it ever occurred to you that the children in replaying trauma might find a way to express their own? That the simulacra of grief, distanced from us, mediated from our own, artificial as they are, allow us to gain a foothold, however tenuous, on the deep-seated horrors that claw at us but to which we do not give names?

Excuse me, Caz, but I, too, have read Aristotle's theory of mimesis. I am talking about actual children, not Ancient Greek stupid drama—how could you watch it all happen, as if the scene, the time, the history has nothing to do with you?

At that, she hit Francisco, who knew better than to respond, and she walked away. He did not follow.

But after that, she left Ludo. She closed her father's house and just walked out on the movie. She did not tell him where she went. She went back to the university. She started reading Proust. She kept rereading a particular moment, the scene of Madame Guermantes and her red shoes, in the third volume, when Marcel recognizes the depths of the Duchess's cruelty in a chapter about making a choice between wearing red or black shoes. In this way, back at the university, she was absorbed, though not happy.

34.

How Could She Know

How could she know the denouement? She did not know the plot. And even his end—how can she put it as she understands it? No matter how terrible it is to recognize the truth, because it establishes her irrelevance in his life, though she was his lover, no matter how terrible it is to recognize it, in the end, Ludo's act, no matter how much she turns it over in her mind's eye, spinning it about until meaning collapses—his act is his.

She thinks, I thought he was whole, a monstrously complete and vital being, and we all were the fractured and fragmenting audience, prey to the director's totalizing gaze.

What she had believed was that the director of a movie commands the world's will.

But he was also a man fused, patched, and growling, so clearly a constructing and reconstructing figure, produced, maybe, by others' needs.

How odd to think—he, too, was unfinished.

But it bothers her though—how she never noticed.

A snap, a wish.

She wished she had noticed it, why he wished to die.

Who knows?

Even her scattershot thoughts, of a woman who loved him, are obscene.

Let him keep them, as he wished to keep them—let him keep his secrets to himself, in his dumb, pale blue columbarium of a box, his secret within a secret.

Eternity, it turns out, is simply this—privacy.

But sometimes the message comes to her like a phantom. She takes it out of the envelope. She opens his letter. He has changed his mind, he says in the letter; he has turned back from the dead, and he will be outside the door, standing by their bookshelf in New York, near the titles P to R. *Perec to Réal.* He was mistaken, he says, and now he has returned. And how good it feels to know that Time, in a reversal of expectation, can in truth turn back.

Then she wakes up.

Semantic recall. Unconscious prompts. It's her limbs that have intelligence: they know when to lift a coffee cup, when to brake the car at street corners. Her wet hands move from face to neck; and once again her gestures reprove her. She has been soaping her body twice over, four arms, four kneecaps, another elbow. She should turn off the shower. She is done.

There is that dissolve on the screen—a splash. Virginie feels that first stirring, when she moves to turn off the tap. She takes a step, thighs parted, so that she opens up to gushing water as she turns—and swiftly, for some reason (the angle? the time of month?), an uncalled memory gathers. That long-dormant pleasure—that clitoral gap. It is the body's memory that moves her: nothing else, apart from dreams, is as strong or real. Not lost conversations, not thinking, not rushes on the monitor, the sudden flash of a man in action, his face just missed, an animal swimming in the water, over and over again, in endless figure eights. No sign contains it. Language does not speak it: this grief that lies every day in her body, involuntary, carried by memory in her skin.

How odd that now, this instant, is the first time she feels that, yes, she remembers Ludo. How absurd, she thinks, her eyes in the mirror strangely looking surprised, how absurd it is to forget that this—this is the core of memory. The body roused. This is grief.

In the stories of widows, they are allowed no vaginas, though everything else has its place. Bernarda Alba has her casa, but no cunt. Novenas, anniversaries, Thank You notes to funeral well wishers that you can buy at Hallmark stores. The library cards go back in the books' card pockets, and she mails his last books to their home. She keeps his jade figures of semiotic Buddhas, each cast in a different posture, the soul's semaphores haggled for at a night market in Bangkok; his mysterious sketch of a jungle trail in Sohoton; this box of index cards with scrambled numbers that she thinks has a code, but he kept it; and the last shirt he wore before he stepped into the bath, a rugby shirt in blue, white, and yellow, with the scuffs on the collar, left in a heap by the tub.

It is a shirt with faded blue and yellow stripes. It used to hang on his thinning frame whittled to nothing in the tropics. He used to leave it untucked over the sheer butt of his white soccer shorts.

In the tropics, he liked to play keep-away with the soccer ball while figuring out his movie's scenes. They had bundled up the clothes in a paper bag. They gave it to her, the wife, the first of kin. It was too early in the aftermath, and no one knew what to throw away, the messenger, a shy man, said. Without thinking, she had taken out the shirt from the bag. Its cotton collar was worn, dulled to dirt gray at frayed ends, and frayed, too, were the cuffs of his sleeves. It was not his favorite shirt, she thought. Just a convenient one. But now it is a symbol. Anyhow, he never bothered with minor details, his clothes or matching shoes, though there was one scarf he favored, a pale blue tissue-thin thing. Now she wonders where it is.

What struck her was that she had never noticed it.

That his shirt was frayed.

It's these matters—these posthumous signals of her ignorance of him (ordinary enough if he were alive)—that challenge the hubris of a wife. Her arrogant belief that she knew him turns her body warm, as if her life were a lie.

The other things are packed, taped into a box, and shipped off.

She takes her toes in hand and pats them. She dabs at her calves, then thighs. A naked woman weeping in a bathroom has no epic counterpart or remedy. In the *Odyssey*, it takes time before some readers believe that Odysseus will come back, despite the prophecies of the gods, because Penelope's mourning for his death is so convincing.

But, of course, Odysseus returns.

She misses him. He will not be back.

1.

The Blood

No one wipes the blood. No one solves the problem of the father and child on the highway, with the culprits, the speeding motorbike with the men riding in tandem, who had shot them, shot them, shot them, gone with the breeze of the habagat, and the two policemen have lost the prize ransom they will not make from the two weird women, chattering over a box. The stocky one is spooked by the discovery anyhow that he had been holding the ground bits of a dead body, he did not know it could have that texture, he had never held it, a body made of a handful of dust. Bodies were rotting, soiled, and waiting for his percentage, at the funeral parlor, at the drug war scenes. He is a Christian man, that is not a Christian body. He crosses himself with his good arm then begins to take notes, writing out descriptions of the child—tongue, purple, lollipop, cherry, arm, broken. He has all the words. But he keeps feeling it on his phantom palm, his hand that cannot feel—the pebbly grit of a human soul, pulverized into nothing. A bunch of dust. A sudden, tight pinch seizes him, in his testicles, it runs to his nipples, it is a sexual arousal—the way realization comes to him, his erotic lash of knowing. This is who he is, Sergeant Bernardo Gustavo Randols, believer in God and the president. A handful of dust. How strange it is to understand finally who he is. He is a small, festering body of a thing, a nothing, he can already feel his bones in his palms: crumbling under his wrinkling skin. He feels the women's eyes upon him, bearing down upon his dead arm as he takes his notes.

"Officer! Hoy! Hoy! Mister Police!"

"Yes, ma'am."

He is looking down, being busy.

"I want them to have a good funeral," says Magsalin. "I want you to give them a casket. I want you to buy them flowers. I want you to get their names."

Chiara reaches into her Hermès bag.

"I don't know," says Chiara under her breath. "I don't know if this is the right way to do it. I prefer justice."

"I know," says Magsalin, pulling the director to her side, her whisper coming out in a hiss. "But do you think you will exact it in the middle of the road in a town where no one knows you, a woman in short shorts and bloody platform sandals, with even your continuity in question, do you think that is your role right now, to be the avenger in a time that does not give a fuck?"

"No," says Chiara.

Magsalin motions to Edward.

"Yes, ma'am."

"You will remain behind, here in Samar, Edward."

"Yes, ma'am."

"You will take the money from Chiara. You will make sure it happens as I say. You will do the best for the father and child."

Edward's smile is shy but proud.

He lifts his Uzi to attention.

Magsalin stares at the blood on it, at the wax square of blood on the rifle's butt like bits of a candle, and pebbles stuck into its flattened design.

She stares at the tableau of return behind him, clutching the box.

She feels in her that uselessness, that cry, so deep it cannot be excavated, and it is so familiar, the weeping in her body, its slack sick weakening, the way her limbs feel like a hot wind has rushed through them, and she is harrowed and hollowed—this familiar, involuntary scraping of the body, a scythe through the blood.

She is so tired. It is never gone. This untold grief.

"Yes, ma'am," says Edward, "I will do everything for the father and child. I will do it! I will do my best!"

31.

The Fabulous Portage

Silent rivalry over who should take over the fabulous portage, the
sacks and bundles from the boats—there is a brief exchange of
glances between lieutenant and captain.

Bumpus gestures to the grinning boys carrying the mail.

Bumpus salutes the captain.

—Mail, sir! It arrived in Tacloban last night. Padre Donato
told me about it, and I kept it a surprise.

—You know it was wrong not to let me know, lieutenant.
Imagine the relief I could have given the men.

—Captain, they would have died from waiting if they knew.
They're loony enough as it is.

—No one is loony here, lieutenant. Mind your speech. What
is the news on Scheetherly?

—Scheetherly is all right, sir. The doctor, too, says he is not
loony, sir. It is only a state of being on the islands. So says the
medico. The harvest of the war in the shape of thousands of sick
and wounded and insane wrecked in body and mind. It is only
the state of being on the islands. Scheetherly will be transported
to a hospital in Manila. He is still singing about Christmas, the

fucker. They will ship him back home, the lucky duck. Here are the orders.

The captain takes the papers.

What Connell really wishes to do is take a mailbag from the porters and snatch at the piles until he finds his name.

But he restrains himself.

Bumpus can be silent no longer:

—Sir! Captain! I also bring bad news.

Captain Connell stares at Bumpus, who is holding out a newspaper.

—McKinley has been shot.

Bumpus, suddenly the oracle, kind of enjoys his role.

The captain looks at the headline before him. It is almost a month old.

Oh my God. Jesus, Mary, Joseph. God protect us on these islands.

Captain Connell crosses himself.

Bumpus shakes his head.

—Of all the ways to go. To be shot by a loony, an anarchist in Buffalo.

—Don't be impertinent, lieutenant. I am from Buffalo.

—Oh, I am sorry, sir! Captain! I am sorry for your loss.

32.

Casiana Nacionales

She has staked their place in the forest with their names.

Fra + Cas.

Cas ♥ Fra.

But he finds her by her smells—the incense of fruit, of mangoes, atis, guavas, and pomelos, that lingers everywhere this lady goes, also bahalina tuba, coconut fritters, and marmalade. She sells everything but bestows her smiles only on a few. Poor Benton Prick, her discarded one. He had returned with his cheeks red, but such chastening will only make him a better soldier, serves that Cherokee right. So Griswold the surgeon smirks. Her *fracasos* had only emboldened Frank. It means anyone can try. Try and try again.

Cassandra Chase is amused by the temerity of Casiana Nacionales. We can learn from her, she thinks. She sees the couple, a fused shadow through the grassy slats of her window out there in the clearing by Giporlos. The picture she wishes to take she would call *The Vespertine Pair*, in which the viewer, tricked by the light of dusk, would not be able to discern the wooer from the wooed. The photographer loves the boldness of the idea, the composition, but she understands her audience might not see the logic of it or even be able to imagine that there might be other ways to conceive of love.

Casiana takes him into her carefully, mindful of his trembling. First she had divested him of his foreignness, his hat, his kersey shirt, his gristly shorts. Then she had taken the heaviness out of his pockets—the coins, his flat whistle, a set of prison keys—then she lightened him of his sad underpants and socks. What a hairy thing is a man, so noble if seasoned, so infinite in faculties, in sounds and moving, how pathetic. He heaves, grunts, pulls at the talahib, growls at the ants, mimics a hundred owls. His absurdity makes her feel tender, as if she had made him, after all, in her image, a roiling, disingenuous, shaken thing. A penis. A man. Then she moves, and moves, and her own body, a warm agitator, surprises herself—her ruse is, to her astonishment, twice blessed. Then thrice and quadruply. The multiplying anarchy of her body is a pleasant detour, a secondary matter—a funny collateral of war. But at one point, there it is, it is all that matters, to both Prank Vitrine and Casiana Nacionales, these two orphans of history—a simultaneous assault, one upon the other—but who is to be master? It is a rocking, sighing braid of a shadow, a beast of a snake with twin heads, back and forth, back and forth in the talahib. And then the strangled salutation, a dull heave, and they lie, a heap of coiled hemp, on the grass. Who is to be master? Sleep unites the breathing pair, but Cassandra hears an odd movement, then a jingling sound, and there is a slip of a hand, a slit in a pocket, and the sheen of metal. It is gone.

THE VESPERTINE WOMEN pass like shushed dusk—a shuffling of slippers on grass and rocks, muffled words under the hesitating moon.

—You got them? asks Felisa Catalogo.

—I left the men two stews, dinuguan, and some bulalo soup, reports Tasing Abayan—Hope they have a good fiesta. Haha!

—Tell the men to bring me back my caldero, reminds Inday Duran—It will be good to have it in the mountains.

—Pssh. You talk about your rice pot in a time like this?

—I hope Nemesio fits my blouse, says Puring Canillas.

—You think my Ambrosio will be able to pin the corchetes on my skirt when he can barely take it off me, asks Delilah Acidre.

—Hahaha, laughs Yoying Delgado.

—Stop it, Yoying, says Dolores Abanador—Stop it, or you'll choke yourself laughing to death.

—I am sorry, Mana Dolores, I just can't stop imagining him, my Dionisio, wearing my camisa't saya. He has skinny calves, you know. He looks like a heron in a lake in his shorts.

—Aaaiiieeee, says Tisay Abanador.

—Stop crying, Tisay, says Dolores Abanador—What are you crying about, it has not started yet.

—I can't stop imagining him, my Exequiel. They will notice his hairy legs in the church, and it will be enough to kill him.

—Estupida! says Dolores Abanador—Did I not give my son the knives from our bamboo water carrier—will he not find a way to defend?

—Who will ring the bells?

—I told my Balê to get your Nancio to do it, Marga, and your son Dong, Puring, says Dolores Abanador.

—Ay, Jesusmariajosep—Nancio knows how to ring a bell—says Marga—I told him, he better not sleep in and forget his job, or he'll be ringing none of *my* bells again.

—Haha, Marga, that is just what I told my Ambrosio—

—Sssh, says Dolores—That will be enough, the two of you, Marga and Delilah! My God, all you can think of in a time like this!

—I hear the children are up in the mountain now, every single one.

—They are with Mayet Cañetes—off to pick some guavas for fiesta, reports Tasing Abayan—Mayet told everyone, including her boyfriend, that young one Meyer the musician.

—Ah, the teen-edger, Meyer the butiki, the one with the smooth face of a lizard.

—Yeah, she told him so no one will miss them.

—You got them, Casiana? whispers Felisa Catalogo.

—I have them, says Casiana—Don't worry. It will be done. I will be back in town to hand them to the Chief.

The women rustle like migrants into Egypt, mice scuttling through the forest leaves, up toward the mountains beyond Giporlos.

33.

The Keys

Frank Betron cannot find his keys. He knows where he had them last. In the forest. He will not tell the captain, who has sent him to seek the priest. Frank looks for the padre in the dim church with its recessed shrines to peeling saints. Casiana had taught him the lives of her saints. San Antonio de Padua. Santa Teresa de Avila and San Martin de Porres, who both look shamefaced. The blackface of San Martin is graying with time and weather into albino shards. How sweetly she once showed him the relics— but he must keep a lid on it, don't think of that. Santa Teresa's stern gaze has battled with heretical rains, erasing her views of unspeakable acts. Only San Lorenzo Martir, the patron saint, yet to be burned in his Roman pot, looks comfortable, painted in fiesta garb.

The bell ringer Nancio has not seen the priest, nor has the priest's helper, that cool cucumber, his amiga, Casiana Nacionales.

Silent as the saints, the bell ringer and Casiana stare at Prank Vitrine.

Frank Betron looks her in the eye when he asks the question.

She is no wilting lily, that Casiana. Whatever happens in the forest remains in the forest. *Fuck you, gecko, get out.* She is smirking at his military demeanor, his official pose. She watches him clutch the Krag's bayonet dangling from his belt.

—Ah. *Un heroe,* Prank Vitrine.

—My name is Frank. You know it. Can you tell me where the padre went?, he asks again.

Both Nancio and Casiana shake their heads.

—Come on, Casiana. *Mi amiga.* Remember the tree, what you carved—oh don't be like that.

—I am no one's amiga, laughs Casiana—Who told you that? I am enemiga. That is what I am.

—The captain wants a word with the padre. There are rumors women are wandering in the woods. Do you know why?

—Aswang, she says—witchcraft. But that is an old wives' tale. Don't believe anyone when they say you can find women in the forest with their split bodies, one for sleeping and one for flying, and if you find one of them in your dreams, you die of bangungot. Men do not die of dreams. Do not believe those women!

—Also, I can't find—I am also missing—did you find it last time—I mean—

It is Frank Betron who blushes, while Casiana holds his glance, not quite a Piero della Francesca angel, hands over her chest, hanging on to the rosary at her neck.

Who is to be master?

Answer: a woman.

—I mean, maybe we can talk it over tomorrow? Casiana —no—don't be like that—

—I guess, she says—sure. Tomorrow is another day.

The Chief arrives at the confessional booth: Prank Vitrine is no Holy Ghost, in his kersey trousers and foreign hat.

—No padre here, the Chief says. He shoos him away from the church—Padre *no hay aqui.*

Casiana holds up before Frank the secret in her clasped hands. But it is not the keys to the men's jails that he is looking for. He sees her rosary. She is mouthing words, as if in prayer. She shakes her head and bows solemnly toward her palms raising the white beads, an amulet, a warning, she is smiling, *santa maria an im' iroy ka nga dios nga yawa ka,* she's an imp, that Casiana, he should have never gotten involved, but he was so lonely, really, and really she could be very nice to him, that Casiana.

Betron backs away at the display, whether it is mockery or devotion he can't tell, after all, he does not know her, though he wishes to. Tomorrow is another day. And he lopes back to the plaza, his boots spraying dirt, marking a path from church to bivouac that the men of Balangiga will retrace.

He does not see Casiana's look as he walks away, the way she stares at him, her rosary in her hand, watching him go, memorizing his pale kersey shirt, the same dissolving color of his eyes—the way his absurd hat fell over his face, so that she had this urge to pull it back with a sorcerer's hand, so she could see his face again, she remembers years later in Balangiga.

The priest is not in the sabong, where the fighting cocks are being groomed for the evening affair, when the roasted pigs and the dinuguan and the pancit will be eaten and the men will be dumb with wine. Under the guise of a piss or a smoke, his men will leave camp at night, such is the looseness of duty in the tropics, Frank knows. Frank Betron passes a party going on at Dong Canillas the tuba maker's hut. The fiesta day of their saint has given the penned laborers from the surrounding towns a reprieve. They raise their cups before Frank Betron: "*Tagay, Joe!*" Back at the plaza, Bumpus calls on Sergeant Irish for more candles so he can keep reading his mail.

—No can do, Irish shakes his head. He raises his own unread letters—Even I will have to wait till tomorrow.

Sitting in darkness, the soldiers read the ghost messages they have already memorized, then they turn in to their dimmed bunks. When the sentry passes, their shadows rise to meet up with their hosts, to leave camp for fiesta, the stuck pig, and the dark wine.

34.

Breakfast in Balangiga

Of course, there is no tomorrow. The next day, at breakfast, they all die. Except for a few survivors, who get the message. The people of the Philippines want them dead. During the official investigation, what the Americans ask Cassandra is how could it be that the photographer had no clue. She rents the hut of that insurrecto, that Geronima of Samar, Casiana Nacionales.

That instigator, the rosary bandit.

Out there in the childish garden of dense anahaw, gumamela, and bougainvillea, Cassandra spends her days watering the orchids, watching the sunset, and so on, and putters about in her petticoats at dusk, a vespertine maiden, in her tropical artist's retreat.

How could she not know?

Did she not witness how Casiana had the keys that unlocked the laboring men's jails?

Were the screams of the American soldiers a dream?

The soldiers, hung over from the fiesta feast, eager in the morning light to read again their letters from home, are slaughtered at breakfast. It is the only time in the day that the Americans carry no guns.

The men of Balangiga are already gone from their jail, released overnight.

The men had rushed off to the convent to dress with the other ones, the hired men of Guiuan, San Roque, Lawaan, Giporlos come to help the Chief and the captain for the garrison's inspection by General Jakey Smith. So the Chief had explained their presence to the captain.

They all came for the cleansing of Balangiga.

The men massed together in the church, dressed in women's skirts and wielding bolo knives and, later, the Krags stolen from the garrison.

They attack at the sound of the bells.

A woman, they say, stood outside the church. At the sound of the bells she raised her rosary. She waved it over her head, like a lasso, the prayed-for noose of the Americans. And she waved her holy lasso and began whooping like Geronimo.

It was the signal for the Chief's shout.

Sulong, Balangiga!

That bumbling oaf, that mumbling linguist, that chess nut and arnis grandstanding master, Valeriano Abanador, the Chief—what an actor! He had tricked them all with his sheepish ways for two whole months. He came howling with his sundang in one hand, in the other a bolo, to lead them, a thousand strong, bands of men headed for their jobs—men to hack at the barracks, men to hack at the mess hall, and the best men to go after the officers in the kumbento. They hacked them, hacked them, hacked them.

Bumpus the lieutenant with his poor weapon in his hand, a candlestick stuck in a zinfandel bottle, and letters from home scattered on his bed. Shot with a Mauser, beheaded by a sundang. Knifed to death by the vice-mayor, Andronico Balais, a softspoken man.

Griswold the surgeon, dreaming of Yosemite National Park, Tuscaloosa Pig Festival, the pineapple gardens of Hawaii, scenes from his placid stereo cards, which Dong Canillas pocketed in a hurry after he hacked him, hacked him, hacked him (but the young man forgot the prize, the Holmes viewer).

Connell the captain, praying his novena to the Virgin. Who did not give a damn about him. It was the Chief who found Connell, oddly childlike in his undershirt, his naked, vulnerable thighs the first to show blood. But it was the fifteen-year-old Nemesio, that sleepy misfit, that narcolept, who stabbed him, stabbed him, stabbed him. Then his guts spilled out, and swear to God—that bloody Chief, that villain of arnis, that master of native military arts, reached in and grabbed the heart.

There is a void in the captain's body where his heart should be.

Swear to God.

Not a single officer survived.

Sergeant Gustav Randles, kalabera nga layaw, Corpse at Large—felled while eating saging na saba.

They say it was a woman with a Krag bayonet, rosary beads around her neck.

The teenage musician, Meyer the bugler with the smooth face of a butiki, a lizard—killed as he drank fresh buko. Shot by the son of Felisa Catalogo, a boy also in his prime.

Markley the orderly defended himself with a fork against Benito Nacionales.

Markley died.

Prick and Prank, wounded in the barracks—though one escaped.

Walls the cook, thrown into his pot by Nancio Balasbas the pious bell ringer. Who chopped him, chopped him, chopped him like stew, like a malunggay tree, with a bolo knife.

While rushing and shrieking and hollering Kapitan Abayan, no longer deaf and dumb, ran about the plaza crowing like a just awakened rooster in a skirt.

As the people of Balangiga, the prisoners and the laborers and the washerwomen and churchgoers and the cooks slashed them, slashed them, slashed the americanos.

Damn damn damn the americanos, cock-eyed, kakiac ladrones, underneath their starry flag, civilize 'em with a Krag, and return us to our own beloved hoooomes!

Turn them over—they were done.

Forty-eight American lives lost.

It is the worst incident in the annals of the Unites States Army since the Battle of Little Bighorn!

Barbarians! Deceivers! Beasts!

Didn't you know why there were no women in town? Didn't you see how they had all escaped to the mountains at vespers the day before, taking even their pots and pans, leaving only their skirts? The men pretended to be women, that old guerrilla trick, so no one would be the wiser in the morning when they all massed up at church, crossing themselves for their sins!

Even in your pictures—did you not see those women were not women—they were men costumed in their wives' holy habits!

They are women, not men, Cassandra says, they only look like holy warriors.

How could you not know?

I was busy looking at their art, Cassandra says.

Cassandra Chase slept so peacefully in the hut on the edge of Giporlos that when survivors of the uprising come upon her in her rented hut near the home of the vanished rosary bead rebel, that insurrecto—Casiana Nacionales—of course the Americans arrest the photographer.

Her deep sleep alone is complicit, they say.

—Casiana is no insurrecto, Cassandra corrects the man who arrests her.

She looks at his name, a soldier who survived.

Sergeant Frank Betron.

—She is an insurrecto, she is part of their plot, she stole my— keys!

—If she is part of their plot, says Cassandra, she is no insurrecto. She is a revolutionary.

Much later, the woman's prepared testament is a rant, so the senators in the congressional hearing only skim it.

—We told them we would free them from Spain. We lied. We took the islands for ourselves. We commit the crimes we say we abhor. We outdid the savagery for which we claim a just war. We reconcentrated their villages. We penned them up like cattle. We jailed their men for no reason they can fathom. We gave their people the water cure. We burned their crops. We burned their villages. We burned their pigs. We burned their children. O what a tangled web we weave—this damned plait of abaca rope we have braided ourselves—this war, this benevolent assimilation, this Manila hempen hell. When first we practice to deceive—we deceive ourselves first—can't you see? Have you not read Mark Twain?—

But to Frank Betron, she was brief.

—It is their country, sergeant. You only hold the keys.

In the end, her evil tongue almost kills her but her connections save her. She is the black sheep of her family, but she is also a Chase. The Chases of New York are friends, after all, with the new president (they sold glass with his dad, and as a child Cassandra once had dinner at his grandfather's place, near Union Square, and they visit him in summers in Oyster Bay). She carries a wrinkled note in the hand of the old undersecretary of the navy—good thing, because now he is in charge of the world.

Anyway, she's only a woman, with no business being a photographer, a job for the vulgar. In this way, Cassandra remains in
the forest, an itinerant artist in Samar, as the Americans retaliate
for the harrowing of Captain Connell and his men by the people
of Balangiga.

35.

An Apotheosis

Cassandra Chase's pictures of the dead villagers in Samar cause a sensation in 1902. America is riveted, as pictures of dead Filipinos in coconut fields are described in smuggled letters to the *New York Herald* and the *Springfield Republican*. They are like bodies in mud dragged to death by a typhoon, landing far away from home. An apotheosis of ten thousand. Figures hanging from trees like crosses, their scrupulous realism shaping a vertiginous city, some shining city on a hill.

Propriety bans the pictures' publication, but damage is done.

The pictures have no captions: *Women cradling their naked babies at their breasts. A woman's thighs spread open on a blanket, her baby's head thrust against her vagina. A dead child sprawled in the middle of a road. A naked girl running toward the viewer in a field, her arms outstretched, as if waving. A beheaded, naked body splayed against a bamboo fence. A child's arms spread out on the ground, in the shape of a cross. A woman holding the body of her dead husband, in the pose of the Pietà.* The congressional hearings on the affairs of the Philippine Islands, organized in January 1902 in the aftermath of the scandal, hold a moment of silence.

True, the photographer's fame is split.

Cassandra Chase gives her oral testimony before the senators, but it is in camera, because the witness of a woman, such a base story from a lady with her good name, is too vulgar to repeat in public. Her unpatriotic display ruffles even the thundering anti-imperialist, Senator Hoar, and her blistering delivery of the facts of conquest, painted as it is with irrelevant asides on Renaissance art, shocking talk of venereal diseases, frank portrayals of insanity among the Americans, plus a long list of useless names—Puring Canillas, Dolores Abanador, Delilah Acidre, and above all, she says, that Geronima of Balangiga, that Casiana—she of the noble name, she repeats—Casiana Nacionales—so many names no one need pronounce correctly—

You must remember her name.

In truth, her story gets on all of their nerves, Republican and Democrat alike—Beveridge of Indiana who storms out of the room twice in protest of her language, Culbertson of Texas who listens with his one good ear, the right-wing one, Allison of Iowa who interrupts her twenty-four times, Burrows of Michigan who contradicts her count of the dead, Proctor of Vermont who asks her to repeat the name Balangiga twelve times, then asks her to spell it, then continues to mispronounce it, prolonging the agony of everyone in the room, Rawlins of Utah who listens kindly, Patterson of Colorado who debates Burrows' count of the dead, and Lodge of Massachusetts who says not a word then suddenly pronounces, you have said your piece, now that is enough, be off or we'll kick you downstairs!

And the three volumes of *Affairs in the Philippine Islands, US Senate Hearings of January 1902*, do not include her witness, for after all she is only a woman, and her pictures will be redacted, and no one will be the wiser, and the people of Samar, after all, 'need to rest in peace.

Ora pro nobis.

After the hearings, history does not hear much from Cassandra Chase. Who knows if her story is also a mirage. Is it wishful thinking that the enemy might be a reliable witness? The troubling, doubling quality of her Tru-Vision prints goes out of fashion, and the world moves on to other fare—praxinoscopes, Brownie cameras, moving pictures—in her world's search for a way to view itself whole, given the limits of human stereopsis.

1.

The Women Give Each Other

In the Pajero, the women give each other their rightful bags. In each, of course, is a script.

"I've changed my mind," says Chiara.

"You do not need to get to Balangiga."

"No, I don't."

"I could have told you that from the start."

"I am done. I know the ending," says Chiara.

"Good for you," says Magsalin.

"I am tired," says Chiara, suddenly feeling the need to weep.

"It's okay. I am also tired. I know my ending, too," says Magsalin.

"We can turn around now. Let us just turn and go back."

And so the Pajero goes back over the whole trip, doubling back along the coast as the vespers bells ring and the sea is memory and the sense of a ghost across the strait on the way to Balangiga in the days of the habagat—that secret, metastasizing thing—the story she wishes to tell, an abaca weave, the warp and weft of numbers—traces the need to forget. Its molting spirals move along the smooth, unscathed road down

Maharlika Highway, across Samar, past Allen into Matnog, and down through the Bicol region toward Southern Luzon Expressway, with the coastal breeze growing fainter and the habagat receding as they drive in the dawn past decrepit, cramped cement blocks of shops, into the insoluble puzzle at the heart of the labyrinth, the secret within the secret, the untold grief, toward Manila.

35.

Sorrow Is a Weave,
a Sinuous Braid of Manila Hemp

They keep moving. All over the place. New York. The south
of France. How was she to know the denouement? She leaves
and returns. She expects to see him in his studio, rearranging
his index cards, reading a book. She cannot stay in one place for
too long. Memory suffocates her, she says. She has dizzy spells.
Their child keeps missing her father. They live in hotels. She
hates remembering. Hotels are her way of forgetting. She has
this thing now—about embracing the present. *One must embrace
the present, Chiara—it is all we have!* She will try Buddhism,
hatha yoga, even the optimistic premises of Catholic resurrection. When they receive the package in Antibes, addressed to the
child, it is the mother who opens it.

A picture of the couple in Las Vegas, the woman in her brocade frock and stiletto heels. A fur stole on a chair. A blurry, too
far away figure of a man in a white suit on the stage, a wavering
tassel of white—one of those concert snapshots that fails to reg-
ister the thrill of the moment. A curly headed child on a beach,
holding up a pink toy trowel. Another picture of the child, going
around on a painted carousel, eating her gelato.

And a wrapped box, a package within the package.

There is a card on it. It is in Ludo's hand.

For Chiara, her mother says.

It is for you.

She will bury the facts of his life's script the way he has stuck in details of the biography of Gus the Polar Bear, his unmade movie, into his colossal, subsequent films—curious details of desolation with resonance only to him. The secrets of her life with him she will also carry to her grave, with perhaps some details peeking through in rough spots, she can't help it, but her choice is to be that life's only reader, because what does anyone else have to do with it? It is nobody's business. Not even the creator can know her part, that mystery writer Magsalin who draws her thin characterization—a rich widow in the South of France with unstable vision whose vagrancy is the mark of her sorrow, though such lingering unease, she thinks, is surely a weave, a sinuous braid of Manila hemp that sneaks through human lives. It must weave through all of us, this sense of horror, this solitude, the secret within the secret, and it is no one's business to know.

Maybe she had found it this time, in a corniche in France, swerving toward the Mediterranean; maybe she had found it in that hotel in Hong Kong. She has no need to explain why a woman would want to seek her place of peace.

And sure, maybe her child will grow up, another desperate mimic, like her dad, to fathom a reason for why anything happens at all. Narrating too many scenes that do not count. When really, all one needs is to bring back the feeling of having once been absolutely loved. That is all. Love is the site of their wounding, these two women, mother and child.

The child tears open the pale blue box.

The child, only six, embraces the present. It is all she has.

It is a Brownie camera.

36.

Finally, the Karaoke

The karaoke strains at midnight are no surprise to the neighbors. The three brothers, Nemesio, Exequiel, and Ambrosio, have that good-natured carelessness that marks some drunks, but if you complain, bad things happen. The neighborhood tries not to rock the boat anyhow. Many are dockhands at Manila's ports, smuggling all sorts of things that nearby merchants appreciate— televisions, rubber slippers, unbroken vases made in Japan. This makes friction in the area inconvenient, since anyone might squeal. Chiara's realism is scrupulous, and she sends the prop girl Fionnuala to nearby shops before mentioning the above detail. Sure enough, the enterprising girl finds in the boholano stores ceramic pigs with bobbing heads; Danish troll dolls made in Macau; sextuplets of semiotic jade Buddhas, each cast in a different posture, a series of the soul's semaphores; and those Chinatown lace fans that unfold to show watercolor scenes of Spaniards flamenco dancing, all under lock and key in the merchants' glass cabinets.

To be honest, late Elvis is not Magsalin's style.

"What is that?" Chiara asks.

"Finally, the karaoke," says Magsalin. "I warned you my uncles were coming to get you if you didn't watch out. You know Chekhov's rule—if you mention karaoke in the first act, you must turn it on at the end."

"Hah! The Filipino Chekhov's rule! Not to mention Elvis."

"Ditto. If at first you mention Elvis, you must try and try again."

"That's easy—his songs are earworms," says Chiara. "I love that song,"

"It's the soundtrack of my life," says Magsalin. "I hate it."

"Oh come on," says Chiara, "'Suspicious Minds' is not the worst Elvis. Though it is atypical, the disco beat. At first he didn't want to record it."

"Hah. Even Elvis thought it was corny," says Magsalin. "That's saying something."

"If you think it's so gruesome, then why make it the theme song for my movie—for *Insurrecto*? I mean, it's prominent in your version, that rewrite you gave me of *Insurrecto.*"

"I was haunted by a gruesome history."

"You mean the story of my parents' marriage?"

"I wasn't making that connection. I'm sorry."

"I don't get it," says Chiara. "In your version, you tried to understand your country's history by taking on the point of view of someone you disliked. Why use a nineteenth-century Daisy Buchanan, some New York socialite photographer with no clue? The white savior story. I don't get that."

"I did it for you," says Magsalin. "It's the only way you could have read the story."

The filmmaker falls silent.

Then Chiara says, "You tricked me."

"I know very well whose story it is: I know whose story is being told."

Chiara falls silent again.

"But you're right," Magsalin says, "I failed. It is terrible how grief is a glutton—it swallows everything in its path. History, revolution, bloodshed. I wanted to write in a voice strange and distant and foreign—I wanted to get outside of myself. A different lens. And I wanted to write about this unfinished thing—this revolution. A story of war and loss so repressed and so untold. But all I did was dwell on trauma that only causes recurrence of pain."

Magsalin's voice is rising, and Chiara can see how this is a moment when the film should just run, then review the rush in silence.

"In the end," Magsalin says, "I could not even show the climactic horrific scenes she witnesses, the gruesome deaths of the people of Samar—which after all is the reason for the photographer's story. I told, I could not show. The history of that war is beyond my powers to add or detract from the terrible pictures it left behind—those stereo cards in your manila envelope."

"But you're right," Chiara says. "It is Casiana who matters. Her story is the point. And history barely knows her name."

"But now you do. The insurrecto. Casiana Nacionales."

"Maybe it is enough to know it, the past," says Chiara. "Maybe change lies outside the story, in the countries we are still making up. I mean, can the exchange of our stories be a way of redemption?"

"No."

But Magsalin smiles. Maybe one day she'll like her, this spoiled brat.

"I also failed," says Chiara.

"It was a valiant attempt," concedes Magsalin. "Your story made me sad. I mean, in some parts."

"I tried to understand why my father did not follow us when we left Manila, choosing to start a new project instead of saving his marriage. I tried to see him from the lens of the villagers who had witnessed his obsession with his film. I tried to imagine a grown-up world, the world of messed-up people making films, because my memory of him is so childish. About my father, I only remember the state of my being absolutely loved."

"But that is a gift, is it not?"

"I wanted him to be resurrected, but in my script my father still dies. I am not even sure if in the final version I should just tell a lie—maybe, say, his death was an accident. Sometimes I imagine he died from the despair I have, the horror of not knowing him. In the end, I guess, everything is just self-portrait. I could not create a portrait of my father. There is only what I wished. I even put in my anachronisms, my own obsessions that I wanted to share—I guess with him. The details of Gus, the Central Park bipolar bear—what a weird story, I was obsessed with it in my teens. My limited memory of going to school with those Chinese toddlers while he was making his film in Lubao, Pampanga. My discovery is, writing my script—I should let him rest. No one will know why my father died. He kept his secret. Let him be."

"I am sorry."

"At least I tried. I was only six, after all, when he died."

"I didn't know you were so young when your father took his life."

"He was young. He was thirty-six."

"But your story is about you, isn't it, your mourning?"

"I guess so. My mourning, my mother's—they're braided together, they're twisted in a spiraling knot. In the very beginning of my script, I tried to imagine her, Virginie, my mother, in New York, in Las Vegas. I gave her mourning to the schoolteacher in the script. But she will take her stories to the grave. She never speaks of him."

"But you have clues?"

"A few photographs, Polaroids of concerts, my parents at premieres, a package shipped from Manila, stuff like that."

"And the Brownie camera?"

Chiara sighs.

"As the writer," Chiara says, "can you at least give me that? To have something from him, my last gift from my father?"

"I will give you that, as the writer," says Magsalin. "A wish is still a thing."

Chiara is silent.

Magsalin asks, "So did you figure out why he died making his last film, out there in Samar?"

"Oh no. He didn't die in Samar. My father never got to Samar. That is just my story, my script. He died in our home in the Catskills. When he came back from the Philippines, after finishing his film. He was alone. In the middle of writing a new script. It is unfinished."

"I see," says Magsalin. "So to write the story you were back at the place where he died."

"That continuity is still a problem," says Chiara. "In my version, I must believe that his death was unintended. That in a different moment, he would have lived for me."

"It is correct to imagine so."

A BURST OF song crashes through the dark as the door opens to admit Magsalin's uncles Nemesio, Exequiel, and Ambrosio, all red from drink and from their maniacal insomnia, heedless of the sleep of their household help and the goodwill of their neighbors. They turn on the lights in the dark mahogany room, the karaoke machine behind them, and they stride toward Chiara and Magsalin.

They are caught in a trap, they can't walk out. Because they love you so much, baaaa-by!

Clearly, the three brothers are well versed. They have sung this song too many times. Ambrosio is the leader. Ambrosio's improbably silken voice, a haunting, high baritone, reveals the reason for their musical habits. They are good at it. They have two okay tenors and one singer who has been compared to Elvis throughout his life (which has not been good for his vanity or the peace of his barangay). Ambrosio, who otherwise sells fish at Punta Market, has a rich, honeyed liquid in his diaphragm that draws out from his listeners a coil of pain. His favorite is *Ave Maria*, but deep at night he chooses variety, and even in his stupor, when it is his turn, he will stand erect, as if offstage adoring Elvis, and his voice elicits a gravitational pull that surprises the director, Chiara. She lifts a hand, stops Magsalin from editing the scene, and she listens.

The silence seems like a flourish.

Exequiel and Nemesio sing out the doubling chorus, their lovely tenors in wavering pitch, one of them, the eldest, Nemesio, trying to out-tremolo the youngest, Ambrosio. But Ambrosio's power will not be denied. The flushed trio stands in the sala, in this harshly lit house on that shadowy street in Punta—a fishmonger, a smuggler, and a pharmaceutical salesman beaming at their homecoming niece and her underdressed friend arrived too late to choose their own song.

The three stand in a row belting out the ending, their hands folded before them in practiced pose, not quite Piero della Francesca angels, in their undershirts and ismagol, their boholano-smuggled slippers, and their faces with that grave piety that always comes over them when they sing Elvis. Their smiling faces, weathered by wine and the troubles of a sad republic, are garishly lit under the fluorescent bulb, so that pieces of their cheeks jerk and make them look unhinged instead of, as Chiara thinks they are, charming. Chiara wishes to adjust their lighting.

We can't go on together—with suspicious minds!

The song is over, and Chiara speaks.

"It's odd," she says, "how neither of us needed to make a script."

"Why," asks Magsalin.

Woe-ooh-wooooe!

Magsalin groans. Elvis's song will never end. She sees the words on the karaoke reappear on the shaking wall that is their screen, and Nemesio, Exequiel, and Ambrosio are at it again. They are belting out sideways now, in the doo-wop mode of national singing competitions, in which clearly they are also well rehearsed.

"What do you mean he said everything already," says Magsalin, her voice above the machine. "Do you mean—to both colonizer and colonized?"

But Chiara is already dancing.

Chiara and Magsalin join the song.

The End

Notes

Magsalin went on to publish a brief monograph, "Fragments of Film, Fragments of Transnational Dysphoria: The Wild, Wide Lens of Cassandra Chase," in *Structure of the Postcolonial Unconscious, Not Really a* Langue *or a* Parole, ed. Dr. Diwata Drake (Oxford University Press). Only a few more pages, and her mystery novel will be done.

～

Stéphane Réal wrote twelve novels, 7,200 lists, and sixteen manuals on various topics, including the swimming habits of bears, hunting for truffles, and orchid planting. His last book, *Two Minutes*, condenses the entire seedy French colonial history of an unnamed African country into the time it takes an assassin to gun down the protagonist, a mystery writer, also named Stéphane Réal. The clues to his death are found in the mystery Stéphane Réal is writing, but he never finishes it. Coincidentally, Stéphane Réal (the real Réal) also dies before finishing his mystery. Mourns his editor: he should have written about winning the lottery.

～

Chiara Brasi is on location on an island somewhere in the West Philippine Sea.

~◡

Muhammad Ali is the Greatest. He received a sequined robe from Elvis Presley in 1974 emblazoned with the words PEOPLE'S CHOICE. An error, as Ali was People's Champ. Ali was a saint for refusing to be drafted into the Vietnam War, saying: "I ain't got no quarrel with them Vietcong." He also said, "My conscience won't let me go shoot my brother, or some darker people, or some poor hungry people in the mud for big powerful America. And shoot them for what? They never called me nigger, they never lynched me, they didn't put no dogs on me, they didn't rob me of my nationality, rape and kill my mother and father. Shoot them for what? How can I shoot them poor black people, babies and women? Just take me to jail."

~◡

In the build-up to the **Thrilla In Manila, 1975,** Ali said, "Anybody black who thinks Frazier can whup me is an Uncle Tom." This makes Joe Frazier mad because, after all, he had secretly given Ali cash during the time Ali was stripped of his heavyweight title and lost his living because he refused to go to war in Vietnam.

~◡

After the Thrilla in Manila, **Joe "the Gorilla" Frazier** never forgave Muhammad Ali. When Ali lit the Olympic torch in 1996, Frazier said, "It would have been a good thing if he would have lit the torch and fallen in. If I had the chance, I would have pushed him in." In his biography, Frazier said of Ali, "I'll open up the graveyard and bury his ass when the Lord chooses to take him."

But the Lord took Frazier first. Frazier died of liver cancer in 2011. *RIP*, Joe Frazier! You are still loved, even by the fans of Muhammad Ali!

~

The traffic hellhole that is Cubao in Quezon City, Philippines, is at the intersection of the MRT and LRT lines, partly privatized trains that have ruined the sanity of working people and destroyed their faith in progress. The management of the railways is marked by incompetence, blatant graft, and criminal negligence, all of which harass commuters daily; hence the *traffic hellhole that is Cubao*. Used to have good bookstores, though.

~

Gus, the famous polar bear of Central Park Zoo, died in New York in 2013 after three decades of celebrity. He moved from Toledo, Ohio, to New York at the age of three and thereafter needed a therapist. He had two loves, Ida and Lily (also polar bears). At the death of Ida, zookeepers observed him swimming in desolate figure eights, at one point for twelve hours straight. His therapist pronounced him "just bored and mildly crazy like a lot of people in New York." A sympathetic businessman gifted Gus the polar bear an endless pool for his endless sadness. Even so, Gus the polar bear had to take Prozac. He became a symbol of the city.

~

Prozac, manufactured by Eli Lilly and Company, is a brand name for fluoxetine, an antidepressant that first appeared on the market in 1987.

～ᴐ

The **Colt .38** was useless against the magical people of Samar.

～ᴐ

The **Colt .45**, on the other hand, was legend. Here is a description of the death of a Filipino in *Muddy Glory: America's Indian Wars in the Philippines*: ". . . he was finally felled by a .45 slug through both ears . . . he had thirty-two Krag balls through him and was only stopped by a Colt .45—the thirty-third bullet." Huzzah! The US Army replaced the useless Colt .38s and shipped new Colt .45s to the Philippines in 1902. Experiments on "both cadaver and livestock" to determine the best bullet were undertaken in 1903: "It is desired that the board [of ballistics experimenters] convene at the Springfield Armory . . . to draw up . . . a program of experiments and tests which it shall desire to make." Turns out the minimum caliber acceptable on cadaver and lifestock was, of course, the .45. (Great thanks for the exacting, clinical research by John Potocki in his book *The Colt M1905 Automatic Pistol*! ☺)

～ᴐ

Juramentado, popular in the lexicon of Americans in the Philippines, comes from the Spanish word *juramentar*, to swear. Spanish priests coined the term for their Moro problem, the Muslim population in the south whom neither Spain nor America broke (or even the current Philippine government for that matter). Juramentados were Moros sworn to kill Christians invading their Moro lands, hence, juramentados were *all* Muslims, according to the priests. A similar misapplication arises with the term jihadist.

～

Colt .45 and juramentados go together. The United States Army shipped Colt .45s as the only weapon effective against the juramentados, i.e., all Filipinos, who were hell-bent on killing all Americans, et cetera et cetera.

～

The Krag-Jørgensen rifle was the subject of a jaunty tune sung among members of the Military Order of the Carabao during their annual Wallow, or convention, when they used to wear bow ties and dinner suits—and presumably take along their Krags. "Civilize 'em with a Krag!" was their anthem, a delightful hymn with resonant lyrics:

> In the days of dopey dreams—happy peaceful Philippines!
> When the bolomen were busy all night long!
> When ladrones would steal and lie, and Americanos die
> Then you heard the soldiers sing this evening song!
> Damn damn damn the insurrectos!
> Cross-eyed kakiac ladrones!
> Underneath the starry flag, civilize 'em with a Krag!
> And return us to our own beloved homes!

～

In 1900, at the Army-Navy Club in Manila, the **Military Order of the Carabao** was founded to lampoon a snobby bunch, the Order of the Dragon, officers who survived the Boxer Rebellion. However, carabao.org notes, "as with most jests, it contained a serious ingredient which gradually eclipsed the initial joke." The Military Order of the Carabao "came to epitomize the camaraderie that grows among members of the armed forces who face the dangers and privations of extensive military service far from home." You can apply for membership now to relive "those days of dopey dreams." You can be Veteran Carabao if you served in the Philippines between May 1, 1898, and July 4, 1913, or between December 6, 1941, and July 4, 1946. Or you can be an Expedicionario Carabao, a status reserved for "those who served overseas in support of an officially recognized military campaign, such as Operation Desert Storm." And so on and so forth, given the eternity of American wars.

～

The **carabao** is a beast of burden on Philippine farms. It was also used to figure out the correct caliber of bullets to kill Filipinos in the Philippine-American War. *See* **Colt .45**. Killing a carabao is just as bad as burning rice. *See* **Burning Rice**.

～

Professor Estrella Espejo's penchant for history-worms has a new home, *The Trials of Paz Chiching Luna*, her Snapchat handle, but her sublime posts keep disappearing. Her essay, "Echolalia: Repetitive Spirals in Philippine History," has been downloaded once on academia.edu.

～

Underwood & Underwood, maker and distributor of stereo cards and other visionary equipment, was founded in 1881 by brothers Elmer and Bert, not of Sesame Street but of Ottawa,

Kansas. At one time Elmer and Bert were "the largest publishers of stereoviews in the world with ten million views a year." *See* **Brownie cameras** and **Holmes viewer.**

～

Holmes viewer was named for the great Bostonian, Fireside poet, philosopher, and eloquent scientist, Oliver Wendell Holmes Sr., not to be confused with the other great American, his son, Civil War general, chief justice, and member of the Metaphysical Club, Oliver Wendell Holmes Jr. Apart from his essay extolling the wonders of the stereoscope, Holmes Sr. wrote such tracts as his great triplet set on the evils of Western quackery—his thunderous "Astrology and Alchemy," which made him persona non grata among several scarved seers on Minetta Street; his scathing taxonomy of Occidental ignorance, "Medical Delusions of the Past"; and his most elegant screed, "Homeopathy and Its Kindred Delusions," in which he called his subject a "mingled mass of perverse ingenuity, of tinsel erudition, of imbecile credulity, and of artful misrepresentation, too often mingled in practice." His work on hygienic prophylaxis, that is, the need for surgeons to wash their hands, was ahead of its time. He also invented the word *anesthesia*, an antidote to trauma.

～

Brownie cameras made Underwood & Underwood obsolete. Once even children could take their own photos of pineapples, unclothed women, and such, stock prices for the Holmes viewer went down.

⁓

The **Caves of Sohoton** are natural limestone bridges near the town of Basey, Samar, famous as a tourist landmark since the Jesuits started bothering the locals in 1565.

⁓

Ludo Brasi died in 1977 on an uncertain date in April: his body was found too late to determine the exact time of death. His obituary in *Cutchogue Clammer's Digest*, clearly written by an anonymous childhood friend, privy to such minutiae (Peter Horn, is that you?), notes that he graduated from Harvard College, magna cum laude, with a major in History & Literature; his thesis, on terza rima in Dante's *Paradiso*, linked the poet's rhyme scheme to the infinity of hexagons and pentagons in a contemporary fútbol, a profane notion that makes his advisor, the world's leading expert on the medieval poet, Dante Cancogni, sadly shake his head. As a graduate student in Baltimore, Ludo worked on a lengthy, heavily footnoted paean to the detective stories of Edgar Allan Poe. In his gap year, he traveled through France, Italy, Greece, and sneaked through what was then Yugoslavia, making friends mainly by mentioning names of soccer players, e.g., Ferenc Puskás or Alfredo Di Stéfano (though of the Real Madrid player he was no fan). He loved the city of Trieste, where he made his first film, a stop-motion animation masterpiece clarifying a moment in *Ulysses* regarding the mysterious recurrence of "the lanky-looking galoot over there in a mackintosh" in the chapter "Hades." He favored stop-motion-animated Danish troll dolls in his early work. Everywhere he went, so the anonymous biographer adds, whether in Bhutan, Mount Athos, or Manila, he always found a pick-up soccer game. He liked swimming. He packed light. He is survived by his wife, a daughter, a number of animal-rights thrillers, an unfinished script of a forgotten war, and a cult classic, *The Unintended*.

~

Chaya Sophia Chazanov Rubinson, also known as Madame Rubinson, began in the New York theater world as seamstress then set designer Cassandra Chase, her nom-de-scène. She caught the eye of an investor in the 1933 Broadway flop, *Mrs. Ida McKinley Gives Her Regards*, a one-woman show. Synopsis: the epileptic widow of the fallen president gives a long and excruciating monologue while crocheting slippers as she talks to her dead husband, who is in paradise. An avant-garde performance, *Mrs. Ida* climaxed in an abrupt and completely unexpected seizure onstage, bringing down the house, as people left the theater to avoid the "stark, vulgar display of rabid melancholy and unbearably extended, high-pitched, squealing noises of mourning," or so the *Times* reproved. Despite rave reviews from a few discerning people in Brooklyn, the show shut down after fifty-three days (to the relief of the ingénue actress, Sylvie Plato, who reported in an interview that "it was not just my vocal cords that were at stake, my fingers were getting numb from all that pretend-crocheting"). Cassandra Chase was in charge of producing the historic slippers Ida kept making until she followed her husband to his (one hopes cozy) grave. At the end of her life, visitors to her home in Canton, Ohio, marveled at how Ida McKinley's rooms had too many cro-cheted slippers in them to shake a stick, or even a Krag-Jørgensen rifle, at. Cassandra Chase, on the other hand, married her true love, Hermann Rubinson, in 1934 and lived happily ever after. They had one child, Virginie Ida Rubinson. *See* **Virginie Brasi**.

Rubinson Fur Emporium was often confused with Russeks Fifth Avenue, another fur emporium also owned by Russian emigrés. Rubinson Fur Emporium became a major investor of the movie world, under the guidance of its peripatetic heiress, Virginie Brasi, until Virginie was disowned for betraying her forefathers by con-verting to Roman Catholicism. *See* **Virginie Brasi**.

Diane Arbus, née Nemerov (1923–1971) was a photographer and a granddaughter of furriers, the Nemerovs of Russeks Fifth Avenue. Like Rubinson Fur Emporium, Russeks Fifth Avenue boasted progeny of cultural significance—in Russeks' case, Diane Arbus and her brother, poet Howard Nemerov.

Piero della Francesca was an Italian painter of the Early Renaissance. He grew up in the hills of Umbria. One can find his masterpiece, *La Madonna del Parto* (The Lady of Partu-rition), in the town of Monterchi, a stone's throw over from his birthplace Sansepolcro—on the way to the Prada discount store, near Florence.

～◦

Freddo of Gubbio, Italy, for the last few decades has tried making a film, a four-minute homage to Piero della Francesca, arranging abstract pale pigments against the background of the painter's favored shade of blue, *blu oltremare*, once obtained by crushing lapis lazuli. The color is not obtainable in CGI.

～◦

Cassandra Chase, born in 1872, brought her reflecting, clanking Zeiss glasses to other historic battles, including the war for Montenegrin independence (which bore her one son, Franz-Gyorgy) and the battle for the cooperative movement in America, located in Connecticut in the glorious philosophical years of the movement, the 1920s. Her autobiography, *Times I Have Seen, Scenes I Have Captured*, 1905, is out of print. A self-published album, *Women at War*, 1907, and her manifesto, *The Collective Hope*, 1921, are best printed on demand. Her masterpiece, "The Vespertine Pair," has yet to be found, or so Professor Estrella Espejo has lamented on FB.

～◦

Virginie Brasi, née Rubinson (1945–), wished to take the veil after converting to Catholicism in 1981. But she had a change of heart going through Cambodia. In a passing moment in September, Virginie heard a song on the radio as she moved through haunting ruins in Phnom Penh. Beneath the high, nasal wail of the country's old Khmer opera, she heard an ancient grief, something spoke to her, that faint tinkling of bells, from her childhood. She found herself swerving into the path of a farmer and his cow: she stopped the car. It was the tinkling of the bells at Central Park Zoo, misplaced in the sunlit, dying fall of the sounds of Khmer, but then the song transformed into a disco tune from the seventies, the preferred Western music of all the dead revolutionaries of Cambodia. It was an unnerving confabulation, and for a moment, she wished she were Buddhist.

～

Balangiga, Samar, has been the eye of many storms. It was razed to the ground by Americans, following a people's uprising on September 28, 1901, and by a supertyphoon, on November 8, 2013. The 1901 uprising of Balangiga may have been plotted by President Aguinaldo's general in Samar, Vicente Lukban, but opinions are divided. Nevertheless, historians admit that the town's daring action is fit for a costume zarzuela, with cross-dressing revolutionaries, divinely inspired heroine, chess maneuvers, and excellent use of ancient martial arts. The Americans found no women in Balangiga after the people's successful attack on the US garrison, despite evidence of the women's presence the night before when the great Chief, Abanador, got people drunk at a fake fiesta. Who knows who those women were, measuring out rice and bibingka to the unsuspecting soldiers? The legend is garbled. In retaliation, Americans burned all the huts in Balangiga, having found no one in them except a lone woman, a foreign photographer; then they also burned the outlying towns, Giporlos, Guiuan, San Roque, Lawaan, Quinapundan. The body count is debated.

Numbers of the dead range from 2,500 to 50,000, depending on who is doing the counting, blamer or blamed. American forces in 1901 killed more people in Samar than history's most powerful supertyphoon, Yolanda, also known as Haiyan.

~⸱

The statue of the valiant **Valeriano Abanador**, the Chief, or the Hero of Balangiga, remains standing in Balangiga despite the ravages of time, oblivion, and Typhoon Yolanda.

~⸱

The martial arts of chess and arnis saved the day. The great chronicler of the Balangiga incident, Professor Rolando Borrinaga, credits the intellectual arts of chess and arnis, the twin obsessions of Valeriano Abanador, the Chief, with the shadowy moves of the townspeople's actions and the martial arts stealth of their plot. An impartial scholar, Borrinaga also notes how some absent-minded person left the door of the kumbento open and allowed some Americans to survive. Kudos and bravo to you, Professor Rolando Borrinaga, for your scholarship! History salutes you!

~⸱

Casiana Nacionales continued trading root crops and braided baskets of sinuous Manila hemp after the war. She died a pious old woman, with secrets. No one can find her tomb.

~⸱

Geronima of Balangiga is the historic term of praise for Casiana Nacionales, whose life is chronicled by the Leyte-Samar

Historical Society, most pertinently in Glenda Lynne Tibe-Bonifacio's "Deconstructing Maria in Geronima: The Balangiga Story," which is hard to find. On the plaque of the plaza in Balangiga registering revolutionary names, Casiana's feminine struggle stands alone. However, the ghosts of the washing women, cooks, gihay sweepers, water carriers, bolo women, female warriors, and so on who were part of the Philippine revolution also lie behind her august name. Women of war salute you with tears in their eyes, Geronimas of Balangiga! And kudos and bravo to you, Leyte-Samar Historical Society! Keep it up!

~

Miss Spain, Amparo Muñoz, was crowned **Miss Universe of 1974** at the brand-new Folk Arts Theater in Manila. Beauty pageants, boxing matches, the backdrop of films—*The Year of Living Dangerously, The Unintended, Platoon, Apocalypse Now.* The country in the seventies is a theater, a spectacle, a screen for global enterprises of war, fantasy, and sex. Curated by capitalism and dictatorship, the spectacle is watched over by another theatrical couple, the dictator and his wife, the Marcoses. Eleanor Coppola in her documentary *Hearts of Darkness* captures the times. She films her husband's helicopters for his Vietnam film, rented from the dictator's army, as they are recalled without excuse in the middle of filming. These dictator stunts ruin her husband's budget, not to mention her wifely peace of mind. However, the length of the filming gave her an excuse to do her own thing, her documentary.

~

Communists in real life in 1974 were being killed by **Marcos's machines**, paid for by the **American military machine**, in turn framed and also parodied in **Coppola's cinematic machine**, which in turn is an art spectacle we subsequently pay for and watch, et cetera. *The Unintended*, Professor Estrella Espejo points out, pushes the envelope: within the spiral of war and loops of art is an unknown war wrapped in another, **a ghost in its machine**.

~

The bells of Balangiga, stolen by US soldiers as spoils of war, have still not been returned to Samar by the United States Army. Shame on you, men of Fort Warren in Cheyenne!

~

Burning rice is not a good thing. The sacredness of rice can be seen in the numerous terms one may use to denote it. Just as there are a hundred names for God, the terms for rice include the following: **sapaw** (budding of rice grains on the stalk), **tukol** (overripe rice grains not harvested), **ipa** (chaff of rice grains), **kumag** (fine powder sticking to polished rice), **tahip** (the shaking of grains to remove husks or chaff), **palay** (unhusked, freshly harvested rice), **bugas** (uncooked but husked and polished rice), **kan-on** (cooked and boiled rice), **am** (broth made from boiled rice), **goto** (rice porridge with meat), **suam** (rice porridge with fish), **bahog** (generic broth mixed with rice), **apa** (wafer made of rice), **busa** (popped rice), **ampaw** (sweet puffed rice), **malagkit** (sticky rice), **kata** (rice bubbling as it starts to boil), **saing** (boiling rice), **bahaw** (leftover rice), **tukag** (burnt rice left at the bottom of a pot). There is no word for deliberately burned rice.

~

General Jacob "Howling Wilderness" Smith was court-martialed in 1902. Theodore Roosevelt despised General Jacob Smith as a cursing, rabble-rousing drunk who ruined the army's name. The general was also a financial speculator, a gambler, and a future convicted swindler. Roosevelt gave him a slap on the wrist: Smith was retired but not jailed. No Americans were harmed in the making of their colony, the Philippines.

~

Balangiga has been called "the worst massacre of Army soldiers in the decades after Custer's defeat" at the **Battle of Little Bighorn**. Sites of trauma for Native Americans are linked to Balangiga: General Jacob "Howling Wilderness" Smith served at Wounded Knee, and many American soldiers were battle-tested in the Indian Wars, of which the Philippines was treated as an extension. However, many Civil War soldiers, Union and Confederate alike, were also happily reunited to exclude genocide in the Philippines. General John Pershing, chief of the US Expeditionary Forces of World War I, began his shining career in Mindanao. He was a Veteran Carabao. *See* **Military Order of the Carabao**. Balangiga contains *analepsis* (flashback) and *prolepsis* (flashforward) of the US military history of which it is part.

~

Demonio nga yawa nga iya iroy is a phrase in Waray, the language of Leyte and Samar. Never say the phrase before your mom. *Demonio* means devil, and so does *yawa*. *Iroy* means mother. It means, "you devil who are a devil who is your mother." Mothers get the brunt of it, no matter what language you speak.

~

Hermès bags can cost up to one hundred thousand dollars.

~

The anarchist in Buffalo who killed President William McKinley in 1901 was a sad-eyed, unemployed factory worker from Cincinnati, Leon Czolgosz, son of Polish immigrants. He is allied in history with such enigmatic men as Sante Geronimo Caserio, Italian anarchist who killed French President Marie-François Sadi-Carnot in 1894; Michele Angiolillo, Italian anarchist who killed Spanish Prime Minister Antonio Cánovas in 1897; and Luigi Lucheni, Italian anarchist who killed Empress Elisabeth of Austria in 1898. What's with the Italians?!

~

William McKinley was an excellent husband to his wife, Ida.

~

Theodore Roosevelt is an American. Progressive and imperialist, conservationist of Western lands, proud hunter of African animals. Charismatic Theodore Roosevelt had complexes. His father paid two servants to join the Union Army in his place, and his doting son, Teddy, never got over the shame. *RIP,* Theodore Roosevelt! You deserve America's eternal gratitude for the national parks! For the taking of the Philippines, not so much. History shows that Freudian impulses produce trauma on all sides, on colonizer and colonized. Anyways, water under a bridge.

～○

Mark Twain told William McKinley to stop it, but McKinley didn't listen. The Anti-Imperialist League spread Mark Twain's broadsheets against American expansion in 1898. His most eloquent screed was "To a Person Sitting in Darkness." Everyone should read it, especially before reading *Huckleberry Finn*—his overt stance against imperialism during the Philippine-American War sheds light on all his work.

～○

Elvis Aaron Presley, born gorgeous and brooding in Tupelo, had an identical twin, Jesse Garon, who died stillborn.

～○

Insurrecto is a misnomer. Revolution is a dream.

～○

The Philippine-American War is unremembered.

Acknowledgments

This book would not have been written without Ken and Nastasia.

There is no way to thank them, so I put them first.

I am indebted to Benedicto Cabrera—BenCab—for his generosity in giving us his painting for the cover of *Insurrecto*. Without knowing him at all, I wrote to tell him *Woman with Fan* looked so much, to me, like my insurrecto, Casiana Nacionales, the Geronima of Balangiga. The simplicity and grace with which he gave us his Woman with Fan marks also his tremendous, transforming art. The art of BenCab is, simply, a human address to the world. It is an honor to have for the cover of this book a Larawan by the Philippine National Artist for Fine Arts.

My thanks to early readers of the book: my agent, Kirby Kim; my editor, Mark Doten; Ken Byrne; Nastasia Tangherlini; Lara Stapleton; Sabina Murray; Viet Thanh Nguyen; Paul Nadal; Darren Wood. To Nerissa Balce and Kiko Benitez, scholars who offered key sources for history: salamat!

Special thanks to Nastasia, expert in readership, whose advice fixed my ending.

Kirby Kim deserves his own line: the sharpest of readers, he took the book to its correct home.

Mark Doten sees what the book is and makes it what it should be: he gave me everything one needs in an editor: a writer's spirit, an artist's eye. I'm so deeply grateful for his faith, his humor, his friendship—and his Paul.

To everyone at Soho Press—a miraculous group of empathic people: you have offered me the comfort of your community, my own private patron saints who have taken this complex, not quite describable book (is it a mystery? a history? a dirge? a comedy? why the hell is it all of the above??) into your fold. To Mark Doten, Bronwen Hruska, Juliet Grames, Rachel Kowal, Janine Agro, Amara Hoshijo, Steven Tran, Paul Oliver, Abby Koski, Kevin Murphy, Rudy Martinez, Monica White—I witness your vocation, your compact with books. You are heroes to me. You are revolutionaries in the publishing world.

As always, this book is for Arne: one more gesture of remembrance.

Stories are all we have.

Arne, I steal your stories not because it does not hurt to tell them but because in my body, they endure.

And for the people of the Philippines, for whom this book tries to keep memory, a history of revolution vital for our surviving: to tell the story of our resistance when our leaders pervert our past and to speak so that the world will know it, too—this book is also for you.

About the cover artist
BenCab (Born 1942 in Manila, Philippines)

BenCab is a National Artist for Visual Arts in the Philippines. His works have been the subject of four books, *Ben Cabrera: Etchings 1970-1980*; *BenCab's Rock Sessions*; *BenCab Nude Drawings*; and the definitive book on his life's work, *BENCAB*. He established the BenCab Museum in 2009, in his mountain home of Baguio, to house his personal collection of tribal art from the Cordillera highlands, as well as contemporary Philippine art. In 2015, a career-spanning retrospective, "BenCab 50 Creative Years," was hosted by eight museums, each highlighting a different aspect of BenCab's work.